Ripper

A Love Story

Lance Taubold & Richard Devin

<u>Praise for RIPPER – A LOVE STORY</u>

*"Lance Taubold's and Rich Devin's **Ripper; A Love Story** is a fantastic read! A wonderful and intriguing take on a story that has fascinated us for years. Wonderful characters, a plot with all kinds of twists and turns and elements. I love this book--a true keeper!"*
Heather Graham, New York Times Best Selling Author

"Queen Victoria would not be amused--but you will be--by this beguiling combination of romance and murder.
Is the Crown Prince of England really Jack the Ripper? His wife would certainly like to know....and so will you."
Diana Gabaldon, New York Times Best Selling Author

13Thirty Books

www.13thirtybooks.com

We would like to acknowledge Heather Graham, a great friend and great author, Debbie Richardson for her friendship and editing skills, Kathryn Falk, Ken Rubin, Carol Stacy, and the staff at the Romantic Times for all their years of support.

PROLOGUE

Whitechapel, London, August 31st, 1888

Polly watched the blood flow along the cracks in the paving stones to the gutter at the end of the alley. She heard the light tread of his fading footsteps.

Why had he done it? He'd seemed like such a gentleman, so refined and so handsome. He was nothing like the coarse, foul-smelling blokes she usually rutted with.

She'd just been standing admiring herself in a dirty butcher shop window, angling her head so that it caught the light from a nearby gas lamp, when she heard a seductive baritone. "Miss," the voice whispered. She peered around the corner of the building into the darkened alley and saw *him* standing there, casually leaning against the wall, his gloved hand holding a brass knobbed walking stick. There had been something different about him. Too late, she cursed herself. She had found out just how different. He had even admired her new black straw bonnet, which now lay broken and misshapen just inches from her rapidly numbing hand.

As she stared at the bonnet, bought with dear farthings she could ill afford, her eyes began to glaze over. Why had she wasted those farthings on a bloody bonnet? A princely sum to pay. Vanity. It would be the death of her.

It was.

Her sardonic laugh came out as a gurgle. She tried to reach the bonnet, mere inches from her, but her muscles wouldn't respond. Then, as her eyes closed, a final thought struck her, *I know him.*

CHAPTER ONE

Butler House, Ireland, June, 1888

"Mother, you can not possibly expect me to wear this!" Coren tossed the gown to Jenny, her maid, who dashed to keep the lace and silk garment from falling to the floor. "I simply cannot go to the Duke's ball in a..." Coren hesitated a moment to find the right words, "in a hand-me-down!" She cocked her head slightly, her emerald eyes glistening with tears. "Perhaps, I shouldn't go?" She cast a furtive glance towards her mother.

The game was suddenly afoot, this game of wits between mother and daughter. As they had been so many times before, the battle lines were quickly drawn. The long-standing rules of this battle were understood by both and simultaneously put into action. Though Lady Butler knew exactly how to play the game. And she knew how to win. Coren was ready.

As unmoving as the rosewood highboy positioned steadfastly along the wall behind her, Lady Butler stood motionless, stalwart, a stern expression on her well-lived face, looking as if she were contemplating a declaration of war, which Coren surmised, she was.

"Jenny, please bring the dress to me," Lady Butler intoned.

Jenny strained to keep the long flowing train of Irish lace and pure Cantonese silk from dragging across the wooden floor and snagging. "By all the saints, if this dress snags it will cost me a year's pay," Jenny mumbled under her breath as she carefully made her way past Coren to Lady Butler.

"Bring it here to the window, Jenny," Lady Butler said as she measured her steps, pausing in stride to add, "I need the light. My eyes are not what they once were."

Lady Butler played the game like no other. She had the master's touch. It was, after all, her game, learned from many skirmishes she had had with her own mother. With Coren as an opponent, the playing of the game had been honed to a fine art; there had never been a student like Coren nor an instructor, like Lady Butler. Even though Lady Butler had taught most of the fine art of battle to Coren, as a player, she had reserved several key ploys for herself.

Jenny handed the dress to Lady Butler. It was a truly magnificent gown. Magnificent by anyone's standards, anyone's that is, excepting Coren's. The iridescent silk garment shimmered hypnotically in the sunlight.

Lady Butler caressed the soft fabric between her fingers. "Perhaps, you are right, Coren," she said, a veiled hint of sadness in her voice.

"Oh, Mother, thank you." Coren hurried to her mother's side, hugging her shoulders, kissing her lightly on the cheek. "We should leave for Dublin this minute."

Coren had won and she wore her victory triumphantly. A faint glow, a winner's effervescence, emanated from her smile. "I know of a lovely milliner in Merrion Square," she said, her perfect white teeth set against the soft peach complexion of her face now alive with the rosy glow of excitement. "I am certain we will be able to have a proper gown in time for the Duke's ball." She strode about the room as if she were the winning horse at the Derby. "Mother, this will be such fun!" she squealed, falling upon the bed in the middle of the room. Then, tossing her blazing deep red tresses that cascaded in curls and waves around her shoulders, she said, "We will, of course, make a stay of it in Dublin. Jenny, have Mother's maid pack a trunk right away, and I will need one as well."

"Yes, miss," Jenny said, hurrying to the door. "Oh, Miss Coren?"

"Yes, Jenny."

"What would you like me to be doin' with the gown?"

"Give it to charity." A glint of triumph flashed in her eyes, emeralds sparkling.

"I should think you would not want to do that, Coren." Lady Butler stared out the window, taking in the vision of verdant rolling hills and kaleidoscopic gardens that surrounded Butler House.

Coren knew her mother all too well. *Maybe all the cards had not yet been dealt.* "Mother, I will not be needing the dress." A tingle of trepidation shot through her veins, and echoed in her voice, as the realization struck that her mother had been all too quiet.

"But, you will." Lady Butler turned from the window and watched as Coren fought to keep the smile on her face.

"Where could I possibly ever wear this dress?" Coren's composure slipped another notch, the rosy glow beginning to fade.

"I think perhaps then, you are right." Lady Butler strolled from the window to the doorway of the dressing room absently tossing the gown to the floor. "You should not go to the Duke's ball."

Coren hurried after her mother into the dressing room. "But Mother, I must go. All of England will be there." Coren felt the child inside slipping out. The little girl who rode the Connemare ponies inside the Great Hall and played with dolls in the toy room was always ready to burst forth whenever her mother trumped her ace. Not this time, Coren thought, fighting to stay the woman she wanted to be.

"You gave me a choice, dear, and I chose." Lady Butler opened the door to the hall and stepped halfway out. "Now, so must you." Winning was something Lady Butler did quite naturally. "I really must go now, dear. Let me know what you decide." She glided out of the room down the long hall to the marble staircase with the confidence and grace of a winner.

Coren could not believe the turnabout of events. Just when she was sure that she was winning, Lady Butler had turned the tables. *Now, all the cards had been dealt and Coren found herself holding a losing hand.* "Mother! Mother!" she wailed uselessly. Coren threw herself on the chaise that the French King, Louis the XVI, had given the Butler family a hundred years earlier, and pounded her fists into the finely woven damask. "Bloody hell!" she screamed.

"Nah, miss, I don't think the Duke would be likin' to hear those words."

"The Duke's not going to hear anything from me! I'm not wearing that bloody dress and I'm not going to that bloody ball!"

"Should I take the dress back then, miss?" Jenny asked, suppressing a smile.

"I don't care what you do with it! Just get that rag out of here!"

"Yes, miss, I remember myself what it was to be eighteen. I struggled a bit dealin' with me own mother. 'Bloody hell' indeed," she chuckled.

"There will be other battles." Coren fought to hold back the tears of humiliation. "And Mother will not win them all," she whispered to her reflection in the mirror, *though that is of little consolation to me now.* She cocked her head slightly as this sobering thought weaved its way through her mind.

However, Coren, had no choice, and she knew it. As the only noble Irish family invited to the Duke's ball, she must go. Father would be insistent upon it and the Queen would never tolerate her refusal.

The truth of the matter was, the ball that Queen Victoria was giving honoring her grandson, the Duke of Clarence, was going to be the event of the entire season. The Queen had planned the ball for a date when most of society had already quitted the city for the country or foreign lands. The season had, of course, ended some weeks earlier. There was no mistake in the timing of the event, however. Queen Victoria knew quite well that having this ball out of season would make it the most mandatory social event of the decade.

What would the Queen say if she found that Coren's father and mother were attending her grandson's ball . . . without their daughter? Coren toyed with the thought for a moment. The great rift between the Irish and the English had been deeply ingrained for generations in both peoples. Lord Butler hand been handpicked by Queen Victoria to help put an end to this ongoing struggle.

Coren's scheme began to unfold.

It would be the smallest of insurrections but, it would reverberate a thousand fold, ringing throughout every hill and vale in Ireland ... and England. Coren, the daughter of Lord Patrick Michael Shea Butler had refused Her Majesty Queen Victoria's invitation to attend His Royal Highness, Prince Albert Victor, Duke of Clarence's ball. To the Irish it would be seen as a resounding slap in the face of the English. It would be a small inroad toward Irish independence. She straightened noticeably, pulling a brush through her hair. She would be a heroine to all Irishmen for decades to come. Her emerald eyes flickered at the thought, the very first of Irish nobility to stand up to the English. This one simple act would bond her countrymen to her and they would revel in her. Statues would be raised. Squares and villages would be named in her honor. Parades of Irish peasants would flock to Butler House, and there, wait anxiously for her next pronouncement.

Her hand stopped the rhythmic brushing as the sobering thought of her parents disowning her insinuated its way into her reverie. All that she knew: from the etiquette and deportment handed down from her mother, to the simple Irish folk tales told by Jenny, through the wisdom, integrity and leadership exemplified by her father, all that made her what she was, and what she would become, had been gleaned within the walls of this house. If her parents disowned her, she would no longer be able to effect the changes that would bring Ireland her freedom. The time would come, she told herself, but not yet.

"Jenny?" Coren shouted then paused, a long moment of silence. An idea began to dance in her mind, teasing her, asking her to venture into a dangerous game. Would she dare to accept the invitation? Could she? Coren cocked her head. "Leave the gown, Jenny."

"Aye, miss," Jenny said suspiciously, raising one eyebrow. Coren's eyes and the slightly upraised corner of her mouth spoke volumes.

Now, lost in her thoughts, Coren dabbled with the ideas that jostled in her head, changing them slightly, refining them.

Something's brewing. What kind of Irish stew is the girl cooking up this time? Jenny thought. Then giving Coren a sidelong glance, couldn't help thinking that look had always boded ill for all. Jenny handed the gown to Coren.

Jenny had come into Butler House at twenty-two, when Coren was just eight. She had watched Coren grow and blossom, unfolding like the bud of the Irish lily that opens cautiously, fearing a late frost would burn its tender petals. She knew her charge was up to something.

Holding the dress at arm's length, Coren pronounced, "Yes, I'm sure this will work." She smiled a bit too devilishly. "Jenny, bring me the scissors and the sewing box."

"Yes, miss." Jenny turned, went to the door, and then stopped.

Coren did not notice that Jenny stood poised in mid-exit.

Several seconds passed before Jenny rapped lightly on the finely polished wood of the door.

Distracted from her thoughts, Coren's head snapped around. "Yes, Jenny?" she asked, a slight irritation in her voice. "Is there something else?"

Jenny held her breath. For a fleeting moment she considered saying nothing and simply leaving the room. Still, Coren was under her tutelage and Jenny had to be certain that Coren's actions would not jeopardize her continued employment at Butler House. Lady Butler did not look fondly on Coren's adventures. Many a time Jenny's quick wits and dramatic abilities had covered for Coren's frequent forays from Butler House. On more than one occasion, Jenny rescued Coren from her mother's wrath. Stealing off at midnight to aid in the birth of a nearby farmer's foal or taking bread and potatoes from the larder to stave off the hunger of the local children, were not adequate explanations for Lady Butler.

Jenny was still recovering from Coren's most recent excursion. Tommy, the gardener's youngest boy, was exceptionally fond of his little cat. He had acquired the kitten by rescuing it from a most certain death by drowning in a nearby well. And then, his beloved feline had run off.

Coren, hearing of the kitten's disappearance, felt duty bound to search every meadow and field in Wicklow County for the tiny feline. The fact that Coren had been absent from Butler House for nearly twelve hours without anyone's knowledge of her whereabouts, summoned the greatest performance of Jenny's acting prowess.

Feigning apoplexy, Jenny kept Lady Butler and the other servants occupied for most of those twelve hours, and had actually managed to get Lady Butler to serve her periodic sips of water and replace the cold compress on her forehead. In all the to do, when Lady Butler did question Coren's whereabouts, Jenny clutched her chest and uttered in a weak voice something about a long ride on Coren's prized stallion Gaelic Glory. When Coren finally appeared, she immediately grasped the situation and joined the farcical drama with gusto. Prostrate with grief, she threw herself at Jenny's feet, keening over her ample figure, all the while tickling Jenny's toes till she cried real tears.

"Jenny?" Coren's voice brought her back to the moment.

Realizing that she was still holding her breath, Jenny let it out in a long sigh. "Are you sure, miss, that you know what you're doin'?" Jenny spoke with more than a hint of apprehension.

Coren walked to the window, her back to Jenny. "That is none of your business."

Jenny was momentarily taken aback. "I'm sorry, miss." There was something different in

Coren's demeanor that caused Jenny to think that maybe she should just keep quiet. In the wink of an eye, a new sense of drive and determination had taken hold of the eighteen-year-old beauty.

Coren was becoming a woman. Jenny's eyes pooled with tears and she nodded. "I'll get the sewing box, miss." She opened the door, its well-worn hinges squeaking slightly, and stepped from the room.

"Jenny?" Coren began, then, hesitated. Images flashed in an exploding montage in her mind: Coren, the symbol, Coren, the woman who faced the English, Coren, the leader to all the Irish. "No, I'm not sure," she whispered.

"Yes, miss." Jenny allowed a smile to slowly and knowingly spread across her face. "I thought not." The door closed with one last squeak, leaving Coren alone to her thoughts.

Coren muttered out loud, "What am I doing? What am I doing?" She suddenly realized that she was not playing a game or acting out a harmless childhood fantasy. Coren's developing plan might not be taken lightly. It could even have dire consequences for the Butler family. Yet she felt that she had to do something. Even the smallest of gestures would give a clear signal that the Irish were going to stand on their own. "Can I really make a difference?" Coren spoke aloud again. She was torn between her love of her parents and the dread of being disowned by them.

Coren leaned against the arched window frame, resting her knee on the crimson velvet pillows of the window seat. Her eyes were drawn down to the manicured lawns of Butler House. There, two beautiful peacocks strutted and fanned their great tails in an effort to gain the attention of one very meek and timid peahen.

Sunlight flickered and bounced off the plumage of the peacocks, casting iridescent rainbows. Coren was mesmerized by the peacocks' displays. Yet despite the stunning, strutting glory of the peacocks, the hen failed to show an interest. The peacocks fluffed their wings, spread their tails and drew their shimmering bodies up to their fullest height. And yet, the hen simply ambled away. For every move that the peahen made in an effort to evade her pursuers, the peacocks countered.

As Coren watched nature play itself out on the wooded grounds of Butler House, her scheme blossomed. The hen moved away, but Coren noted the bird never took flight. Instead, the hen meandered in the opposite direction of the peacocks, occasionally stopping to peck at the ground in a poorly disguised endeavor to allow her suitors to catch up. Once the cocks had caught up, the hen lingered a moment and then moved off. *That*, Coren thought in an exploding realization, *is exactly what I must do!* Prince Edward Albert Victor, the Duke of Clarence, was the most sought after bachelor in England. His father, Edward, the Prince of Wales, would succeed Queen Victoria to the crown and Albert would be next in line to the throne.

Queen Victoria had invited only the most eligible and appropriate young ladies from society and royalty to attend the ball as prospective brides for the Duke. Lord and Lady Butler were not any different from the rest of the parents who would attend this ball with their daughters firmly in tow. They hoped that the Duke would find Coren to be suitable as his future wife, a thought that Coren did not share. She wanted a husband and a family, but she wanted to choose them for herself; an English Prince would never be one of her prospects. Shivers coursed through her. Coren, the symbol, the leader to all the Irish, would never marry an ... <u>Ugh</u> ... Englishman. She was going to the Duke's ball. She had no choice in that. What she could choose is what she would do once she was there.

Coren leaned closer to the window, the slight imperfections in the glass pane warping the outside view. The peahen stopped and looked directly at Coren as if she sensed her thoughts. And agreed.

A knock at the door brought Coren out of her musing. "Come in," she said.

"I've the sewing box and scissors, miss," Jenny said as she entered the room closing the door behind her. "Now, what sort of tomfoolery would you be up to?" she asked. Not sure if she really wanted to know, Jenny quickly added, wagging her finger, "Now, don't be tellin' me if it's gonna get the Irish up in your mother!"

Coren hesitated, thinking a moment, a slight smile coming to the corners of her mouth. Then with a wave of her hand said, "Oh, Jenny, there is no need to fret."

What she was about to do with the gown would not make Lady Butler mad. But, if all went well, what she was going to do to the Duke would drive him insane. "I will be very happy to adhere to Mother's ultimatum to wear this dress ... once we recreate it, that is.

The gown was not the only recreation that Coren was thinking of. She, too, would be recreated. Coren would become the coy little hen, strutting carelessly around the floor of the grand ballroom of the palace. Her cock would follow, but she would take no notice of him. Perhaps she would glance his way or wiggle a tail feather in his direction, or she might not. She started to giggle at the thought. Coren's mind danced with images of the Duke's eyes following her every move, ruffling his plumage, stretching his wings and Coren simply strutting past. She would preen languorously and coo, just loud enough for him to hear. Coren could contain herself no longer. The scene in her mind sent her into a fit of laughter.

"What? By the blessed Virgin, has come over you?" Jenny bleated. "Are ya ill? Are ya daft?" She felt Coren's forehead and cheek.

"Nooo, Jenny," Coren said, still reeling with laughter. "I'm perfectly fine." She turned to Jenny, composure in place. The green of her eyes lit up like emeralds. "I've never been better!"

CHAPTER TWO

"Grandmother, you can not possibly expect me to attend this ball!" His Royal Highness, Prince Edward Albert Victor, the Duke of Clarence, and grandson to the queen, said as he paced the length of the enormous grand hall. "I will not be paraded about like some randy stud before a herd of brood mares," he continued, cobalt blue eyes flashing.

"My dear grandson, of course you will." Queen Victoria spoke evenly. "It is for the good of the crown. And what is good for the crown is what must be done." She stamped the royal seal into the purple wax on the last of the invitations.

"But Grandmum? What about what is good for me?" The Prince sat down next to the Queen. His broad shoulders slumped.

Still not looking at him, Queen Victoria said, "Eddy, I do understand your reservations about this ball. But you must trust me. This is the fairest manner for you to meet those amongst society whom you have not had the opportunity to meet."

"But Grandmum ... a ball? You know how I loathe them."

"Yes I do." Queen Victoria lowered her voice. "If you had attended any of the previous affairs this season, there would not be the need for this one."

Prince Albert smiled wryly; recounting the various excuses he had used to explain his absences from this seasons balls and parties. He was particularly fond of the brilliant excuses he had come up with to avoid the seasons last two – and most important – balls. Both The Lady Barrow and the Grahams' of Scotland balls were well attended and a must for all of society. All except for one that is. Instead of using the common, headache and sniffle excuses, Albert had informed his valet to report to Her Highness, that the Prince was indisposed because of a rather annoying itch in his private area. The Queen was appalled and none too forthcoming with sympathy for her rascal of a grandson. The balls continued without the Prince, much to the dismay of young ladies in attendance. Now, however, the Queen would accept no excuse and seemed to revel in her revenge on him.

The Queen stirred Prince Albert from his musing. "Eddy. Please listen to your grandmother. You know that I love you very much. I am now asking you, as a personal favor to me. Please attend this ball. I must tell you, I have a strong intuition that this ball will be very special occasion for you. I feel that you may find your true love there, for that is what I know you are looking for. But you must be receptive to it. I know that this is the reason for your reluctance at attending these affairs. And truth be told, I do not have a fondness for them either. But that is neither here nor there. They are necessary." The Queen looked directly into Prince Albert's dark blue pools. "You will attend?"

Prince Albert stared back, seeing a love that he knew was reserved only for him. How could he refuse? "Yes, Grandmum, I will attend."

"Splendid." The Queen regained her regalness. "Now, be so good as to summon the butler for the delivery of the final invitations."

"Yes, Your Majesty," Prince Albert said as he stood and bowed with no air of deference. "I would be most happy to." He strode from the room but just before completely exiting, paused at the doorway.

The Queen, following him with her eyes as he exited, now

cocked her head at him quizzically. "Yes, my grandson?"

"I seem to have some difficulty . . ." the Prince hesitated, waiting for the Queen to take the bait.

"Yes." The Queen reluctantly grabbed the hook.

"Whatever am I to wear?" Prince Albert roared with laughter as he exited the room.

Queen Victoria shook her head, gazed skyward and whispered, "I do love him. And I hope he finds his true love as I once found mine." She clutched her hands in prayer, "Ah, Philip. How I miss you. Please guide your grandson to his heart's desire." Her eyes misted.

CHAPTER THREE

Coren had been to the great city of London several times. Each time she had done so, it had been in the company of her mother and of course, Jenny. The two-day journey began with a ferry from Dublin to Cardiff, and then by rail on to London. Coren marveled at the speed at which people now traveled.

On her first visit, when she was eight, Coren, Lady Butler and Jenny had spent two weeks in the city. It was a fondly remembered visit, as it was the first time that she and her mother had gone off to a faraway place without the presence of Lord Butler. Of course, they were not entirely unchaperoned, as Lord Butler had entrusted their well being in the care and home of his great friend Sir Robert Talbot of High Gate Hall. That particular trip to London had been to purchase clothes for the start of school at Trim.

And buy clothes they did. Coren and Lady Butler, with Jenny firmly in tow, stopped at every reputable milliner, haberdasher and bookshop they could find. Coren was to begin attending boarding school in the Irish city of Trim. A place - Coren had been told - that lay just outside the ruins of a huge castle. The castle's decaying walls stretched over acres of gently sloping hills. Its enormous tower rose hundreds of feet into the sky and could be seen for miles around. Coren was almost delirious with the anticipation of climbing that tower the moment she arrived at Trim, an idea that she did not share with Lady Butler at the time.

Coren's mind whirred again. Trim Tower. It wasn't until many years later, well after Coren had graduted from Trim Boarding School, that she had revealed her secret. Coren smiled, even now, at the recollection of that *discussion*.

"It was a dare, Jenny. I had to do it," Coren spoke matter-of-factly.

"No miss, ya' didn' have to climb that tower. Ya' coulda' broken yer bloomin' neck!" Jenny's chiding continued, "A dare or not, tis no reason to risk yer life and if yer mother found out about this she woulda' . . ."

Yes, Jenny I am aware of Mother's feelings. That's why I did not tell her or for that matter, you." Coren paused for a moment gauging the reaction from Jenny who stood with arms crossed over her ample bosom, a scowl covering her face.

"Lucky for me then, that I did find out," Jenny huffed.

"I wanted to tell you, but,but I was afraid that you would be upset."

"I am upset!" Jenny said, nearly shouting.

"See then? I was right." Coren said, in an attempt to add a touch of levity to the situation.

It did not work.

"Don't think ya' can joke your way outta' this one." Jenny sighed. "All right then, who dared ya' to do such a foolish stunt? And before ya' answer that, what's the real reason you did it?" Jenny's eyes grew wider in anticipation of the truth. She knew her charge too well.

"It was for money." Coren said.

"Money? Money?" Jenny intoned. "But, yer father sends you more than enough monthly allowance. Why a family could live on what he sends ya', it could."

"And it does," Coren added.

Jenny frowned.

"Do you recall the Murphy family?" Coren asked.

"Sharon and William and that crop of little ones?" Jenny

said. "Yes, I do. We met them outside of Trim that time . . ."

"Yes Jenny, we did," Coren interrupted. "In a letter to you, I explained how they, and several other families here in Trim, lost everything when the river flooded its banks. And how they were all in desperate straits."

"Aye, I remember." Jenny paused, the realization of Coren's action suddenly becoming apparent. "So, of course ya' had to help them out and give them yer allowance."

"Naturally," Coren said. "But it wasn't near enough..."

"So *that's* why you took the dare to climb that bleedin' tower?" Jenny said, shaking her head.

"You're angry." Coren turned away. "That's why I didn't tell you then, and why perhaps, I should not have told you now," she spoke with her back to Jenny.

"I'm not angry with you, child. I'm concerned that you mighta' been hurt, that's all." Jenny wrapped her arms tightly around the young Coren's waist. "There are other ways to raise the money to help those in need, you know?" Jenny squeezed a little tighter. "In all my thirty some years I never seen anyone the likes of you, I haven't. Yer a special one, Coren. A very special one indeed."

As these recollections dissolved, the memories of , her first trip to London, whirrled back into place, and her thoughts now turned to Lady Butler's proclmantion that Coren would be allowed to accompany her mother to tea. Coren had always wondered at the goings on inside these dens of adulthood. She imagined tearooms to be dark, secretive places where people met for mysterious rendezvous, identities hidden in the concealing shadows.

She was, nevertheless, not in the least bit disappointed to find that there was nothing mysterious about tearooms. Instead, they were bright and airy places, very much like having tea in homes she had visited in Ireland. Well-dressed and mannered people sat in large overstuffed chairs or at small intimate tables sharing tea and small sandwiches.

In the hansom cab on the way back to High Gate Hall,

Coren enthusiastically rambled on to Lady Butler about the wonders of the tearoom and how she would like it very much if they went to tea everyday.

"I'm afraid that would not be in an eight-year-old young lady's best interest," Lady Butler had said.

Coren was never really quite certain what her mother had meant by that comment.

Not even Jenny understood. "I think your mother means well, miss." Then, Jenny confessed as she saw Coren wrinkle up her brow and purse her lips, "But, I can't be sure, now, what she meant."

Excited and overwhelmed by the countless packages containing the shoes, hats, and dresses that Lady Butler had purchased for her, Coren concluded that she could do without going to the tearoom everyday. At least for now while a young lady under Lady Butler's watch, but that would change when she was married and on her own.

Even though past trips to London with Lady Butler and Jenny were remembered affectionately, this trip, made especially for the Duke's ball, would be Coren's first trip as a woman.

A woman.

The thought stirred mixed feelings in Coren. On her first trip as an eight-year-old, Coren was afraid of being swept up in the tide of people that ebbed and flowed through the London streets. Now, she could hardly control her desire to plunge in amongst that tide and feel herself awash in the energy with which the streets abounded.

Coren's childhood, well into her late teens, had been spent living at the boarding school at Trim. It was an exclusive place where the very privileged few of Irish society sent their daughters. Coren excelled at school and enjoyed the friendships she'd developed there. These friendships eased the tensions of being away from family and familiar surroundings. As much as Trim Boarding School had become a second home to her, she always anxiously anticipated the holidays where she would again be reunited with her beloved family at Butler House.

The Butler family, although well established, was not the wealthiest of Irish families. "Far from it," Lord Butler announced when Coren, who was only ten at the time, asked. "And finances are not for the concerns of a young lady," he added before going back to his books of accounts.

But Coren was determined.

"It seems as though we have everything we could ever want, Father," Coren said innocently.

"Yes, but it's only because I sit in here checking the accounts every day," her father explained.

"But, Father . . ." Coren paused to situate herself next to him on the overstuffed arm of his desk chair. "How do you know which families that work the land are producing and prosperous and which ones are not." She began to play with her father's furry sideburns.

"Producing and prosperous?" Lord Butler said, surprised. He twitched his cheek at Coren's caressing and sighed. "Ah, Macushlah. . ."

She had him.

Whenever her father used that endearment "macushlah"she knew he was hers.

Coren went to her father's study everyday and after a few months was actually able to take over some of the messier aspects of the accounting. She was very quick with figures and showed an amazing aptitude for projected income and loss. But most importantly, Coren was able to determine which families would be in need of some extra help if their crops were not doing as well as expected. Then she would make a casual visit to said needy family on the pretext that: "Oh, I'd heard it was little Jamie's birthday" or "But I was sure that I heard Mrs. Donovan had taken ill." Then she would unload the several baskets of food she had brought, usually with Jenny in tow. The poor families would declare: "There's enough food here to feed the entire county!" Coren would just smile and tell them to eat what they could and store the rest because she could not possibly carry everything back.

Coren's childhood and her time as a young lady were very sheltered, other than her interactions with the local farm workers. Between Butler House and Trim Boarding School she was not exposed to much of what outside life was like. She was a happy child, given every amenity that her family could supply, but living removed from the hardships of life and having grown up in a sheltered existence, made the yearning for knowledge of all things outside her world, even more intense.

At eighteen Coren looked considerably more a woman than a child. Her once slim and uncurving figure had blossomed. She was striking by anyone's standards, tall, with a sculptured body that held her salient breasts high and firm. She was poised, crowned with rivers of flowing crimson hair, a fact that was not easily missed in the confines of the steamer from Dublin.

The many blatant stares she gathered, as she traversed the ship's decks, caused her to ask Jenny, "What is wrong with me?" Coren turned around in a circle trying to see behind her. "Do I have a tatter in my dress?" she asked pulling at the hem.

Jenny circled her, lifted up the hem of Coren's dress and examined her waistcoat searching for a tear or smudge of dirt. "No, miss. I don't see anything."

"There must be something, a stain or an insect in my hair. Look again, Jenny! Dammit!" Coren snapped. "I am getting all sorts of looks from strangers." She rubbed her hands on her face and checked the pins in her hair.

Jenny stepped back, watching her charge for a moment, and then burst into laughter. "Why, miss, don't you know?"

"No, *I don't know,*" Coren mimicked Jenny's working class

brogue. "And I'll ask you to stop laughing at me, and tell me what it is."

Jenny roared with laughter. "You must be havin' me on, miss." The sun deck was crowded with people milling about, taking in the sight of the great Irish Sea. Jenny's laughter did not go unnoticed. A couple strolled close by, lingering for a moment before they walked off.

A gull's cry in the distance echoed Jenny's peals of laughter. Coren searched the skyline for the bird, cursing it silently, watching it rise and fall on invisible currents of air spreading the laughter to all at sea.

Coren gritted her teeth, pressed her lips tight and scowled at the laughing maid. "Jenny, I demand you tell me why people are looking at me!"

After a few moments Jenny's laughter subsided. She glanced at her charge and raised an eyebrow, "You really don't know?"

Coren became silent. She was hurt and angry that Jenny, her life-long maidservant and friend, would laugh at her in a public place with absolutely no remorse.

A gust of wind blew up from the waves carrying with it a fine salty spray. Jenny, recovered now, glanced over her shoulder, and sure that no one could hear, leaned in close to Coren. "I'm sorry, miss, if I angered you, but it is not a speck of dust nor a tear in your dress that causes the looks," she paused. "Tis you."

"Me?" Coren took a step back. "What do you mean? Tis me'?"

Jenny reached out taking hold of Coren's hand and placed it in her own. She at once noticed how soft and white Coren's hands were. Jenny suddenly became conscious of her own hands, rough and worn from years of labor. "My child." The tone in Jenny's voice at once put Coren at ease. "People look at you not out of disgust, but out of envy." Jenny watched Coren for a moment waiting for her to react. "You are beautiful, child. I would dare to say the most beautiful woman in all of

Ireland."

A tide of love washed over Jenny. She loved Coren as if she were her own daughter. Jenny had taken care of Coren for over eleven years. She'd accompanied Coren on all of her outings, and stayed with her while Coren was educated at Trim Boarding School for Girls. Except for the infrequent times at Trim, when Jenny was required at Butler House, Coren was rarely out of Jenny's sight.

Yet their relationship was much more than that of a maidservant and charge. They were true friends. In the past eleven years they had shared much together. Jenny was an only child, losing her father, when she was just three, to the Famine, some thirty years ago. Then losing her mother on Jenny's twentieth birthday. Coren was now Jenny's family and Jenny was Coren's.

Coren was all the world to Jenny.

Now, silent for a moment, Coren recalled the words her father had often said to her. "Macushlah, you are as beautiful as all of Ireland." But surely, she thought, all fathers must think their daughters beautiful. Yes, she had admired the color of her hair during her nightly ritual of combing and brushing. She thought it her best feature when she looked upon her reflection in the mirror. She would watch the light of the gas lamp change the hues of her hair as the brush flowed through the strands, deep red becoming auburn, then fiery scarlet.

Could it be true? Coren thought. It had never occurred to her that she could be beautiful. When she gazed upon her reflection in the mirror, the image she saw was that of a little girl, not a woman. Let alone a beautiful woman! She wanted to believe that it was true. "Are you quite sure, Jenny?" Coren held her breath, not daring to believe Jenny's obviously biased words.

"Ah, miss, I am quite sure."

As she and Jenny slowly ambled along the sun deck, Coren caught the reflection of her face in a porthole window. Behind her the sun broke through the clouds and captured her reflection vividly in the glass. She cocked her head slightly and furrowed her brow as she now concentrated on each of her features. Her full head of red hair tumbled about her shoulders, framing a face that had a sculptured jaw, high cheekbones, and a rather too large forehead. Well, perhaps not, it did seem to go well with her other features. She also noted her large green eyes, a pert nose and full lips with a strong chin, like her father's. Her complexion had a somewhat peachy tone highlighted by a darker pink in her cheeks.

A thin eyebrow arched and curved perfectly over each eye. *Nice features*, she thought. She pursed her lips thinking, perhaps they're a little too red, but then maybe it was just the effect of the sea air. *But what of that little indentation in my chin! That was certainly not beautiful!*

Looking at her face as a whole, she decided, even with that…dent in her chin, she was pleasant to look upon. Dare she say … beautiful?

No! That was ridiculous.

Coren knew women, or girls really who were beautiful. She could count many of them from her friends at Trim. Maureen O'Farrell, she was beautiful. Everyone knew it. And all the girls had agreed that, Katie McKnight was an exceptional looking young lady. But as for herself…well perhaps she had grown into her looks.

Then a thought struck her. *Did men find her beautiful? Men that she did not know. Would they genuinely find her attractive? Do they?*

Should she ask Jenny? Then, answering her own question, thought, no. How would Jenny know what a man finds beautiful? Besides, Jenny would of course think that men would find her charge appealing.

Coren had hoped that by altering the gown that Mother was forcing her to wear to the Duke's ball, she would make herself stand out. If the gown was more striking than the multitude of silks, satins, cottons and velvets that adorned the throngs of the other contending ladies, then she would be able to draw the attention of His Royal Highness Prince Albert Victor, the Duke of Clarence, away from them and to herself.

Now, as Coren considered that she could possibly be beautiful, a new scenario began to play out in her mind. She envisioned the Duke, swooping down, taking her into his arms, becoming completely entranced by her. Blinded by her beauty, he would see no others. His Royal Highness would be hers alone and she would...she had no idea what she would do.

The sudden realization occurred to her, if a man makes advances to a woman, how does the woman respond? Lady Butler and the instructors at Trim had been most indulgent at instilling the proper behavior, deportment and decorum for young ladies. But neither had even broached the subject of what to do in the matters of relations. Of course, simple matters of courtship were explored, what one was to do when a gentleman asked her to dance and how a lady reacted when polite conversation became too familiar. But the question that now plagued Coren, overshadowing any visions of princely swooping, was what would she do with a man after she became married to him?

Matters of this kind had not been discussed in the Butler household. A few of the girls at Trim Boarding School had talked some about what a wife was expected to do with her husband. But, they had been girlish conversations filled with moments of laughter and embarrassment.

Surely no one at Trim spoke from experience, only from rumor and gossip. The girls at Trim did not really know anything about life with a husband, except for what they had witnessed between their own mothers and fathers, or had overheard from a stablehand or plowman. Coren would have to find out for herself, she realized. A twinge of dread and a tingle of excitement surged through her body simultaneously.

What would it feel like to have a man's body pressed up against hers, to feel a man's lips pressed tightly against her mouth, her lips unwittingly responding? His hands would caress the small of her back as she lay naked beside him, his breath hot on her neck. Her hands would stroke the taught muscles that formed his perfect torso. Her eyes would devour his nakedness.

An unexpected surge of warmth crept between her thighs and a spasm of intensity coursed through her. Her knees buckled and Coren grasped for the deck railing to steady herself. "Oh my!" she cried.

Jenny whirled around from her position at the outer rail of the deck, "What is it, miss?" Jenny moved quickly to Coren's side taking hold of her arm.

"It's nothing, Jenny. Perhaps, I just got a little too excited."

Emerald eyes sparkled with desire.

CHAPTER FOUR

The clarence, drawn by two brown and white paint percherons, rolled through the cobbled streets of London on its course to Sir Robert's High Gate Hall, Coren's view of the city was different than it had been during her past visit. She was no longer an awestruck child seeing the wonders of a big city. Today, Coren was seeing the English capital through the eyes of a woman. The streets, the shops, the people, were now more vivid than her childhood memories. It was no longer a child's fantasy. It was a woman's reality. This would be Coren's trip. She would find herself here. She would challenge herself to all that life had to offer, especially men, and one man in particular, His Royal Highness, Prince Albert Victor, the Duke of Clarence.

The upcoming ball would be her trial. Her plans had been made and she would see them through. The stage was set. The players were in place. The work on the dress had long since been completed. Coren, with Jenny's reluctant help, had put in many secret hours changing the dress to suit her needs. Now, as the fingers of doubt began to creep into her thoughts, Coren internally begged, *"Please God, let me be right!"*

As the beat of the horses' hooves slowed to a walk, the carriage came to a stop in front of "Uncle" Robert's High Gate Hall, anxiety rose up from Coren's stomach. She began to question everything. Was this just the fantasy of a child wanting to be a woman? Wanting to change the world? Her heartbeat quickened. Coren felt herself grow faint. She searched her inner thoughts to find answers; answers that she was sure lay there hidden from her.

"Coren." A voice sounding distant and faint called to her. "Coren! Sir Robert is waiting. Would you kindly come out of the carriage?" Lady Butler glared at her daughter.

Coren shook her head, regaining her senses. The shards of panic slipped silently away, falling back to the recesses of her mind. "Yes, I'll be out straight away, Mother." She gathered her handbag and wrap and stepped down from the carriage.

"Coren, dear, is something the matter?" Lady Butler reached for her daughter, helping her down from the cab.

"No, Mother." Coren thought quickly, not wanting to concern Lady Butler or upset the trip. "I'm just caught up in the excitement."

"You must rest then as soon as we get settled." Lady Butler motioned to the manservant. "Kindly help my daughter into the house."

"Oh, Mother, I'm fine," Coren said, brushing the dust from her coat. "Truly. I feel fine."

Lady Butler was undeterred. "Nevertheless, you need to rest. It is a big city, my dear, and much has changed since you were here last." Lady Butler studied her daughter's face— searching--then continued nonchalantly, "Come along, now."

Coren realized that she wasn't hiding much from her mother. Lady Butler was too astute to let this lapse go unnoticed. Coren was startled to find that she could become lost in anxiety so quickly. She had allowed the fear to creep in and engulf her. That must not happen again. Her senses still reeled from the experience.

What kind of a leader will Ireland have if I give into panic so easily? Her resolve strengthened. She cleared her mind of the thoughts from a moment ago. She drew herself up and strode through the archway of High Gate Hall.

Sir Robert Talbot came rushing as quickly as his squat legs

could carry him down the long corridor to the entrance of High Gate Hall. "Lady Butler! How perfectly delightful to have you in my humble home again. You always make it feel so much more inviting, even to me and I live here!" He chuckled. "You do look wonderful, just wonderful!" Sir Robert fumbled for his glasses. "And where is that precious child of yours?"

"I'm afraid she's not a child any longer." Lady Butler lowered her voice, "If only they would learn to stay babies, wouldn't that be grand?

Sir Robert laughed and nodded in agreement.

"Mother, I heard that!" Coren said, stepping into the marbled foyer.

"It cannot be! No, it simply cannot be!" Sir Robert held out his hands to Coren. "Look at you! What happened?"

"I told you, Robert, that she wasn't a child any longer," Lady Butler said smiling broadly. Her daughter was glorious and Lady Butler swelled with pride.

Sir Robert danced around Coren, gushing over her. "You look just as your mother did when I first met her." He shot a quick wink at Lady Butler.

"Now, Robert, don't you try that blarney on an old woman like me," Lady Butler said falling into their familiar banter. "You've had ample opportunity to marry."

"True. True. But Lord Butler had already captured the most beautiful woman in society for his wife." Sir Robert's his eyes twinkled with merriment. "What was I to do?" He raised his hands in a gesture of mock surrender.

Sir Robert loved to bandy words with Lady Butler. He looked forward to their word play whenever the Butlers visited. Theirs had been a warm, enduring friendship and one he treasured dearly.

High Gate Hall was mammoth. Its expansive halls and extensive chambers could contain several houses the size of Butler House. Yet the great dimensions of his mansion could not swallow up the warmth and joy of life that Sir Robert exuded.

Over the many years while the kinship between the Butlers and Sir Robert had grown, High Gate Hall had become a second home to the Butlers. Sir Robert would have it no other way, and the Lady and Lord Butler always stayed in the great mansion when visiting London. There was a comfort in the familiarity of the guest rooms. Sir Robert saw to it that they were always kept clean with freshly laundered linens and fragrant blooming flowers for the unexpected visit from a Butler family member.

Sir Robert's friendship was truly valued by the Butlers.

Lord Butler and Sir Robert had become steadfast friends when the two men had attended Oxford University. They formed a tight and long-lasting fraternity with one another. One that even the sometimes-awkward discussions on Irish independence could not shake.

Lord Butler believed strongly in Irish independence. And, like all Irishmen, hoped that it would come about without a single drop of blood being shed. He was a true gentleman and scholar, firmly believing that any conflict could be resolved with intelligence and discussions. He always chastised the young scholars he spoke with, begging them to remember that: "Battles are for the ignorant and swordplay is strictly a pastime good for keeping one's reflexes honed."

Sir Robert mirrored his friend's feelings. He, too, believed that there should be an independent Irish state and vowed that he would do all he could to prevent even the smallest drop of blood from being spilt. A servant of the Queen, Sir Robert was duty bound to support the Crown's decision. Yet, he felt honor bound to show the Crown that the two nations could coexist for their mutual benefit. To demonstrate his belief, he often pointed to the long friendship between himself and Lord Butler.

It was only a month ago that Lord Butler was in London for a week of debate with several members of Parliament, Sir Robert included. One evening, when the discussions had been continued at The Yellow Rook, a favorite pub of both Sir Robert and Lord Butler, Sir Robert shakily hoisted himself to a tabletop, and waving a tankard of good Irish stout declared, "If we can make this friendship, this brotherhood last for forty years...surely our two countries can do the same." He raised his glass high above his head and shouted to his close friend, "Am I not right, Lord Butler?"

"You're damn right, Robert," Lord Butler averred heartily, joining his friend atop the table.

They made quite a pair, Sir Robert a short, squat and jolly man and Lord Butler, the tall, squarely built and considerably serious man, balancing along side each other. Then they laughed, slapped each other's backs and ordered another round for the house. Several draughts apparently loosened up even the staunchest conservatives in the Parliament. Both men felt that Lord Butler's frequent visits to Parliament were beginning to wear down even the Crown's most steadfast anti-Irish independence voices. Together Lord Butler and Sir Robert were insurmountable.

Upon returning to Butler House from London, Lord Butler would sit with Coren in the library and talk for hours. He would fill his daughter's ears with each detail of the trip. Well, not quite every detail. Lord Butler would edit the portion of the trip that had drinking and standing on tables.

Coren would be enrapt, as her father recalled the often-heated arguments that he and Sir Robert and the members of Parliament would become entwined in. Every word that her father spoke filled Coren's thoughts and inspired in her the desire to be like her father and to pursue his dreams, which were now becoming her own.

Coren standing in the great entryway of High Gate Hall gazed fondly and with great respect at her "adopted" Uncle. She wondered if Sir Robert was lonely living here at High Gate. He had never married, preferring to spend his time with a few select friends and his seven beloved boxers. The parents of the dogs had been a gift from Lord and Lady Butler years earlier. Now the puppies of those original two roamed the great house in a pack that created loving havoc wherever they went. Surely, Coren thought, a man of Uncle Robert's convictions and commitments would not be scared away from the vows of marriage. However, maybe he had never truly found the love of his life. Or had he? Coren paled at the thought. Lady Butler? Mother? Had she been Uncle Robert's great love? If true, how terrible for him! All these years being around Mother, while she was married to his best friend! Coren fought back a tear. Life could be so cruel. Yet, she had never seen anything but honest love and affection from her Uncle toward herself and her parents. Perhaps she was wrong and Uncle Robert's great love was just around the corner. Her eyebrows arched and a sly little smile grew on her face as she thought, and perhaps, so is mine.

As Coren reached the landing at the top of the curving staircase, she paused with her hand on the smoothly worn newel post before continuing along the hallway to her room. A mental image came to her of an eight-year-old . . . brat -- Coren smiled, thinking, yes, she ertainly was -- peeking through the balustrade at the glorious dancers in the ballroom below. How many times had she had to scurry back down the corridor to avoid being caught by a wandering party member? She loved the look of the richly varnished walls, burnished to a deep auburn. She could almost see her reflection in the highly polished wood as she ran her hands along the panels, loving the feel of being in this home.

The suite of guest rooms that Coren and Lady Butler usually stayed in had not changed since their last visit, except for the spray of heather and thistle that adorned a bedside table. Sir Robert was not one to change something just for the sake of change, but the addition of the carefully chosen dried flower arrangement made Coren aware that Uncle Robert was always thinking of them.

The old decor could not diminish the grandeur of High Gate Hall. Actually, it enhanced it, Coren noted, as she pushed open the bay window. A warm breeze lofted into the room, carrying with it the flowered scents of summer and something more

The gardens below the suite of guest rooms in the east wing were well kept and although not quite as colorful as the gardens at Butler House, they were teeming with life. Birds fluttered about, chasing insects and each other. Butterflies on wafer-light wings danced among the yellow and orange tiger lilies, and purple snapdragons. The garden spread out into the narrow patch of woods that surrounded High Gate Hall. Beyond the woods in the center of London rose the towering clock at Westminster.

Coren marveled with awe and elation as new smells and sounds greeted every turn of her head. Distant stacks billowed smoke, forming great gray clouds of ash that spread out on the horizon, molding and bending the light from the sun. She imagined ghosts ascending and falling away, blown by the wind over the rooftops leaving in their wake a snowy dusting of ash.

Coren wondered what kind of people lived in those ash-covered buildings? What was their livelihood? Why did they stay?

She knew of poverty, of course. The men, women and children who worked the land back in Ireland frequently had very little to live on. She felt deeply for the poor souls that tilled the land in Wicklow County. As often as they could, Coren and Jenny rode out to the surrounding farms to hand out food and clothing. It was not much, but it helped fill the immediate needs that continually plagued the farmers. Sadly, Coren realized that just as the hungry were fed, they were hungry again. It was a cycle that she alone could not break. It would take the efforts of many people and many years.

As her thoughts returned to the distant view of London, Coren could see how the poverty of this city was kept well away from the rich and royal. Pondering a moment, she considered that it must be the same in Dublin, but that Lady

Butler had never allowed her to see it there, nor would Mother allow exposure to it here in London.

I should like to go to that place.

The idea struck her causing her to look around as if someone else had said it. The thought lingered. Chills of excitement raced through her and goose flesh rose on her arms. She rubbed them to chase the cold away. Would she dare? The answer came quickly. She asked herself over and over in an attempt to change the response. But, *yes. Yes,* continued to reverberate in her head.

She remembered Father telling her of the dreadful places and havens of iniquity in London, where prostitutes and drunkards filled the lanes and children ran unattended. A place where people slept in doorways or out in the street; where sailors went to spend their money and women waited to take it. A place where only the desperate dared to travel. And only the forgotten dared to live.

Whitechapel.

CHAPTER FIVE

"Jenny, please go and hurry Coren along." Lady Butler glanced at the ancient clock standing against the library wall. "We shall be well past respectable time if we wait much longer." Lady Butler checked the clock again as if time had suddenly sped forward.

"Yes, My Lady." Jenny hied from the room, closing the door silently behind her.

Now, as time quickly passed and there had been no appearance by Coren, suspicion began to creep its way into Lady Butler's thoughts. Her daughter might be up to something. Ever since their little tête-à-tête over Coren's gown, Lady Butler had been wary. Coren had been nothing but charming and agreeable, a dangerous combination. Well, Lady Butler thought, whatever that something is, it certainly will not keep Sir Robert and myself from arriving at the ball on time.

Lady Butler raised Coren to regard such formalities as timeliness with the utmost of importance and, for the most part, Coren had adhered to that rule. The set of rules that Lady Butler had laid down to Coren many years earlier had included timeliness as rule one, and making a good first impression as rule two. Lady Butler had every intention of making a grand first impression at the Duke's Ball. However, Coren it seemed, was not cooperating. Lady Butler noted to herself that she would have to remind her daughter, first impressions were everything.

Lady Butler leaned on a high-backed leather chair, switching her weight from one leg to the other. Her face was stoic masking her growing anxiety.

The grandfather clock chimed a quarter past. When the hammer struck the last note, there was again silence.

Alone in the worn mahogany paneled library surrounded by hundreds of books that filled every shelf and lined every wall from floor to ceiling, Lady Butler contemplated, *How odd it is that a room filled with millions of words can be so silent.*

In defiance the clock dared to break the quiet with a chime.

Half past the hour.

The doors to the library swung open. "My dear, I hope that I haven't kept you too long." Sir Robert, dressed in tails and carrying a top hat, said apologetically as he weebled in. "There are always so many things to be taken care of in this great house. If it wasn't for the fact that this manor has been in my family for so many generations, I would sell this place and move into something less grand."

"Oh, but Robert, how could you ever want to leave High Gate? It is one of the grandest houses in all of England." Lady Butler punctuated the statement, sweeping her arms wide open, emphasizing the great girth of the estate.

"As long as there are ladies in this house such as yourself and Coren, I will stay." He moved to a small shelf behind his writing desk and poured two glasses of brandy from a crystal decanter.

"Well, then, we must visit more often." Lady Butler smiled slyly. Her eyes shifted to the door for a moment hoping that Coren's entrance would soon follow Sir Robert's.

Sir Robert handed a snifter to Lady Butler. "Ah, then, my plan is working." He sipped the brandy, drinking in the rich aroma before the burning tingle of the alcohol hit the back of his throat. "And might I add my dear, you look wonderful!" He gestured for Lady Butler to turn around so that he might take in the full effect of her charms.

"You are good for my vanity, Sir Robert." She slowly turned around, being careful not to spill the brandy on her deep azure gown.

"And you are good for my image." He winked at her. "Lord Butler doesn't know what he's missing tonight." He held his glass high above his head. "I salute him, his fine daughter and his exquisite wife. And I thank him for allowing me to accompany them to the Duke's ball." He tossed back his brandy and turned to pour himself another.

"I'm sorry he will miss it," Lady Butler said, her eyes glazing over. "But the Queen's business must be taken care of."

"Yes, quite right. And Patrick is the right man to take care of it," Sir Robert said as he finished the second brandy.

"Oh, Mother, Sir Robert, forgive me for keeping you." Coren bounced into the room. "I'm sorry, but I wanted to make sure that everything was just..."Her voice trailed off.

Lady Butler and Sir Robert both stared at Coren with strange expressions, the likes of which Coren was quite certain she had seen somewhere before. "Is something wrong? Mother, are you all right?" A hint of worry crept into Coren's voice. "What is it?"

Lady Butler placed the crystal snifter down onto the small table beside the chair. "Saints preserve us, Coren! You are stunning!"

"Stunning? My dear Lady Butler, that is an understatement!" Sir Robert said, pouring himself another brandy. "You, Coren, are extraordinary. A most beautiful woman." The glass trembled slightly in his hand as he set it down on the tray.

"My darling, what ever have you done to that dress?" Lady Butler circled Coren, feeling the fabric of the gown, inspecting the hem and seams.

Coren stood rigidly as her mother circled her. She watched Lady Butler carefully; unsure of how to read her reaction to the changes she and Jenny had wrought to the dress. Speaking softly, Coren said, "I hope you are not angry, Mother, but I just couldn't wear the dress the way it was."

She waited a moment for a response. Coren had removed entirely the fine lace from around the neckline, causing a décolletage which was just shy of indecency, but still respectable all the same, or so Jenny had told her; Coren still had her doubts. She had also removed the two layers of lace from around the capped sleeves, leaving just a whisper now of one elegant layer. All the lace: neck, collar, and hem had been dyed the lightest of greens, complementing the richer hues of the body of the dress, which couldn't be discerned as one specific green, given the iridescence of the silk, and every movement of the dress brought new shades forth, all of them enhancing Coren's skin tones and ever-changing hues in her own burgundy tresses. She was the shimmering vision of an Irish fairy queen, mysterious, enchanting, and indomitable. Glorious.

"I only made a few slight changes to the hem and…"

Lady Butler wrapped her arms around Coren and hugged her. "Coren, you are even more beautiful than I could have imagined." Tears welled in Lady Butler's eyes.

Coren returned her mother's embrace. They held for a moment, until Lady Butler pulled away, yet still a slight awkwardness lingered. "Look, now I've gone and wrinkled my gown," Lady Butler muttered as her hands rubbed gently over the moiré silk, removing the imagined crease.

"Mother, you couldn't possibly put a wrinkle in anything." Coren twirled quickly. "So you do like it!" She laughed, a child's laugh, and spun around again. The gown flew up around her legs and twisted in the air, floating for a second before coming down. "I feel just like a princess in it," she said giddily, her voice breaking, causing her to laugh even harder.

"Coren, it is smashing! Perfectly smashing!" Sir Robert trumped in. "But the gown pales next to you, my dear!"

"Oh, do stop," Coren said, not at all meaning it. "You will

embarrass me."

"Not bloody likely, my dear."

"Robert, really!" Lady Butler chided.

Sir Robert blushed as he refilled his glass. "Just stating the obvious," he said sotto voce. He downed the brandy. "Oh dear, look at the time. Shall we go? I can not wait to see the look on the Duke's face when he sees you, my dear." He placed the glass onto the tray and headed for the door, swaying slightly as he grabbed his top hat and cane. "Après vous, Mesdames."

The liverymen had polished the white carriage of brass and glass to such a gleam that Coren felt like royalty just riding in it. Sir Robert had the coachmen dressed in white tails and top hats. White silk tassels adorned the length of the reins to the heads of the pure white Arabian horses. Brass and glass oil lamps had been hung from each corner of the coach, their lights casting an enchanting glow.

Coren stood at the bottom of the steps unmoving, awestruck. "It's just like a fairy tale," she spoke, barely above a whisper.

"It's all for you," Sir Robert said. "I wanted this ball to be perfect."

As the carriage rolled down the lane, pedestrians stopped and waved. Several young boys ran in pursuit, craning to get a look inside.

It was all going so well that Coren wondered if it could possibly continue. It was a great relief that Mother liked the changes to the gown. Coren had fretted about that. If Mother hadn't acquiesced, what would she have done? It would have demanded that she change everything. Her whole plan would have had to be reconsidered. It would have meant … she dismissed the thought. No need to think of it now.

The streets and lanes to Westminster became more crowded with people and coaches as they approached the palace. A warm summer breeze whispered its way through London. It was the perfect night for a ball.

His Royal Highness, Prince Albert Victor, Duke of Clarence would find a wife tonight. At least that was what all of Society was saying. Whether that would happen or not was yet to be determined. Coren had her doubts. There were certainly eligible women in society who would love the chance to marry the man who would be king, if only for the title. But to find one's wife at a ball struck Coren as too much like a . . . circus event. She would try, of course, to get her share of the Duke's attention, to please her mother. But she would, in no uncertain terms, not allow the Duke to select her like a carnival souvenir. If he had even the slightest inclination that Coren could be won in such a manner he had quite a revelation coming. However, she was certainly not above being wooed in the proper manner.

Princess Coren Catherine Elizabeth Butler. She liked the sound of it. But then who wouldn't want Princess . . . or Queen before her name?

Oh, what was she thinking? There would be hundreds of eager, beautiful young ladies at the ball. Surely any chance that Coren had to actually impress the Duke would be infinitesimal. With so many vying for his attention, she didn't even know why she was bothering to attend. Then, she reminded herself, she wasn't going to be vying for his attention.

The carriage began to slow. They had arrived.

The entrance to the Palace was festooned with tiny kerosene lights. A long red brocade carpet luxuriously cascaded from the entrance steps to the ornate gate at street level. Guards in full regalia stood at attention lining the route from the gate to the entrance.

The carriage door swung open and the coachman assisted Sir Robert, as he pried his way unceremoniously through the tight carriage opening. Lady Butler closely followed.

Coren sat still. *What am I doing? This is ridiculous! Impossible!* The consequences of her well thought out plans, suddenly consumed her. "I can't do this. I can't do this. I can't do this!"

"Of course you can, my dear."

Coren's head snapped in Lady Butler's direction. Had she read her thoughts again or had she just spoken aloud?

"It's all possible. I'm sure the Prince will be most charming. Come now. We do not wish to be the last to arrive," Lady Butler admonished. "Your eyes, my dear, give it all away." She finished as if in answer to Coren's unspoken question.

Coren nodded. "You're right, Mother. It is all possible!

Under the gaslight, the glittering diamond dust cast a shimmering spray across Sir Robert's hand as he placed Lady Butler and Coren's invitation along with his own onto the receiving salver. The invitations had been written in gold ink on silk and cotton paper. Diamond dust was sprinkled around the borders and pressed into the purple wax of the royal seal.

The herald's white-gloved hand removed the invitations from the tray and he announced Her Majesty's subjects: "Sir Robert Talbot accompanied by Lady Catherine Eleanor Butler and her daughter ... " His voice caught in his throat as his gaze found Coren standing just behind her mother.

Several others standing by looked up to see what had stopped the herald's pronouncement. They followed his gaze to Coren, their faces frozen in an expression of bewilderment. Conversations sputtered to a stop. Movement ceased as heads turned and eyes lifted to the spot were Coren stood.

The herald, regaining his composure, continued, "...and her daughter Miss Coren Butler."

Coren stepped around her mother and stood at the top of the wide marble staircase, motionless. She observed the people below. *My subjects,* she thought, suppressing a giggle. And then, slowly, as though time would not tick another second until she had made her way to the bottom of the stairs, she took a step forward.

Coren's eyes unhurriedly swept over the grand ballroom. Women, who had only a moment ago thought themselves beautiful, gaped in awe and faded back into the crowd. Men edged forward aching to get a closer look at this ethereal beauty descending the stairs. While each step drew Coren closer to the throng, many of those observing her would swear, at subsequent social gatherings, that she seemed to radiate more and more with each step, until some had to turn away, as if they were afraid they would be blinded by her beauty.

A group of young ladies standing off in a corner of the ballroom began a conversation of contrived gossip in a gesture of defiance, until nearby gentlemen hushed them, their faces slapped with the theatrical hand of shock. They assumed expressions of amazement and indignation at being told to be quiet and to make way for this crimson-haired harlot.

At the last step Coren paused, looking out over the sea of admiring faces. She smiled brilliantly, triumphantly, ensnaring even the most jaded males in the room in her web of glory. Then, she descended the last step and glided across the marble floor. The bodice of silk and lace hugged her figure. Cut daringly low, the neckline revealed more than ample, firm high breasts that tapered to a narrow waist, before flaring out over perfectly proportioned hips. Emerald earrings swayed and dangled from her ears as though a constant soft breeze curled itself around her neck. A necklace of diamonds clustered around emeralds hung just above the straight line of her décolletage, daring any man to follow it with his eyes.

"Well, my dear, you certainly made an entrance." Sir Robert chuckled as he and Lady Butler came up behind Coren.

"Yes, my dear, you most definitely did," Lady Butler added. "And I couldn't be more delighted. It was splendid, simply splendid." Lady Butler tried to remain discreet, but her pride was threatening to overcome her. "Oh, I wish that your father were here to see this."

"I'm sure he will hear about it." Sir Robert chuckled again. Then reminding them, "Come along, we must present ourselves to the Queen."

Queen Victoria was seated on a high-backed, red-velvet chair that stood on a raised dais, near the far end of the ballroom. Two enormous pillars flanked either side of the platform, purple and red draperies hung from them spilling onto the floor around the Queen. Several attendants and guardsmen stood nearby.

Sir Robert stepped forward and bowed. "Your Majesty, may I present Lady Butler, your loyal and faithful servant from the Irish lands and her daughter, Coren."

Lady Butler and Coren curtsied and dipped their heads.

"It is always a pleasure to see you, Sir Robert, and how gallant of you to accompany Lord Butler's wife and daughter." Queen Victoria spoke in studied tones as though she had rehearsed for many years. Then, addressing Lady Butler, "Your husband is a great asset to all of England and we appreciate him and his fine work very much. I am only sorry that his duties for the Crown have kept him away from this event."

"Thank you, Your Majesty. It is our pleasure to be here, and my husband, Lord Butler, sends his warmest greetings." Lady Butler curtsied again. "This, Your Majesty, is my daughter Coren." Lady Butler turned to Coren and lightly grasped her elbow, encouraging her to come slightly forward.

"My dear, your presence in this room is known already," Queen Victoria said, motioning Coren forward with a royal wave.

Coren took a timid step closer.

The Queen studied Coren for a long moment--inspecting her, searching for a weakness, some place soft, where an enemy could gain a foothold. "You are the embodiment of Ireland my dear," the Queen said admiringly, her inspection apparently over. "My grandson, the Duke will be most pleased to meet you."

"Thank you, Your Majesty," Coren said as she again curtsied. "I am also looking forward to meeting the Duke." *It wasn't a lie*, she justified to herself. He could be very useful to her.

"I am sure you are." The Queen's words carried a vague hint of intuition, as though she knew something of Coren's thoughts. "He will be here momentarily, I expect."

Queen Victoria knew too well of her grandson's aversions to social occasions, this ball in particular. She had used every means she possessed, which were considerable, to coax him into attending, and she could still not be certain that he would be here. She eyed them a moment longer. "I hope you will enjoy the ball."

"Thank you, Your Majesty, we will," Sir Robert said, apparently dismissed, as he escorted the ladies away.

Coren sat down on a nearby settee, in an attempt to slow her rapidly beating heart, thankful to be away from the scrutinizing eyes of the Queen. Had the Queen been able to detect something in her eyes? Could she possibly know of her hidden agenda? Coren thought about it for a moment, and then dismissed it, refusing to let doubt slip into her mind.

Coren had thought her plan through. She would attract the attention of the Duke in a way no other woman at the ball could. She would bedazzle him. Blind him. He would want her and only her, forsaking all others who might desire him. What would he be like? Would she want him? Yes, but only for the betterment of Ireland.

As Coren sat, a line of gentlemen began to circle around her, snaking its way through the ballroom. Sir Robert joyfully introduced the many gentlemen, whom he knew were anxiously waiting to get a closer look at this most amazing woman from Ireland. Several of the gentlemen that were paraded before her, Coren considered very attractive, with fine thin bone structures, showing impressive English breeding. They were dressed in finely tailored eveningwear of silk and wool. Coren soon learned that most of the gentlemen at the ball were also in search of wives, just as the women here, were in search of husbands. Should the Duke overlook any of these fine young ladies, there would always be an eager throng of gentlemen waiting in the wings to comfort them. Any of these gentlemen would be a fine prize for any woman.

Any woman, but Coren that is.

As politely as she could, Coren indulged each of the men in innocuous conversations. By the sixteenth or seventeenth admirer she had heard all she cared to: "My, what an enchanting dress." "Oh, how green your eyes are." "Your hair is like fire at sunset." None of these compliments, as pleasant as they were, intrigued her. She had her plan and she was not about to deviate from it.

It was difficult to receive so many compliments in such a short span of time and not, at least, be flattered. Admittedly, Coren was becoming embarrassed. She was not used to such unabashed compliments, especially those that focused on her womanly attributes. She thought, 'they actually like me.' She giggled at her musing, looking into the eyes of a decidedly handsome young man as though he was charming to her.

"You seem to be having a fine time, Coren," Lady Butler spoke when the young man had moved away. The orchestra began the strains of a lilting waltz. "Wouldn't you like to dance with one of the gentlemen? I believe they are playing that Strauss waltz from Die Fledermaus."

"Mother, that opera was so inane. It seemed it would never end. The only reason I stayed awake, was for that wonderful Italian tenor. He was quite comical." She stared at her mother a moment. She knew that look. The game was being played without Coren's cards being dealt to her. So, it seemed Lady Butler had a plan of her own. Coren would have to humor her. "Oh, Mother, of course I would like to dance." *With the Duke*, she thought, then continued, "But I'm a little overwhelmed at the moment." Coren played her ace.

"Don't waste your evening on one man, dear." Lady Butler

looked into her daughter's eyes and smiling, trumped Coren's ace.

Coren cocked her head and smiled back. Mother knew, she realized, then quickly played another card. "I wouldn't think of it," she said watching Lady Butler for a reaction.

There was none.

Lady Butler turned to Sir Robert and his small gathering of friends and fell into conversation with them without missing a beat.

She's good! Coren shook her head amazed by her mother's understatement. Lady Butler had a way of surprising Coren at every turn. *There is much to learn, Mother, and I am the perfect student.*

Her thoughts were disrupted by a voice in the distance. At first it was indistinguishable from the chatter that filled the ballroom. Music from the orchestra floated among the pillars clouding her perception. Then as she strained to hear, the voice wound its way down from the high ceiling, as though someone spoke just loud enough for Coren to hear. She cocked her head and searched for its origin. Again she heard it, reverberating from the arch of the ceiling, followed by giggles of girlish laughter. Coren stood up, eyes skimming over the throng of well-dressed society players. She could clearly hear nearby gentlemen speaking of politics and finances. Ladies gathered about the gentlemen, whispering of trivialities, sipping punch from small crystal cups that bore the royal seal. Several servants rushed by carrying trays of highly polished silver, offering punch and champagne. Another pushed a cart of gold and glass piled high with finger sandwiches, its wheels squeaking on the marble floor.

"He wouldn't dare!" a female voiced shrieked.

Coren heard it clearly, as though someone had been standing next to her, speaking each word directly into her ear. Cautiously, her eyes darted left then right.

"What would the Queen think?" The voice sounded, again feminine but not the same as the first.

And still another countered in haughty tones, "Well, I wouldn't presume to imagine."

It had come from above!

Coren looked up searching the balcony. Her eyes swept from the marble floor to the mammoth pillars up to the ceiling across the dome and down the other side of the room. Her eyes stopped at a purple, brushed velvet settee where five young ladies huddled, animatedly talking.

Coren's eyes narrowed as the vainglorious society ladies spoke. She watched their hands gesticulating and their lips curve into Cheshire grins. Then a second later she heard what they were saying, just as if she were standing in the middle of their conversation. The words were clear. Each nuance in the voices, perfectly understood. The dome of the ballroom ceiling caught the voices, swept them around the arch and delivered them to the other side of the room. Right to where Coren stood.

"I shouldn't think that any of us would possibly have any concerns. The Duke would most certainly not marry an Irish woman." The speaker was tall and very slender, brown ringlets of hair hugged her gaunt and angular face. She was older than the rest, twenty-two or three and dressed in a shimmering, olive satin gown.

And she was speaking of Coren.

"We are all aware of the Duke's desire to marry, but good heavens, Buffie, he's not desperate!" It was Emmeline Cotswold. She and Coren had met as young girls while their mothers visited one another. Emmeline had aged, yet looked identical to when she and Coren had played together. Except for the fact that she was several inches taller, Emmeline had retained her boyish figure and stark countenance.

The "Buffie," Emmeline referred to, was a rather short plump creature with red blotchy cheeks. She was draped in a red velvet gown, reminding one of an overripe strawberry.

The young ladies surrounding Emmeline Cotswold, looking much like Christmas trees, with jewels hanging from their necks and ears, broke into gales of laughter. The laughter echoed round the dome, crashing into Coren sending her spinning into emotional pain and confusion.

She fought back tears of humiliation that welled up inside her. Coren could not believe what she was hearing. How could she have been so naive? She whirled around not wanting to listen to their derision anymore. The thought that the English Duke would not want to marry an Irish woman had never occurred to Coren. Her only thought was that this Irish woman would not want to marry an English Duke!

Coren bit down hard on her inner lip. Humiliation gave way. A void opened and determination rushed in. The pain and shock that had overcome her ebbed. Her composure restored and Irish temper in full flower, Coren turned back to the pack of women on the other side of the room. She would not let anything or anyone ruin her plans.

Their conversation continued. Coren didn't listen. *To the devil with them all!* She inwardly decried. And with fury dripping from her veins, she drew up her long gown and marched directly towards the group. Cutting across the dance floor instead of around it as etiquette dictated, Coren's sights were set. Undaunted by the reveling dancers that obscured her from her prey, she headed straight at them. Those in her path scurried out of her way. She stopped for no one.

A squat, rather plain girl on the edge of the group suddenly gasped, and her eyes ignited in fear as she saw Coren charging toward her. She raised her hands to her mouth tossing the forgotten flute of champagne into her own face and yelped in shock.

"Enid! What on earth...?" Emmeline didn't get to finish the sentence. It was too late. Coren had arrived.

She stopped and stood right beside Emmeline Cotswold.

A strangled gasp gurgled its way out of the mouth of a nearby girl. The others turned to see what it was she was looking at. Then froze. Deep lines of disbelief etched onto their foreheads.

Coren let the tension build, staring at each one in turn. She did not blink. She just stared. "My name is Coren Butler," she said thickening her brogue in an imitation of Jenny. "I was standing on the other side of the room, there, just below the dome and I heard this laughter." Coren gestured to emphasize the point. "When I looked around I saw that it was coming from your circle." Her tone was matter of fact.

The young ladies waited. Some swallowed hard, others coughed. Enid stood frozen, champagne dripping from her nose and lashes. Buffie's mouth hung open while her hands strangled an embroidered napkin.

Coren smiled. "It appeared that you were having such fun, I just had to come over to introduce myself. I hope I'm not intruding, but I simply must know what was so amusing?" Coren fluttered her eyes and put on a most ingratiating face. "Oh, please tell me. I really must know." She turned to Emmeline Cotswold, who had not yet moved, or for that matter, breathed. "Oh, won't you tell me?" Coren said, as she cocked her head slightly.

Emeralds sparkled.

CHAPTER SIX

Within moments, only Emmeline Cotswold remained. Her fellow cohorts had, using one excuse or another, been able to step away. Emmeline's face held a blank expression, as if there was not a single thought behind her eyes. Coren knew better. She recalled the days when she and Emmeline had visited together while their mothers shared tea in the parlor. They were never the best of friends, hardly friends at all. They were two little girls, forced together by their mothers' associations. Emmeline and Coren had made the best of the situation playing in the game room off Emmeline's bedroom. And yet, even then Coren had been aware of a strange jealousy that Emmeline exuded. It was scarcely noticeable at first, but as time went on and the glib cutting remarks Emmeline made trying to be humorous, began to show themselves for what they truly were. *How sad that the petty jealousies of a little girl had grown into the spiteful remarks of the woman she now faced.*, Coren thought, narrowing her gaze to the still blank expression on Emmeline's face.

"Well, it certainly is a blunderful wall," Emmeline blurted out, then quickly untied her tongue. "I mean, a wonderful ball!"

"Yes, it is turning out to be," Coren said, a hint of mockery in her voice. "You don't remember me, do you?"

Emmeline's lips curled downward while she squinted her eyes, scanning them up and down Coren, searching for a clue as to when they could have met. "I'm afraid I don't," she responded, barely concealing her contempt, as she thought, *No one would ever forget meeting this woman.*

Then, smiling hopefully, she asked, "Was it at the Winter Garden Ball? There were so many people in attendance that it is terribly difficult to remember everyone one meets." It was all she could say to avoid being further embarrassed by this Irish woman. Emmeline was sure that they had not met before. Her eyes scanned the crowd, searching for an escape. Seeing an opportunity, she waved to Sir James McCardle, a man she hardly knew, hoping for a response.

Any port in a storm, she thought. But he took no notice of her.

"My name is Coren Butler. My father is Lord Butler. My mother is standing under the potted palm on the other side of the hall speaking with your mother."

Emmeline forced a smile and felt her eyes grow wide. "Oh, my word!" she gasped. "You can not be the same child I once played dolls with!" She could not hide the astonishment that that little girl – who'd barely even been cute – had grown up to be this woman. This woman that every man in the hall wanted. And every other woman envied.

"Well, you have certainly . . ." Emmeline stuttered, breathlessly hunting for the proper word, not wanting to pay Coren a compliment, "you have certainly ... grown." It was the only word she could think of.

"Yes, I have," Coren said smiling. "And you, Emmeline Cotswold, have not changed a bit. I would have recognized you anywhere. "You've always looked so . . . "she paused, choosing just the right adjective, "mature for your age."

Emmeline's jaw dropped. The barb stung. She knew she couldn't possibly look the same as she did at nine. Her thoughts swam randomly through a pool of emotions, immersing her first into disbelief and then plunging her into the reality of how Coren Butler had recognized her, yet she had failed to recognize Coren.

"Well, I did enjoy our little chat, but I really must be on my way." Coren's voice carried with it an intentional sarcasm. "Perhaps we shall see each other again." Coren turned from the stunned Emmeline and glided away.

Several short blasts resounded from the trumpeters outside Westminster, echoing throughout the ballroom. His Royal Highness, Prince Albert Victor, the Duke of Clarence, had arrived. The Royal Coach and procession stopped directly in front of the main gate. The red velvet carpet that stretched from the massive palace doors to the street had been swept clean. Not a footprint or speck of lint could be seen on it. Footmen, trumpeters, butlers and guardsmen lined the walkway from the Royal Coach to the top of the stairs just inside the main entrance.

The trumpets' fanfare sounded for a second time, startling a flock of pigeons from their roost in the eaves of the roof.

Then a third fanfare was played, with long, brassy notes ringing out high and pure. The orchestra stopped in the middle of, yet another, Strauss waltz. Ladies and gentlemen came to an awkward halt on the dance floor, politely thanked one another and stepped away to join the groups forming in anticipation of the Prince's arrival. Men and women rushed to form a corridor at the bottom of the stairway.

Losing all sense of decorum, the young, bright, eager, and beautiful, women who dreamed of becoming the Prince's bride, pushed their way to the forefront. Now, at every step along the path the Prince would take, he would see nothing but dress-shop tableaux of nubile femininity. Gowns of every hue and fabric, from rich silk to spun cotton, formed the wall of this border. Every woman was smiling and posing. Some, less attractive than others, fanned themselves with ornate paper fans, in hopes that they would catch the eye of the young prince. Every woman in the ballroom took her place in the serried ranks.

Every woman.

Every woman, but one.

Coren stood alone peering from behind a pillar that occupied a corner of the ballroom. She had a completely different strategy from all the other young women in attendance. Coren's plan was to quietly wait in the wings, and then, after the others had done all they could to impress the Prince, make her simple but grand entrance.

As she surveyed the young ladies, she was reminded of the fillies jockeying for position at the Sweepstakes, each one trying to nose her way to the forefront and into the winner's circle where she would be "crowned" by the Prince himself. Coren watched with amusement as one by one the young ladies struck a pose that each was sure would impress. Heads held high, cleavage on display, their necks craned for that first glimpse of the Prince.

"Bloody hell!" Coren bit her lip to keep from shouting, as it dawned on her that she had never seen the Prince. She thought for a moment, trying to remember if the Prince had ever made a visit to Ireland. No. Coren could not recall one. So how would she know what this most eligible man looked like? Why had this not occurred to her? It irritated her that she could have gone to the trouble and time to alter her gown and come to England for this ball to entice a man without even knowing what he looked like. Suppose he was a . . . hunchback! Didn't that run in his family? Or perhaps he was like the doctor in a book she wasn't supposed to read but had anyway . . . a Jekyll and Hyde? It was a nagging question that

bothered her, perhaps more than it should. She realized that she had never thought of him as anything but a handsome prince. Coren simply never pictured anything less than a perfect man. All the books she had read growing up always had a handsome prince. Even the ugly frog had turned into a prince that had bedazzled the princess. Was there such a thing as an ugly prince? What a naive fool she had been! And now it was too late. He would be coming down the same long row of stairs that she had made her entrance on just hours ago. Would he cause the same stir that she had? She would soon know.

A final blast from the trumpets and he appeared at the top of the stairs. "Make way for His Royal Highness, Prince Albert Victor, the Duke of Clarence."

Coren strained to get a clear view of him. The column that hid her from the view of the others also obstructed her line of sight to the Prince. But what she saw pleased her. Very much. Prince Albert was dressed in the white formal attire of the Royal Cavalry. A sword in a bejeweled scabbard hung from his waist. Medals pinned to his jacket lined the left side of his wide, solid chest. A gold sash stretched from his broad shoulders, down to narrow hips, dangling just above powerful, long legs. Even under the layers of the uniform his finely muscled body seemed to ripple as he moved.

Prince Albert strode down the stairs barely casting a glance at the young ladies lining his way. He headed directly to the Queen. "I thank you, Your Majesty, for this ball in my honor. And may I say that there are a great many, beautiful young ladies here, one of which I am sure would make the Crown happy as my bride."

Queen Victoria looked at him archly. "The Crown does not need to be happy. My grandson does. We are pleased that you have found time, in what must be a very busy schedule, to be here for us."

"Your Majesty must forgive me for my untimeliness, as I was predisposed." Prince Albert bowed slightly.

Queen Victoria smiled, shaking her head. "You are forgiven, Eddy. However, you must absolve yourself to the young ladies here. It is their time you have wasted. I expect that you will find the opportunity to dance with each and every one of them." Her eyes widened awaiting his response.

"That would be impossible Your . . ." He trailed off as he took note of the formidable look on his grandmother's face.

She fanned herself slowly, awaiting the correct response.

"It will be my pleasure to dance with as many ladies as possible, Your Majesty."

"Humph! Indeed it shall," Queen Victoria said, sending a disdainful look in her grandson's direction.

Albert had been instructed on every manner of royal etiquette. Refusing the Queen was high on the list of what not to do. And after their prior meeting on the subject of his attendance, he decided acceptance of this less than dubious task was the better part of valor. He was well known in Society for his convictions and for voicing those convictions, whether they agreed with the Crown or not. Albert's father, Prince Edward stood directly in line to the throne. Although he agreed with his son on many issues, he knew when and when not to voice his opinions. Many times Edward had to soothe the bruised ego of a Member of Parliament or an elder Earl who had had his feathers ruffled by the young Prince.

From her hidden corner Coren watched as Prince Albert, Duke of Clarence played out his hand with the Queen. She liked what she saw, a feisty, well-built young man and ... handsome. Her worries of a moment ago melted away as her eyes followed him. He left the Queen and made his way to the line of available young ladies awaiting him. Mothers and escorts stood by the sides of each maiden as they were introduced to the Prince. He took the hand of each and held it lightly, his attendants inscribing every name to a page in a small book as they proceeded down the line.

Coren could now see him clearly. She smiled at the small, thin mustache that adorned his upper lip. His nose was narrow and aristocratic, not at all out of place with his wide, dark eyes, which were accented by arched eyebrows, giving him an inquisitive look. Thick, black hair swirled around his ears and fell onto his forehead. His face was smooth, a bit boyish with a hint of danger just behind eyes--the look of a man one wanted to make love to. Coren startled herself at the thought. *Where had that come from*? She questioned herself and felt the warmth in her cheeks.

"Coren Butler!" The voice boomed from behind her.

Coren spun around in fright, letting out a loud gasp as she did. "Mother! You scared me half to death." Her heart pounded. "Whatever are you trying to do?"

"Whatever are you trying to do?" Lady Butler shot back.

"Well, I was just standing here..." What was she doing? Her brow wrinkled as she tried to explain to herself what she was doing. She had a plan, a well-thought-out plan, and here she was watching this man, this Prince, and daydreaming about him: his swaggering walk, his face, his arms strong enough to pull her to him and hold her there, a muscled form whose weight she longed to feel, strong, hard legs that could lock around her own, squeezing tight ... That was not in the plan!

"Coren? I'm waiting for an answer." Lady Butler shook her head in exasperation.

"So am I, Mother," Coren said, confusedly. She had slipped again. It happened so quietly, so quickly. She shivered at the thought of him. Spasms and tingles, which were at once painful and pleasing, coursed through her. She swore silently that she would not succumb to him. She closed her eyes tightly, locking out the sight of him. But even the mere thought of him sent her spiraling into a chasm of emotions. Both fear and desire rose up and pulled at her, twisting her until she was lost, not knowing if she should fear him or love him.

In the distance a faint voice called out, "Coren? Coren?" Her mother's tone was cautious.

Coren opened her eyes slowly. "Coren, are you feeling all right?" Lady Butler said, the strain of a moment ago easing in her voice.

"Yes, Mother. I'm fine," she replied a little too quickly. "I'm fine."

She wasn't fine.

She was falling in love.

CHAPTER SEVEN

"You are avoiding me." A hand reached out lightly grasping Coren's hand with just enough force to bring her to attention.

"Your Highness!" she gasped, looking up into cobalt blue eyes.

The commotion her mother had brought to Coren's hiding place behind the pillar had attracted the Prince's attention and given Coren away. *Thank you, Mother*! The thought had an edge to it. She glanced to her Mother who, conveniently, had stepped to the side.

Coren tried to jerk her hand out of the Prince's hand. He held tight. She could feel the tingle of his warmth pulsating from his fingertips up her arm, and smell the masculine scent of bayberry. *Thank you, Mother*! This time the thought was filled with true thankfulness. A wave of embarrassment washed over her, and she knew her face must certainly match the hue of her crimson hair.

Prince Albert's fingers gently played on her hand. Surely he must know what she was thinking! A look of awareness, with a hint of amusement, exuded from his face - a face that bore the dark shadows of a beard, defining his jaw line and cheekbones to perfection.

Coren awkwardly flattened the silk and lace gown with the palm of her free hand, then brushed back her hair and tried in vain to think of something intelligent to say.

"It is not very often that I must search behind a column in the farthest corner of the room to find the loveliest woman at the ball." He smiled.

Coren melted. What had happened to her? Her plans? They were completely undone. And he had done it with just one smile. How dare he? Who did he think he was?

"Well, Your Highness," Coren said sweetly. "I am not like the others here. I do not stand in line to be chosen, like a horse at auction." She smiled at him, quite satisfied. "You must have many young ladies waiting for you." Coren curtsied, and turned to walk away.

He tightened his grip on her hand. "Let them wait."

Coren pulled herself up quickly. She was not prepared for this Prince. Why couldn't he be fat or old or ugly, instead of what he was? Perfect. "Oh, I'm afraid I could not agree to letting them wait. You had best be off now."

"A maiden who dismisses a Prince!" He laughed loudly, and those around them, who were not already staring, turned their heads to look. "You are certainly," he paused unsure of the right choice of words, "different from any woman I have ever met."

"Perhaps you have not met any Irish women before?" she said, intending to sting, as well as to extract information.

"You are quite right," he said, as he lowered his eyes following the neckline of her gown to her breasts. "I have met many ladies from Ireland, but now I see that you are the only Irish woman I have ever laid eyes upon." His eyes still focused on her pronounced décolletage.

She brought her free hand to her necklace and fingered it provocatively. "You are very kind, Your Highness, and you may be able to stay and chat, but I must be off. I did promise dances to so many of the gentlemen here." She pulled her hand from his, letting it slip slowly between his fingers, lingering as long as she could.

Albert smiled, and closed his hand around the last of her

fingers. "You can not get away from me that easily," he whispered softly.

Coren leaned in close to hear him. Bayberry and cobalt pools. She pulled back. Albert held her fingers a moment longer, before releasing them.

"Well then, I should not like to keep you from your duties," Albert spoke, with a definite emphasis on the last word, breaking the trance they had fallen into. "The gentlemen you have promised dances to are surely waiting." He turned to Lady Butler, who had remained uncharacteristically silent during their intercourse.

"Good evening." Bowing slightly, he departed.

Coren watched, slightly stunned, as the Prince strode forward, took the arm of Emmeline Cotswold and proceeded onto the dance floor. A bolt of jealousy surged through her. Of all the women in this great ballroom he had picked Emmeline Cotswold to dance with first!

In truth, I was chosen first. But I refused him.

She felt better for a moment and then the sight of Emmeline Cotswold laughing in the Prince's arms brought back the pang of jealousy. Emmeline Cotswold stood in the way of the independence of Ireland. Emmeline Cotswold was destroying the vision of an Irish woman to help her fellow Irishmen to independence. Emmeline Cotswold was dancing with the man who could bring about the change. Emmeline Cotswold was laughing carelessly while Coren stood alone in the corner of the room. Emmeline Cotswold had mocked Coren from a distance. And Emmeline Cotswold was now whispering in the ear of the man that Coren loved!

"I will not stand for this!" Coren said through gritted teeth. "Mother, we must leave!" Coren stormed off, crossing directly into the path of the Prince and his dancing partner, Emmeline Cotswold.

Coren felt his gaze burn. She knew he was staring at her, demanding that she turn around and look into those infuriating cobalt pools. She would not. Coren quickened her pace. Hauling up her dress, she climbed the stairs two at a time, causing quite the spectacle. When she had reached the top landing of the staircase, she stopped, waiting for Sir Talbot and Lady Butler to catch up with her.

"Wait. Please wait a moment!"

Coren turned around expecting Sir Talbot. It was not. His Royal Highness, Prince Albert Victor, Duke of Clarence stood only inches from her.

Breathing heavily from his quick climb of the stairs, he leaned over slightly trying to ease the stitch in his side. "You see," he said, gasping for breath. "I am already aching for you." Albert chuckled at his own pun.

"I do not find this, or anything you are doing, to be amusing, Your Highness." Coren crossed her arms, holding them tightly to her body, afraid that they would not obey her and reach out for him. "I am sorry, but we are leaving."

"What is it that I have done to offend you?" His breathing slowed as he caught his breath. She wanted to believe that he did not know. She wanted to believe that he was innocent of his doings. She wanted to believe that he loved her. "You don't know?"

Albert moved in closer to her. She could feel the heat radiating from his body. She could smell the bayberry mixed with his musky sweat from his sprint up the long staircase. Then she felt the moist warmth of his breath on her cheek. "I truly do not know, my Princess." Genuine pain filled his voice.

She drifted down dizzily deep into cobalt pools. "Oh! Your Highness! I am sorry for your trouble," Coren said, genuinely apologetic.

He burst out with laughter and grabbed her around the waist, spinning her in a tight circle on the landing, coming dangerously close to the stairs. "You are the kind of trouble I have been waiting for!"

Coren screamed with fear of falling head over heals down the stairs and with childish delight, as she hugged the Prince's neck; decorum and etiquette now completely forgotten by the both of them.

She had her Prince.

"May I have the next dance?" Albert raised his eyebrows in a moment of doubt.

"This and every other," Coren assured him.

Albert took her hand in his and held it tightly. Together they descended the stairs, passing Sir Talbot and Lady Butler on the way.

"Coren, dear? I thought you wanted to leave?" Lady Butler uttered as her daughter stepped quickly by.

"Don't be silly, Mother. The ball has just begun."

Emeralds sparkled in ecstasy.

They danced in a dream, as if out of a fairy tale. Prince Albert held Coren lightly at arms length as they moved in time to the rhythm of the music. As the waltz played on, he swept her across the floor ... or perhaps above the floor. She was floating in an effortless glide that lifted her higher and higher. Every step brought on a fury of emotions. Her senses reeled. And yet the two barely touched. Faces and colors spun by in a collage of blurred images. Yet Coren could only see one face clearly.

His.

She lost herself in those eyes, cobalt pools swirling with the reflection of the passing room. Faint flickers of the flames from the gas lamps sparkled in eyes that grew darker with passion, like black diamonds.

He spoke not a word, and yet Coren clearly heard him, "I love you." Those words alone made up the lyrics to the songs she heard. No matter what the tempo, the words were the same.

Coren swayed, lost in a hundred thoughts, a thousand

feelings and a million dreams. Her Prince had come and she wanted him more with every downbeat of the music.

Slowly he drew her upright hand down until it was in close to his body, desperate to close the gap between them. His left hand found the small of her back and pulled her in tight. An explosion of mind-numbing shock waves collided in her as her breasts molded to his powerful chest. His heat penetrated her silk and lace gown, sizzling through the garment.

She longed to tear the garment from her body.

Her head spun.

Her body ached.

Her lips yearned for his.

They danced.

They dreamed.

They made love in her thoughts.

Albert heard those same three words in his mind, "I love you," spoken with the deep, undying passion that he had only read about. Yet her lips never moved. Only her eyes, sparkling emeralds that hypnotized him. He saw only her. There could be no other. He never knew what love was until this moment. It was not the spark that he had thought it would be. Nor was it the simple stirring in his loins that he presumed it to be. It was every sight and sound that man had ever witnessed coming together at once. It was overwhelming and frightening. And now that he had found it, he would never let it go.

They never noticed that the orchestra had stopped playing.

CHAPTER EIGHT

"Jenny, you would not have believed it!" Coren threw herself onto the down-filled bed sinking into the soft, silk-covered pillows, burying her face in them. She kicked her legs like a gleeful child and let out a muffled scream of excitement.

Och, the girl will drive me crazy, Jenny thought, quickly closing the door to muffle Coren's squealing and bustled over to the bed, as morning sunlight eked through the slots in the shutters that covered the windows, casting stripes of light across the floor. It was as though a ladder had been left leading to the window and the sky above. Small specks of dust floated through the sunlight and revealed themselves for a brief moment, and then disappeared into the darkness.

"Well, come on then, tell us what happened!" Jenny begged and plopped down hard next to Coren on the bed.

"Oh Jenny, I wish you had been there! It was the best night of my life!" Coren withdrew the green ribbon from her hair, letting the crimson tide flow. "Everything about the night was enchanted!"

"Was he handsome?" Jenny leaned forward in anticipation.

"Oh, yes! And strong! And he could dance to perfection! It was like a dream." She looked around, lost in some distant thought for a moment. "Jenny, do you think it was a dream. Maybe it didn't happen the way I remember. Maybe he was never really there. Maybe I was never there!"

"Of course you were there! Don't be silly, now." Jenny went to the window and threw open the shutters covering them, flooding the room with warmth and sunshine. "There now, that's better."

Coren turned from the light. A tear found its way from the corner of her eye and slipped slowly down her cheek.

Jenny moved back to the bed, put her arms around her charge, and held her tightly. "I think you're just a wee bit in love."

"I am in love, Jenny. And it scares me so!"

"Child, you don't need to be frightened," Jenny said, remembering the feeling of being in love all too well. Her own heart had been broken by a man she, too, had dreamed about. He had been her prince. Although, he was not a real Prince as Coren's was, he was everything that she could possibly want in a man. Jenny understood Coren's fears and she hoped that they, unlike hers, would never come true.

"What do I do, Jenny? How do I act?" Coren said, as she turned to face her maid. "I have so many questions. I don't know where to begin."

"Well, darlin', what did you feel when you first saw him?"

"That's just it. I couldn't really see his face very clearly, but he stood there at the top of the staircase and looked down at all of us as though he was searching from his perch through a prized herd of sheep for one special lamb, and I thought, why, you pompous ass!"

Jenny squeaked. "You didn't!"

"I did. And he was." Coren rolled over on the bed, pulling Jenny down with her and burst into laughter. "I wanted to walk up to him and tell him what I thought."

"No!" Jenny gasped.

"Good evening, Your Highness. It is a pleasure to make your acquaintance. And my, aren't you looking the perfect pompous ass this evening."

Jenny slapped her hand on the bed. "Tell me more!"

"He strolled down the stairs, strutting, posing, and passing by the long line of young ladies who had gathered to meet him." Coren rose from the bed and strode through the room in exaggerated mockery of Prince Albert's movements.

"Were you the first or the last in line?" Jenny interrupted, as she struggled up from the bed. "Let me see. Begorrah! If I know you, you were the last in line. That's it. I'm sure you were the last one that he laid eyes on."

"Don't be silly. I wasn't standing anywhere in that line."

"Where were you, then?" Jenny's eyes grew wider.

"I was resting under the potted palms." Coren spoke as if anyone with the least bit of dignity would have done the same. "Oh, Jenny, you can not possibly think that I was going to stand in that long line, waiting to meet this Prince?"

"I'm sorry, miss. But I would have done anything to stand in that long line."

"Well, that is where we are different, Jenny. I would never wait to be viewed like a prized filly at a derby."

"If the stud who was doing the viewing was a prince, I'd wait."

"Jenny! That is vulgar! I can not believe my ears."

"I'm sorry, miss." Jenny turned away from Coren. "But it's true just the same."

Coren let out a small scream, startling Jenny, and then fell back on the bed in a fit of laughter.

"Och, miss. I thought I'd said something awful!"

"You did," Coren said in between bouts of laughter. "Awfully true!"

Jenny joined in, adding her high-pitched laugh, bobbing and holding her ample sides as she did. "Awfully true, awfully true," she kept repeating. And their laughter swelled.

A knock at the door brought them both up quickly.

Coren thought, *please don't be Mother.*

"Coren? Coren?" Lady Butler's voice had a slight hint of concern. "Coren, whatever is going on in there?"

Jenny jumped up, straightened her dress, and crossed to

the door as she tried to compose herself. "Coming, Lady Butler," Jenny said, stifling yet another giggle. Jenny pulled the door open and curtsied to Lady Butler, who passed by her without so much as a glance.

"Now, Coren, what have you been up to?" Lady Butler looked around the room, inspecting it. "I have been standing on the other side of that door knocking and knocking. Why I believe I have bruised my hand on that door." She paused for a moment as she inspected her hand. "You have been making such a commotion in here, just like a couple of school girls. It's not proper!" Lady Butler bit the words off, making her point.

"I'm sorry, Mother. I was just explaining to Jenny what a wonderful evening I had last night at the Prince's ball," Coren said, then quickly added, "Here, let me see your hand."

"You are not going to make amends by pretending to have concern over my bruised hand." Lady Butler said, seeing through Coren's obvious attempt at diversion.

Her mother definitely knew her too well. How could she ever get the upper hand?

"I came all the way up here to give you a message," her mother continued. "And now, I may carry a scar to remind me of it the rest of my life."

Coren knew she was taking advantage of a situation and playing it for all it's worth.

"Mother, I am sorry that we didn't hear you." Coren turned her Mother's hand over slowly, looking for some sign of a bruise. "Shall I have Jenny bring a bowl of cold water and liniment for your hand?" Coren asked, not seeing any sign of injury.

"No. Let me suffer." Lady Butler pulled her hand from Coren's inspection. "I shall be fine." She stepped to the door ready to make her grand exit.

"By the by," Lady Butler paused, her back to her eager listeners, letting the anticipation build, Coren assumed. "His Royal Highness, Prince Albert Victor, Duke of Clarence..." she paused once again, as she dramatically perused the imagined bruising of her hand.

"What, Mother? What?" Coren could not conceal her exasperation.

"Yes, I do think my hand will be fine," Lady Butler intoned, as she slowly maneuvered her fingers.

"Lady Butler, please," Jenny interjected, totally forgetting her station.

Lady Butler arched an eyebrow at her daughter's maid, as Jenny's hand flew to cover her mouth.

"Forgive me, my Lady," Jenny muffled as she bowed her head.

"As I was saying," Lady Butler turned to face Coren, "the Prince has called upon you."

Coren stood stunned. She did not blink. She could not breathe.

"His Royal Highness would like your company at the Palace in two days time," Lady Butler announced.

He would like your company at the Palace.

Coren sighed with relief. It hadn't been a dream. For a moment she had lost herself to fear. The fear that he would not want to see her again.

Coren tried to replay every moment of the ball in her mind. She tried to see each face and every expression. She strained to hear the whispers that filled the ballroom. It was a glorious night. Coren's eyes stung with tears waiting to overflow. She wanted to cry. And after her Mother had finished the next statement she would.

"The Queen is having a dinner reception to meet all the young ladies that His Highness has expressed an interest in. I, of course, responded that you would be there." Lady Butler stepped into the long hallway that led from Coren's suite of rooms.

"Wait, Mother ... "Coren began and then froze.

A long pause followed. Both Lady Butler and Jenny looked at Coren, then at each other, not sure what to do.

Coren's face held a blank expression. Her eyes stared

straight out, not seeing.

Jenny reached out a hand and touched Coren's are. "Miss? Miss Coren, what is it?"

Coren turned to Jenny. She had heard her Mother's words and now they were turning over in her mind, spinning a painful web that clouded over the memories of the night before. Now, once again, she was unsure.

"Mother? You said the Queen is having a reception?" Coren spoke slowly, deliberately.

"Yes, dear, she is," Lady Butler said.

"And for whom?"

Lady Butler's face creased as she wrinkled up her forehead. "As I said, for all the young ladies . . . "She stopped, studying her daughter's face. The realization appeared on her face. "Oh, Coren!" Lady Butler cried. "I'm sorry, dear."

"There are many young ladies from the ball that the Prince has invited?" Coren asked with no small amount of trepidation in her voice.

"I only assume there are." Lady Butler stepped back into the room. "My dear child. The Prince is a very important man, and if he is to find a lady suitable as his bride, he must meet with many." She pulled her daughter in close to her. "One can not expect to be the only one invited."

"Oh Mother!" Coren fell into her Mother's embrace and let the tears flow. "I thought that after last night there would be only one." She sobbed. "How foolish of me to let this man into my heart and not expect him to break it."

"Coren, you have only just met the Prince. These things take time."

"No, Mother! Not this time." Coren pulled away. "I love him, Mother. I loved him from the moment he stood at the top of those stairs."

"Hmph," Jenny interjected.

Coren gave her maid a withering glare and rushed on. "He looked down at a sea of young ladies waiting for him. But I know, Mother. I know he saw only me." Coren looked out the window at the green rolling hills that surrounded High Gate Hall and was reminded of her peahen that strolled the gardens at Butler House. "I shall not be attending this reception."

"Coren, you must! I have sent word to the Queen that you would be there," concern apparent in her voice.

Coren turned from the window, her silhouette black against the light of the sun. "We will have to send word to the Queen that there has been a setback ... no, a sudden change in our plans. I must pack immediately! Mother! I'm going back to Ireland!"

"Coren, you could at least give him a chance." Lady Butler attempted to reason.

"Jenny, get my trunk. I don't want to be here a moment longer than I have to be!" Coren snapped the orders.

"Yes, miss," Jenny said, begrudgingly, mumbling something about being daft as she shuffled off to the dressing room.

"Coren, are you sure about this?" Lady Butler asked, her doubt and oppostion now becoming obvious.

"Yes, Mother. I am very sure. I will not be part of this parade of hopefuls for the Prince's attentions. I am Irish, Mother. I am not like these English maidens, ready to line up and be chosen. If His Royal Highness Prince Albert Victor, Duke of Clarence wants to have dinner with me, he will have to come to Ireland to ask me. I will not wait here for him!"

Emeralds flashed with fury.

CHAPTER NINE

Coren stood at her window, transfixed, her eyes vacant. She had no idea how long she had been standing there, staring, thinking of nothing, and feeling empty. It was only the movement of the sun, now high above her, which led her to believe she had been here at the window of her High Gate Hall rooms, for quite some time. Her gaze slowly began to focus. What must she do?

Smoke billowed upwards from the tall stacks in the distance. It was only a few short days ago that Coren stood peering from this same window overlooking the gardens of High Gate Hall. The bustling city of London, then as now, stood in the distance. She looked beyond at a strangely darkened area. That was the place she had overheard her uncle, Sir Talbot, speaking about to her mother. Whitechapel. That was it. What an odd name for such a dark and gloomy district, she thought.

The smoke filled the cold wet sky. The sun struggled to break through the smoke and ash to light upon the Earth. Like fingers of warmth, it would touch on some of the lucky faces of that morbid part of the great city. Its light, however, would reveal the dirt and despair that existed there, sights Coren had a gnawing desire to see, sounds she ached to hear, smells she had wondered about. The desperation and the struggle of those poor souls, whose lives had sadly been brought to this state, possessed a strange allure for Coren.

Coren sighed now as she thought of her own predicament. She had seen her own fairy tale go up in smoke, climbing skyward along with the noxious billows from those looming towers. Last night's dream had become morning's nightmare.

Coren had spoken to no one since this morning's revelation about the Prince and all the young ladies he was interested in. Lady Butler had said it so innocently, as though it didn't matter, as though everyone expected there would be hundreds of ladies that the Prince held an interest in. Coren rationalized, perhaps not hundreds, but several at least! And several were many more than Coren could allow. Did it come as a shock only to Coren? The thought of it sickened her. Her stomach rolled and tossed so much, that she thought she would dare not eat that entire day.

She turned from the window, dabbing at her eyes with a damp hand cloth. She had cried herself dry throughout the morning. *Jenny, dear Jenny,* Coren thought of her friend who had of course, tried to comfort her, but Coren spoke no words, only tears. As hard as Jenny had tried, there was little she, or anyone, excepting His Royal Highness, Prince Albert Victor, Duke of Clarence, could do.

Now, after replaying the events of the previous night, she had regained some of her lost composure. Perhaps, it was all for the best. Coren bit down hard on her lip as that thought played out. Her mind was now set on going back to Ireland to finish the plans she had made. There would be changes, of course. She would return to her homeland, not as a princess filled with dreams, but as a woman resigned to the realities of her life. She had not lost. She had learned. She would go back to Ireland and win the hearts of many. She would join in their struggle and make it her own. She was a winner, even when winning meant losing the man she had fallen in love with. Whether as Princess Coren, or simply as Coren Butler, she would still be able to be a powerful force in achieving independence for her people. Now, she would be unencumbered by a Prince who could not make up his mind. *I will not be laden down by his indecision,* Coren thought.

"Perhaps then, it is all for the best," she said with renewed determination in her voice.

As these great thoughts began to unfold in her mind, Coren moved to the bureau and hurriedly began yanking handfuls of clothes from the drawers, tossing them to the bed. Then doubt found a niche and caused her to stop. Reality took over. What did she really know of life's dangers? What did she know of the struggles that the poor common man wrestled with every day of his life? Looking to the window, she found that the answers were there. The clouds of dark ash writhed on unseen currents of air, beckoning her to come and learn the secrets hidden beneath them.

A whisper of wind sighed with a hushed voice. *"Come. Discover for yourself what man's curse upon himself and his brethren is. See what life is like for those who never dream of marrying a Prince, who dream instead of a single loaf of bread and a day without hardship. Come. Walk the streets where blood flows freely and only the lucky survive the night. Enter the houses if you dare, where rodent and man sleep side by side. Come. Come and be my bride."*

Chills filled her, as though a cold gust of air had smacked into her with the full gusto of an ocean storm. Her legs grew weak and threatened to buckle under her. Her breath caught in excitement. Anticipation rose and swelled in her stomach, replacing the bitter taste of disappointment she had eaten this morning.

She was driven anew.

Fear and curiosity make great bedfellows.

The next ferry from the coast of England to the emerald shores of Ireland would not make its crossing until three days from now. Coren was stuck here in this city, at least for three more days. Three days. Coren's eyes fired with determination. Two days of which could be put to good use. If she couldn't be in her beloved Ireland, helping those in desperate straits there, she could certainly find a way to be of aid to the destitute here. And if it meant walking in the footsteps of despair, and following the trail of smoke and ash to Whitechapel, so be it. Coren avowed, she would find some good to do there! After all, if she could cross the sea, she could cross the city.

Coren spun around. "Jenny! Jenny! I must speak to you at once! She opened the door to the dressing suite and burst in. "Jenny? Where the devil are you?"

"I'm here, miss," Jenny said, tugging at the large trunk she had just packed.

"Jenny! Please stop that now. I need your help."

"By all that's holy! What are you all in a tether about?" Jenny released her grip on the trunk, dropping it unceremoniously to the floor.

Coren's lips slowly spread into a sly smile. She raised an eyebrow and cocked her head slightly to the side.

Jenny looked warily into her charge's eyes. "Ah, miss. You're determined to get me beheaded yet!"

Emeralds sparkled.

CHAPTER TEN

"Whitechapel." Coren barked out the order to the driver, perhaps a bit more aggressively than she should have. It was all she could do to keep her nerve up. She furrowed her brow, mulling over the decision to involve Jenny in another of her missions. She was not about to go to Whitechapel alone. And, she reasoned, who else could she possibly ask to accompany her? Jenny was the only choice. Thus, Jenny now sat beside her in the hansom cab, shielding her face under an old wrap that she had brought along to use as a disguise.

"Miss? I begs your pard'n," the cabby's cockney baritone rumbled. He hesitated before adding, "Whitechapel's no' a place fer young ladies of means. You should 'ave an escort."

Coren could see that the driver spoke out of concern for her. It was the fatherly tone in his voice that caused her to waver in her drive to see the underbelly of this great city. What would her own father think of this excursion? How would he react at the thought of his one and only daughter venturing into the depths of misery and depredation? *I'm being melodramatic*, she decided, and quickly pushed the thoughts from her mind.

"If you are not willing, driver ... " she paused to let the threat sink in, "I am quite certain there are any number of other cabbies who would be more than happy to take us."

The driver didn't speak. Instead he shook his head slightly, as if trying to weigh the cost of his conscience against the profit of the fare.

"Well, driver? Should we step out of the cab?" Coren stared at him, waiting for his response.

With a sudden jerk, the cab pulled forward as the driver slapped the reins on the back of the horse.

"We'll take that as no," Coren snapped at the driver. If he had heard her, he didn't let on. As the hypnotic sound of the clip-clopping hooves droned on, Coren became introspective. This was something she had to do, to gain a knowledge that she must possess. Her father would understand. After all, wasn't he just as driven in his ambition for Irish independence? She knew he would go to any lengths, short of violence, to achieve his goal and Sir Robert was right there beside him in every way, just as her dear Jenny was with her. Well, Jenny was perhaps, not quite right there beside her in the same way as Sir Robert. Jenny had seemed more reluctant of late to join in on Coren's ventures to give aid. *Perhaps, Jenny is getting old,* she thought. *Or perhaps I'm getting too headstrong,* she considered. She hadn't even listened to a word Jenny had said in admonishment and caution. Jenny agreed wholeheartedly with Coren's desire for Irish independence and she, too, would do whatever was necessary to achieve it. Coren knew this. And to this effort, here Jenny was, sitting beside her bundled up in an old-rag disguise. Jenny was there to help those in need, English or Irish, just as Coren was. *Ah, Jenny, you're not old, just concerned and devoted as the day is long.* Coren squeezed Jenny's hand.

Jenny returned a suspicious glare.

The streets of London were crowded that morning. Household servants scurried about from one shop to the next, buying, while vendors crisscrossed their paths, selling. The chants of street vendors hawking their wares: "Ripe, strawberries, ripe! Violets, fresh violets! Knives, sharp knives!" created a cacophonous atmosphere that was at once exciting, and nearly overwhelming.

Men dressed in fine coats and top hats strolled easily up to The Royal Exchange. Clerks darted from the Bank of England, sprinting down the square past The Poultry building and King William Street, delivering notes and drafts to the Safe Bank.

Saint Peter's Cathedral scented the June morning air with the aroma of incense and myrrh. The hansom rolled past Saint Peter's up Cornhill Street. There, buildings began to show the wear of age and neglect and the air took on the stench of hides being tanned as they passed The Leather Market.

Both Coren and Jenny sat spellbound.

Slowly, they rolled up Leadenhall Street. At Aldgate, the cab turned left. Screams of terrified sheep, pigs and cattle assaulted them as they made their way toward Whitechapel Road. Boys crowded the doorways of small shops, watching with grotesque delight, while animals were dragged inside, their hind legs kicking hopelessly at the dogs and men who clawed at them. Blood and urine flowed freely into the street and clogged the open gutters, where homeless dogs lapped at the still warm pools puddled there. Men, wearing what Coren guessed must surely be their best, stepped gingerly around the slippery, reddened rocks.

Jenny watched in disgust, as a group of children gathered entrails that a butcher had flung at them in a gruesome game of dodgeball. With shouts of glee, the children ran off down shadowy streets to deliver the goods to their tired and desperate mothers, who would make a feast from these scraps.

The stench of death was overwhelming. Coren's face blanched to a pure white. "Shouldn't we turn back, miss?" Jenny asked, hope evident in her voice.

Coren could only shake her head no.

Onward, up Whitechapel they rode. Passing women hurled jeers at the ladies, and for a moment Coren thought it would be best to turn back. But the sight of the children, hundreds of children clogging the street outside of the uninhabitable lodges that lined the sidewalks and alleys, kept her going.

The children crowded at them from every direction. "Please give us a ha'penny, miss." Sad and empty faces became a blur as the cab bounced over the roughly laid road, continuing their journey.

At George Street they came to a sudden halt. After a moment, Coren leaned forward to get a closer look.

"Driver? What seems to be the difficulty?"

"Sorry, miss, but the police won' le' us pass." The driver's voice carried a faint hint of relief.

"Why?" Coren asked with frustration.

"Can' tell ya, miss." The driver tied the reins to the hand brake and jumped from the cab. "I'll take's a look."

"You cannot mean to leave us here," Jenny snapped at him, fear rising in her voice.

"Don' worry, miss." Sarcasm seeped into his words. "I'll be close by."

"Driver! I demand that you stay in this cab." Jenny's fear had risen up and now controlled her. She stood to emphasize the point. "Driver? Did you hear me?"

He apparently did not, or else he chose to ignore her as he took a few steps away from the cab.

"Constable!" Jenny shouted to an enormous policeman standing nearby. She raised her voice above the laughter and mock screams of the people who had gathered to vie for the chance to pick a pocket or purse.

The driver returned as the constable approached. "Ladies, this isn't a place for the likes of you," the constable said, horror evident on his pale face. "It would be best if you went back to the many safer streets."

Coren's curiosity got the better of her. "What has happened here?"

The constable's face blanched even whiter. Coren knew that whatever had taken place here was ... well, she would leave the description to the constable.

"I'm afraid there's been a murder, miss." The constable

glanced away, as though the mere mention of it would place a stain on Coren and Jenny.

"Who was it?" Coren asked, as though she had dealt with the murders of people many times before. The casualness shocked even her. But her curiosity overwhelmed her better senses.

"A lady, miss." The constable stared straight at Coren and then corrected himself, "Not your kind of lady, I mean, a female ... a woman. She was found this morning by Bucks Row."

"Thank you, Constable," Jenny cut in. "We had best be off now."

"Righto." The cabby jumped up onto the hansom gathering the reins.

"How was she ...?" Coren began.

"Killed, miss?" The constable seemed to know the question was coming. "They always want to know, don't they?"

"Who are you talking to?" Coren said.

"Oh. Sorry, miss. Just thinkin' out loud. But there's a morbid curiosity to an unnatural death, there is. It's human nature. Even I have to admit that after fourteen years of walking these same streets, I feel the... attraction, if you will." He shuddered, then said, "You don't want to know about this one, miss," but continued anyway, "I never seen the like. All the blood and... I almost..." Regaining his composure, he stated, "It was quite brutal."

Coren read the utter horror on his face. It unnerved her and made her imagination go where she wished it hadn't. "You are quite right, Constable. This is no place for ladies like ourselves." She tried to remain calm but the thought of a murder victim close by, and the chance that the murderer was in this very crowd, sent shivers down her spine and made her legs and arms tingle. It was not a pleasant feeling.

The color began to return to the constable's face as he took on a more official demeanor. "It's best, miss."

"Tha's wha' I been sayin'," the driver piped up, and then

added, "I told 'em, Constable. They shouldn' be 'ere, but red 'ere...she insisted." He pointed directly at Coren. It was obvious that the driver said this to cover any questions that may have been lingering in the constable's mind.

"I've no doubt," the constable said, raising an eyebrow in Coren's direction. He took the reins of the horse and pulled the cab through the crowd, shouting orders to the onlookers to move out of the way. "Good day, Ladies," he said, tipping his hat. "I don't expect to be seeing you in Whitechapel again."

Silence accompanied the ride until the hansom was well out of Whitechapel and back into the more proper squares of London.

The release of tension was palpable.

Coren's stiff shoulders sagged and her lower back eased into the well-worn cushion as she closed her eyes, enjoying the silence.

"I'm certainly glad we're back in a safer neighborhood. This little adventure of yours has taken quite the toll. It was nothing like climbin' up a tower or goin' down a well--both of which were terrors on their own. I musta' been daft to let you talk me into this one. What was I thinkin'? We coulda' been killed. It coulda' been you or me layin' on that street instead of some poor other soul. Your mother will wear me raw with a tongue lashin' when she hears a' this one. What'll she think, miss? What'll she say when we tell her . . . ?"

"We will do no such thing!" Coren snapped and came bolt upright. "And will you please stop rambling on so?"

Jenny paused, puzzled. Then, she raised her head and stared down her nose, looking right into Coren's very wide-open eyes, and said, "Your mother doesn't know that you were going to Whitechapel today?" She didn't need to ask. She already knew the answer.

"Of course she didn't know, Jenny," Coren intoned. "She would never have permitted it."

"An' rightly so!" the driver piped in.

"It would be nice of you to mind your own business."

Coren slapped her hands together to make the point. "But Jenny, you know as well as I do how Mother would react to our ... our little outing."

"Outing! Coren Catherine Elizabeth Butler, your little outing almost got us killed!"

"Oh, don't be so dramatic, Jenny. The murder happened long before we even got there."

"What if we'd gotten there sooner? If we'd had a faster driver...?"

"Aye now, miss. There's none faster in all a' London than ole Dick Dolittle."

"Are we speaking to you?" Coren snapped.

"Sorry again, miss. Won' let it 'appen again."

"Very good. See to it." Coren turned her attention back to Jenny.

"But you was speakin' abou' me an' old Rusty 'ere." The cabbie jiggled the reins as he spoke. "An' 'e doesn' take too well to bein' talked abou' an' all."

"Really. This is too much."

"That's what your mother would say if she knew where you'd been," Jenny barked.

"Aye that's true, miss," the cabbie joined in.

"Mister Dolittle!" Coren almost shrieked.

"Sorry, miss. Forgo' meself. Won' le' it 'appen again."

"Please, don't."

"She's righ' though," the cabbie muttered, unable to stop himself.

"Agh! Driver! Stop this cab immediately!" Coren shouted. "I want to get out. Now."

"Of course miss. We're 'ere. 'igh Gate 'all."

"Oh." Coren swallowed.

Dick Dolittle came down from the front of the cab to help Coren step to the street. As Coren took his proffered hand she said to Jenny, "We will simply tell Mother we've been shopping."

"Shopping? Shopping! Miss Coren, we haven't got a

package with us other than this bundle of clothes and dry goods that you've been collecting from the laundry and larder every day. Lady Butler will never believe we went shopping in the second greatest city in the world and returned empty handed."

Coren raised an eyebrow in exasperation. "You're right."

"Och, Miss Coren, I will really be replaced after Lady Butler hears 'a this one." Jenny closed her eyes in resignation.

"All right then, Jenny. We will go to some nearby shop and make a purchase."

"What shop? Where?" The questions rolled off of Jenny's tongue as she tried to rid herself of any doubts. "What will we buy?"

"Calm down, Jenny. It has never been a problem for us to find something to buy in any shop before. And I don't see that as being a problem now." Coren paused in thought for a moment.

"Begs your pardon, miss. Dick Dolittle 'ere."

"Yes, Mister Dolittle? What is it now?" Coren bit off each word.

"I knows a loverly little 'at shop."

Jenny's eyes sprang open. "Really? Where?"

"An' there's a charmin' confectioner righ' across the way, where you, miss, an' your saucy friend 'ere, can ge' a nice sweet."

Jenny drew in a quick breath.

"Fine. Where is it? We'll walk," Coren said.

"Well, it's a migh' far to walk. But I could gets ya there righ' quick."

"Drive then," Coren said, as she stepped back into the cab ignoring Dick Dolittle's helping hand.

Jenny accepted the help as she looked in astonishment into the cabby's face.

He winked, jumped to his seat and shouted back, "Hold tight now." Slapping the reins into the horses loins – they were off.

Several minuets later, Dick Dolittle pulled the cab to a stop. Coren turned to Jenny and said, "Oh look. There is a fine perfume shop there. We are sure to find something to wash away the smells of today." Coren reached out taking hold of Jenny's hand. "Don't worry, Jenny. We'll be fine."

"Righ', miss. Now watch your step gettin' down." Dick Dolittle extended his hand to Jenny who coyly accepted it. "Takes all the time you wan'. I'll be righ' 'ere waitin' for you."

Coren groaned.

Jenny smiled.

Waves of flowers, spices and fruit scents washed over them as they entered the door to Madame La Fleur's Parfumerie. The strong aromas cleansed their minds of the day's sights and smells, bringing them both back to life.

"Oh, now this is much better." Coren breathed in deeply, letting the commingling scents drown her fears and concerns about her mother.

"Miss, smell this." Jenny held out a small masculine bottle.

Coren breathed the scent in deeply, then wrinkled her nose in disgust. "Oh, Jenny. Really! Bayberry."

"I think it smells lovely, miss." Jenny took back the bottle breathing in another whiff. "Mister Dolittle has been so nice to us. Maybe we should buy him a little gift, some bayberry cologne, I think."

"Oh Jenny, don't be ridiculous!" Coren blurted. "And certainly not bayberry!"

"But, miss, we need to buy something."

Coren paused a moment. "Jenny we need to buy something that we can take with us. Not something that we're going to give away. What will we have to show Mother?"

"Oh, miss. You're right." Jenny picked up a second bottle of the cologne handing it to Coren. "Maybe you should buy one too, miss."

"What ever for?"

Jenny spoke, puzzled by Coren's irritated response, "Why, for Sir Robert."

"Oh. Of course. Sir Robert," Coren said contritely. "Fine. Fine. But not bayberry! Pick out anything else. Anything, but not bayberry," Coren said as she flung her arms wide and made contact with a solid surface.

A loud smack resounded throughout the shop, and heads turned as hand met cheek.

"Oh!" Coren gasped and whirled around.

Emerald green met cobalt blue.

CHAPTER ELEVEN

Coren stood frozen. Time stood still. And before her, stood the man of her dreams. Like an apparition, he appeared and beckoned to her. Her thoughts ran wild. Uncontrolled emotions roiled up and ebbed.

What do I do? What do I do?

That thought echoed in her mind. She tried to move. She could not. She tried to speak. She could not. She tried to breathe, and gasped. The sudden rush of air made her heady. She was trapped by her own indecision.

The man she loved stared at her. His eyes glistened, a slight smile on his face, devilish and coy. The bayberry cologne assaulted her once again, bringing with it feelings she thought she had replaced. She was transported back to the night of the ball. In his arms again, swept up by the strength of him, she'd floated. Mesmerized by him, she had fallen in love.

And now, her prince had come. Twice. Just the sight of him was enough to send her reeling. Only a moment ago she was certain of her convictions and now ... How could just one look transform her feelings? Was she that weak? Was he that strong?

Mother of God, please help me! Her silent prayer went unnoticed. Time passed, hours she felt, before she found her voice. "Is your Highness leaving or has he just arrived?"

Bloody hell, she thought! If that wasn't the most inane comment she could have made. *Coren the heroine? Bah! Coren the insipid!*

"I was just about to leave the shop, but I have just remembered a purchase I still need to make." His eyebrows arched as he waited for Coren to respond. "And you?"

"Oh, I was just about to purchase a bottle of bayberry..." She bit her tongue. "Jenny, my maid, was just about to purchase a bottle of bayberry cologne for a friend ... of hers. She's right here." Coren whirled about, desperately searching among the crowd of gawking women for the ample figure of her maid. "Jenny! Jenny!"

"Aye, miss. I'm but two feet away from you now. You can stop your yellin'!"

"Oh! I ... I would like you to meet His Royal Highness, Prince Albert Victor, Duke of Clarence. Albert, this is Jenny."

With shock and horror apparent on her face, Jenny's head turned slowly to Coren. "Miss Coren!" she said in complete amazement.

"What?" Then realization dawned on Coren. "Oh my God!" She was crimson. "Your Highness, I am so sorry. I should know not to introduce you to the maid."

"And you probably shouldn't have called him Albert, either," Jenny added.

"What!"

"Aye, miss, you did." Jenny nodded her head.

They turned to the Prince. Albert's eyes were streaming with tears. He clutched his stomach and such a roar of laughter issued from him that every head in the store turned, once again. He reached to a nearby shelf to steady himself.

"Your Highness!" Jenny screamed.

Too late.

The shelf the Prince thought would steady him, came crashing to the floor. Intricately cut glass bottles and atomizers filled with expensive perfumes fell. Coren lunged for the shelf hoping to save some of the precious liquid. Jenny lunged for the Prince. A double "oomph" resounded as Jenny unceremoniously landed on the Prince's backside.

A communal gasp was heard in the parfumerie.

"Oh my! Excuse me," Jenny said, trying to right herself.

"No, no. Forgive me," Prince Albert, grunted, pulling himself from under Jenny.

The two sat there amidst bottles and shelves staring at one another.

"I believe I've caused quite an aromatic mess." Albert began to laugh again, taking Jenny in with him. The Prince and the maid rolled on the floor of the parfumerie gasping between fits of laughter.

"Och now, it's all right ... Albert." Jenny guffawed.

They laughed all the harder.

Coren and the remainder of the patrons in the store gaped with open-mouthed horror. The bottles that Coren managed to salvage from the tumbling shelf, slipped unheeded from her hands.

As the Prince and Jenny extricated themselves from one another, Albert stood and extended a hand to Jenny. "Be careful of the glass, dear Jenny."

"Why I certainly will. Thank you, Your Highness."

"My, won't this make interesting dinner conversation this evening," Albert said, carefully brushing bits of glass from his waistcoat and righting one of the few unbroken bottles.

"I had almost forgotten." Sarcasm dripped from every word Coren spoke. "I am so glad that Your Highness has mentioned it."

"As am I." Albert smiled, the same smile that had once brought down the heroine of all of Ireland.

Coren turned away slightly not wanting to lose herself again in that smile. "I am certain the dinner will go exceedingly well and that all attending will surely enjoy the evening."

"That is my hope, my lady." Albert's eyes twinkled as he spoke, "That all attending enjoy the evening."

Coren looked about the shop. The clerks, except for those cleaning up the broken perfume bottles, scurried to help the clientele. While most had gone back to their business of shopping, several still gawked from a nearby corner, averting their gaze as Coren turned their way. There certainly would be interesting dinner conversation tonight in many of the homes of London's society, Coren thought.

"Is that whomYour Highness was shopping for . . . your dinner guests this evening? Some small remembrance of you, perhaps?" This time her eyes twinkled. She would be the victor yet.

Albert's smile faded slightly, before it - the smile - and his admiration grew. He positively beamed. Coren appeared to take no notice. "Extraordinary," he said, "so much beyond simple beauty."

"I beg your pardon your Highness." Coren cocked her head slightly.

"Oh, I'm sorry, just musing aloud," Prince Albert said. "I had hoped to find just the right token to give this evening, but it seems I have made a mess of it." He grinned again.

"Oh, Your Highness is very good, it seems, at making a mess of things," Coren demurred. Only Jenny caught the true meaning behind her words and gave a slight "tsk." Coren shot a glare at Jenny who turned her face heavenward.

"Well, if Your Highness will excuse us, we will be on our way and you may return to your gift shopping." Coren pulled Jenny closer, "It would distress me greatly to be the cause of your dinner guests' disappointment."

"But, miss? We haven't..."

"That's right, Jenny. We haven't finished our shopping yet, so we'd better hurry along," Coren rushed on.

"And what about poor Mister Dolittle?" Jenny added.

Coren's face went blank and then she remembered the cabby. Was she such a ninny that she couldn't remember anything, she berated herself. Really! He wasn't that handsome! She cast a quick glance in the Prince's direction.

Those eyes. That mouth. Those lips. That . . . smile! Oh, yes he was! Goodness, he was laughing at her. Again! He was insufferable. Before he could speak, Coren turned her back and dragged Jenny along saying, "Jenny, dear, why don't you go check on Mister Dolittle."

"Very good, miss. If you say so." Jenny curtsied as she turned to exit.

Coren paused mid-stride. "Oof!" The Prince collided with her.

Coren froze. Again.

"Forgive me!" Albert said. "I was going to get the door for Jenny and I . . ." He stared into the most incredible pair of emeralds he had ever seen. He was speechless.

Breaking the spell, Coren cleared her throat and stepped forward. The Prince moved aside and reached for the door. Coren stepped past, accidentally brushing his hand with hers. She recoiled from the intensity of the contact and hurriedly exited the parfumerie. Glancing over her shoulder she teased, "If your Highness will be staying, I will be leaving."

Coren stepped through the doorway and down to the sidewalk, where Jenny waited arms crossed and a scowl on her face. "Come, Jenny," Coren barked. "We need to find your Mister Dolittle."

"We need to stay here and go shopping with a prince." Jenny stopped quickly looking back to where the Prince still stood in the doorway of the parfumerie. "What are you doing, Miss Coren?" Jenny's brogue emphasized the incredulity in her voice.

"I'm going to another shop, one that doesn't have a prince in it," she spoke quickly, biting at the words and quickening her pace.

"But heavenly Father above, why?" Jenny looked at Coren and then at the Prince. "If I had a prince like him in my shop, I wouldn't mind him checkin' out my wares."

"Jenny!" Coren whispered afraid someone might have heard the comment. "How can you speak like that? Especially out in public?"

"I'm sorry, miss. But it seems to me that he's a right fine lookin' young prince and he's still standin' there starin' at ya, holdin' the door open." Jenny nodded her head in the shop's direction.

"What is he doing?" Coren asked without looking his way.

"He's just standin' there, miss."

"Standing where exactly?" Coren turned slightly hoping to see where he was without him noticing that she was looking.

Jenny shook her head and placed a hand over her mouth in an attempt to disguise the fact that she and Coren were speaking. "He's right there where we left him, miss, in the doorway."

"Well, what's he doing?" Coren asked raising her whisper above the noise of the street.

"He's just standin' there. He's not doin' anything, unless you'd say that lookin' at us is doin' something?" Jenny smiled and nodded again in the Prince's direction.

Coren squeezed Jenny's arm. "What are you doing?" Their pace had slowed to an easy stroll.

"I'm nodding at the Prince."

Coren's eyes grew wide. "Why would you do that?"

Jenny sighed in exasperation, not understanding Coren's obtuseness. She let out a long breath and answered, "To see if he nods back."

Coren moved in closer to Jenny keeping her back to the Prince and the shop. "Well?"

"Well, what, miss?" Jenny raised an eyebrow.

It was Coren's turn to sigh. "Well, did he nod back?"

"I don't know. You pulled at my arm before I could see what he did."

"Oh." Coren thought for a brief moment. "Well, you will just have to nod again."

"Again!"

"Yes. And this time, for heaven's sake, watch what he does!"

"He's goin' to think I have a problem controllin' my head is what he's goin' to think." Jenny pleaded, "Oh miss, I can't nod again."

"All right then," Coren paused. "Wave at him."

"I don't think that will be necessary, miss." Jenny clenched her jaw squeezing the words out.

"Why ever not?"

"Because he's closed the door, miss."

"Oh well, isn't that just perfect!" Coren shouted now, not caring who heard her. "See what you've done?" She brought her hands up, covering her eyes, blocking out the sunlight. "Now I'm going to have to come up with some excuse for going back into that shop." She grabbed Jenny's arm. "Come on!" Coren lurched, pulling Jenny with her while loudly announcing her idea, "I know what to do, we will say that I had to ... "And she walked right into His Royal Highness, Prince Albert Victor, the Duke of Clarence.

"Did I forget to mention that after closin' the door, the Prince was headin' in our direction?" Jenny bit down on her lip as she started to chuckle.

Coren stifled a smile, forcing it into a frown. "You will be dealt with later," she said to Jenny in a feeble attempt at anger, when in truth she was overjoyed. Jenny, dear sweet Jenny, had kept her from storming off down the crowded street. She had secretly hoped that the Prince would call to her, raise his voice over the tumult, and beckon her back to him. Her desire for him was overwhelming. Oceans of emptiness washed over her, creating a void, which only he, her Prince, could fill. She had loved him from the moment she had seen him high atop the ballroom stairs and she had hated him when she had found that there were others he was courting. How could he tease her so, entice her with his smile, bewitch her with his eyes and steal her heart with his tender words and sensual touch? Coren found it easy to despise this Prince when he was a great distance from her, but now that he stood only inches away, she could do nothing, but love him.

"Your Highness has left the parfumerie I see." As soon as she said it she wished she could take it back. Obviously he had left the store. He was standing right in front of her. She wanted to slap herself for again saying something so vapid.

His eyebrows rose in the same little quizzical arch that Coren had noticed when he had first asked her to dance at the ball. "Yes, I have left the shop. It was very nice of you to notice."

The Prince, Coren thought, had his own game and he was playing it now. He gave it away when his brow curved upward and his lips pressed together in a tight beguiling smile. Coren remained composed, at least outwardly. She was not going to let him get away and she would not allow him to have the upper hand. Her retort came quickly, aimed straight for the heart. "I am actually very pleased that we found each other today. You see, I am leaving London on the morrow and I did hope that I would have the opportunity to say thank you to your Highness for a wonderful ball. It was certainly an enchanting evening." She smiled slyly, drawing him in to her game. "For so many of us, I hear."

Coren watched a shadow fall over the Prince's face. It was as clear as the day was bright. She wondered if she had misjudged him. He was genuinely hurt. She replayed the lines in her head and fought an urge to reach out and caress him. Was it all a part of his game, an effort to pull her in closer? To test her? Did he play the same game with all the others? The question lingered. The urge to caress him dissipated and a desire to slap him rose.

"I'm afraid that I am a bit confused," Albert's voice hesitated.

Coren interrupted, "I believe I have made myself clear, Your Highness."

"I understood that you would be attending the Queen's dinner." Albert's voice carried with it a hint of hope.

"Your Highness is quite correct." Coren had him.

"But did I not hear you say, you were leaving for Ireland

tomorrow?" An awkward mix of confusion and anxiety were apparent in his voice.

Coren studied him for a moment. His face clearly showed concern. Did he really want her to be at the dinner or was his pride hurt by her refusal? She could not tell which it was. "Yes, I was invited to the dinner, along with all the others," she said it again punching the words hoping they would knock the breath out of him.

"But as you are not leaving until tomorrow, surely you could attend a dinner this evening." He bowed his head averting his eyes from hers. "Unless of course there is someone..." He caught the words just in time, "Or some pressing affair you must attend to."

Coren looked away and caught Jenny's disdainful gaze. Jenny merely tsked and shook her head.

The Prince was searching for an answer. Coren thought she had already given it to him. Twice now she had tried to get the message through to him, deliberately using the same words that had crushed her, all the others. Yet, he seemed to take no notice. "No, Your Highness, I am not leaving to attend to a pressing affair." She watched him closely noting the small creases around his eyes, the slight dimple in his chin and the pain and lost expression on his face. "I am just tired of London." Coren breathed in deeply and then wrinkled her nose. "I miss the clean, crisp air of Ireland."

"But truly the air in Ireland will be as clean and as crisp on the following day," he said glancing up to the sky.

He's hiding something, Coren thought. Were his eyes really that blue? Did she catch a hint of a tear? She moved to block out the glare from the sun. The Prince held his head angled up. His strong chin and jaw line were accentuated by the positioning. His face, clean-shaven except for the thin mustache, reddened in the hot sun. Coren's eyes followed his jaw line to the dark waves that fell over the tops of his ears, and up the high cheekbones to the soft tendrils that brushed his aristocratic forehead. Her perusal culminated at his eyes.

Eyes that shimmered. Eyes that engulfed her. Dark, swirling pools of cobalt surrounded by the whitest pearls. An odd sensation stirred in the pit of her stomach and arose. Restlessness and passion, emptiness and fear. She shook her head, trying to clear the fog.

The Prince looked down at her. He opened his mouth as if to speak, then stopped. The words would not come forth. Swiftly and suddenly he bent down, wrapped his arms around Coren and drew her to him. His mouth now sought another form of expression and without the slightest hesitation he pressed his lips to hers. The flames from the sun reached down, touching the Earth, scorching their lips, blinding them to all around them.

Jenny let out a cry as the Prince engulfed her charge. She was powerless. She could only watch, dreaming.

Coren did not struggle. How could she? There was not an ounce of strength in her body. Her knees crumbled beneath her. She clung to the Prince for support. His arms tightened and he raised her from the street. His lips seared her; a brand so hot it marked her soul. She wanted to cry out to him. She wanted to tell him to never stop. She wanted to love him like this forever.

When his grip on her eased, Coren pleaded to him in her mind, *Don't let go.*

But he did.

The kiss had lasted only a moment. Or was it a day? Coren could not be sure.

"Forgive me, Coren," he said it, but did not mean it. "I should not have done that." Prince Albert backed away. "Please. Forgive me." He bowed his head slightly while keeping his eyes on this Irish woman.

Coren stood stunned. How could she leave this Prince? Her Prince. Even if he had invited other women from the ball to the Queen's dinner, she could not leave him. She spoke quickly, not wanting him to go. "I forgive Your Highness."

"So do I," Jenny offered from the side where she stood all

but forgotten.

"Thank you," Albert said and added to Jenny with a wink, "thank you, also."

Embarrassed and elated, he turned away. He raised his hand and as if by magic, a carriage of black walnut and red velvet appeared from around the corner. "I wish that you would stay," he said stepping into the carriage. "The Queen will be very disappointed that she will have to cancel her dinner."

"But why, Your Highness, would the entire dinner have to be canceled?" Coren spoke into the shadows of the carriage. "It could not simply be because I can not attend?"

"When the only guest invited can not attend there is little need to have the dinner." His voice was soft and an air of melancholy slipped between his words. "Good-bye, Coren," he said her name in the softest of tones.

The carriage pulled away so swiftly it kicked up a cloud of dust. "But wait!" Coren's cry was drowned by the clattering of hooves. Only Jenny had heard Coren's plaintive plea.

"Oh miss! There were no others. It was only you. Only you all along,"

Only me. Only me.

The words echoed in her heart. Joy replaced sadness. Fear replaced joy. And an agonizing question gnawed at her. *What had she done?*

Emeralds misted over. And teared.

Coren's tears.

CHAPTER TWELVE

Dick Dolittle had scarcely reined in old Rusty, and the wheels had barely come to a stop, when Coren leapt from the black velvet-covered seat of the hansom to the stone-paved drive at the entrance to High Gate Hall. "Pay the driver, Jenny," she yelled over her shoulder without a glance back. She ran up the long, stone walk, in a most indecorous manner, with skirts raised and heels kicking up behind her. She flung open the great doors and disappeared inside, leaving the doors wide open.

"What do we owe you for your kind services, Mister Dolittle?" Jenny coyly batted her eyes.

Dick Dolittle slyly grinned. "'Ow abou' a little trip to tha' swee' shop, I was tellin' you abou'?" His grin grew wider.

Jenny thought for a moment, knowing she should make some sort of false protest, and then came to the quick conclusion, that, at her age, and with the lack of eligible men around, she shouldn't dally about in the briar patch! "Why, Mister Dolittle, I'd love to." She tilted her head and coyly batted her eyes, twice!

"Then tha's all you owes me." He blinked his eyes twice in response.

Jenny slightly flustered, said, "Well, I daresay, we seem to be gettin' the best part of this bargain, Mister Dolittle."

"Au contraire, miss. Ridin' abou' with two lovelies such as

yourselves has made the pleasure all mine." Dolittle tipped his hat.

"Oh no!" Jenny jumped.

"'Ave I offended you, miss?" Dolittle spoke with obvious concern.

"Begorrah, no." Jenny clutched her chest. "But I left the package inside your cab."

"Allows me." Dolittle gave her a slight bow and reached inside the cab to retrieve the package. " 'Ere you are, miss."

"Thank you. You are most kind." Jenny gave him a surprisingly girlish smile. "However, you may keep it. I bought it for you."

Dick Dolittle blushed and grinned back. "Wha' is it?"

"A lovely scent that Prince Albert himself wears," Jenny said proudly.

"I shall treasure it," he said gripping the package to his chest. "Migh' I calls for you sometime soon?"

"That would be lovely." Jenny shyly turned and strode up the walk. After several steps she glanced back and wiggled her fingers in a wave. Dolittle stood staring after her, a boyish smirk of victory on his face.

Jenny closed the doors to High Gate Hall behind her, the color high in her cheeks, a long dormant twinkle in her eyes.

The door to the library sprung open. "Mother! Mother!" Coren called out, as she quickly looked inside. Not seeing her mother there, she hurried down the hall to the sitting room. It too was empty. Coren backtracked along the long lower hallway, and then ran up the stairs to the guest rooms with fury in her stride. She flung open the door to her mother's suite of rooms. It crashed against the wall and rocked the room, as if an earthquake had just struck London. "Mother! Where are you?"

Lady Butler vaulted from her seat next to the warming fire, sending her tea to the floor in a spewing stream of dark brown liquid. A small cry of fear escaped from her throat and her face contorted. "Coren Catherine Elizabeth Butler! By what means do you barge into my room, scaring me to death. And look, you have made me spill my tea."

"Mother! Mother! We must send word to the Queen. Immediately, Mother!" Coren spoke disregarding her Mother's scathing glare.

"Child, what is wrong with you?" Lady Butler moved quickly to Coren, placing her hand across her daughter's forehead.

"Mother, I'm not ill," Coren snapped, pulling her mother's hand from her brow.

"Well, what is it then, Coren?" She paused. Lady Butler's eyes moved slowly across her child's face.

Coren watched as her mother's face went through a series of expressions, first concern, then anger, then back to concern. "Oh, Mother." Out of breath, her words came in fragments. "I am sorry...but we must...act quickly...before all...is lost."

"Before what is lost, Coren? I don't understand," Lady Butler said, now exasperated.

"The Prince, Mother, The Prince!" Coren blurted.

"Will you stop repeating yourself. It is most annoying," Lady Butler said, as she brushed away imaginary drops of tea from her dress.

"We must send word to the Queen that we will not be leaving." Coren dashed about the room as she spoke. "Where are your cards, Mother?" She flung open the doors to the cherry wood secretary that sat in the far corner of the room. "Mother, please, help me!"

Coren was completely undone. She fell in a heap onto the chaise, and tears she hadn't known existed escaped from her. Great heaves and sighs pushed up from within her. Thoughts of love lost, gained hold and strangled her. "I've lost him, Mother." Coren managed to eke out in between the cascade of tears.

"Lost, Coren? Lost who?" Lady Butler stared at her child; her beautiful child lying before her, wracked in pain and sorrow. "Jenny!" Lady Butler screamed down the hallway. "Jenny! Jenny! Good Lord, where are you? Jenny! Come here, quickly!"

Distant cries of servants calling and the clatter of hurried footsteps made their way to the guest suite of High Gate Hall. Sir Talbot's voice could be heard above the others, offering staccato orders.

Jenny could be heard down the long hallway, "I'm comin', but where are ya?'" her brogue, heightened with concern.

Coren's tears had abated some as Sir Talbot made his way into Lady Butler's suite of rooms. "What is it?" His gaze darted between Lady Butler and Coren, concern growing with each moment. "My precious darlings, what is distressing you so?"

"I have no idea, Robert," Lady Butler said, her voice easing a bit. "Coren came bolting into the room, flinging the door open, scaring me half to death and then … this." She used her hands to indicate Coren, balled up on the lounge.

"Coren, my dear, what is the matter?" Sir Talbot said as he eased himself down next her, he began to slowly rub her shoulders and upper back. The tight muscles relaxed a bit. Coren gave a low moan, arched her shoulders, released a deep sigh and buried her face in her hands. "Perhaps we should call for the doctor?" Sir Talbot looked up to Lady Butler, waiting for her approval.

Before Lady Butler could respond, Jenny entered the room, "Lady Butler? You called for me?" Confusion and concern apparent in her eyes. At once she noticed Coren. "Oh my! I told her it was not a good idea. Lady Butler, I told her. Believe me, I did not want to go. I don't mean to sound like I'm savin' my own skin but … Well, I did say that you would not be happy with us…"

"Whatever are you talking about, Jenny?" Lady Butler

turned to her, shaking her head in total confusion.

"I was telling you ... I was going to say..." Jenny's gaze darted back and forth from Lady Butler to Sir Talbot.

Lady Butler finished her sentence for her, "Say nothing, Jenny. Get us some smelling salts. Quickly!"

"And bring us a decanter of brandy from the library," Sir Talbot added, as Jenny hurried down the hall barking the same orders to the household servants.

"I guess it may be for the best that Coren wants us to leave soon." Lady Butler sat next to her daughter in the spot on the chaise just vacated by Sir Robert and continued, "This trip has been, I fear, too much for her."

"Catherine, I'm sure she'll be fine." Sir Talbot was reassuring in his tone, but concern still showed on his face. "She's just a bit overwhelmed, poor girl."

A serving maid, dressed as though she had walked off the pages of the ever-popular *The Queen Magazine* knocked lightly at the door before entering. "I've brought the brandy, sir." She held a silver tray draped with a rich, red-velvet liner. Several small crystal glasses and the crystal decanter, filled halfway with the amber liquid, rested upon it.

"Very good. Please bring me a glass of the brandy," Sir Talbot said. He reached for the brandy and tossed it back quickly. "Another please," he barked to the startled girl.

Coren's deep heaves had all but stopped now. And with her tears drying, the tension in the room eased.

"Here," Sir Talbot said pushing a glass of brandy into Coren's hands. "Sip it slowly, dear. It will make you feel better. It always helps me," he chuckled.

"Brandy?" Lady Butler spoke with a certain indignation in her voice. "Are you sure, Robert?"

"Just a sip," Sir Talbot reassured Lady Butler. "A sip alone can not hurt."

"Robert, she has never tasted alcohol before." Lady Butler said. "Of course I'm not sure of this, but for the sake of my daughter's reputation I feel the need to say it, as, honestly

Robert, I'm not sure what is happening with my child.

"Oh, don't get on so, Catherine," Sir Robert said, waving his hand dismissively in the air. He leaned into Coren and urged her to take some of the brandy. "There now. Just a little."

As Coren closed her hand lightly around the glass, she was surprised at its warmth. Her hand gingerly brought the glass to her lips, tipping it slightly allowing the liquid to gently spill over and onto her waiting tongue. It burned the back of her throat and she widened her eyes in surprise. She could feel a rush of heat rise from the pit of her stomach and bring a flush to her cheeks. Coren paused briefly, analyzing the sensations, and then tipped back the glass, emptying the remainder of its contents. "My, that was rather good!" she said perking up, apparently forgetting her sorrows of a few moments ago. "May I have another, Uncle Robert?" Coren thrust the glass at him.

"No, you may not have another," Lady Butler snapped. "One was more than I intended to let you have in the first place." Then reprimanding her further, "You were only supposed to sip it."

"But it made me feel ever so much better, Mother." Coren's voice took on a new cheeriness.

"Could one more wee glass hurt?" Sir Talbot said, as he took the glass from Coren and poured another from the decanter.

"Yes, it most certainly could." Lady Butler glared at Sir Talbot. "Robert? What are you doing?"

"With this?" He raised the glass.

"Yes. With that," Lady Butler said, more than slightly annoyed.

"It's for me." Sir Talbot downed the brandy. "See?" He gave Coren a quick wink.

"Here are the salts you asked for, ma'am," Jenny blurted breathlessly, as she rushed into the room.

Lady Butler glared at Jenny. "We don't need them now,

Jenny. As you can see, Coren is feeling much better."

Jenny looked to her charge. "Ah, so you are, miss!"

"Oh, Jenny, come here. You must try some of this." Coren reached for the decanter and glass, stealing them from her uncle's hands.

As Coren poured, Lady Butler's voice boomed in alarm. "Coren Catherine Elizabeth Butler! What is going on here?"

"I'm giving Jenny some of this delicious brandy, Mother." Coren poured out another glass of the brandy that Sir Robert had graciously given her. "Here, Jenny. It is absolutely delicious." Coren handed the glass to Jenny

Lady Butler, temporarily speechless, stared in amazement.

Taking the glass, Jenny turned to Lady Butler and Sir Talbot. She raised it high above her head. And in her best full Irish, barked, "Slainte," and tossed the brandy back.

"Very good. Cheers to you, Jenny." Coren took the second glass and before Lady Butler's fretful cries had reached her ears, drained it.

"Might as well join them." Sir Talbot laughed as he poured and drank another glass.

Coren, Jenny and Sir Talbot fell into uncontrolled laughter.

Lady Butler glared at the trio, obviously not amused.

"Cheers to you," Jenny repeated and mimed the motions of the salute.

"Cheers to you," Coren mimicked bursting with laughter.

"Jenny! Robert!" Lady Butler's sharp tongue cut the laughter like a sword. "That will be quite enough!"

Like scolded school children, Coren, Jenny and Sir Talbot wound down their laughter to silence. Each sat or stood with their heads bowed down, afraid that if they were to meet one another's eyes, they would again burst into laughter.

Lady Butler stood silently, almost statuesque, waiting for the respect that she demanded. After a very long minute had passed, she broke the silence. "Sir Robert?" Robert's eyes came up. "Would you and Jenny kindly excuse yourselves? I would like to speak to my daughter alone." It wasn't really a question. That was understood. "And please take that offensive liquid with you."

Jenny bit her tongue to squelch a giggle. "Yes, ma'am." She hurried to the door as fast as her squat little legs could take her.

"Jenny. The brandy!" Lady Butler boomed.

Jenny stopped dead on the spot. "Sorry, ma'am." She returned, picked up the tray, replacing the glasses and with a quick wink to Coren, was out the door and down the corridor.

"Well, then," Sir Robert spoke as though he hadn't been dismissed. "I shall leave you two alone." He headed for the door. "If you should need me..."

"Thank you, Robert," Lady Butler interjected. "I believe you've done quite enough already."

As the door silently closed, Lady Butler began pacing the room. She was angry, yet still very concerned for her daughter. The episode with the brandy had helped ease the tension and Lady Butler hoped that whatever it was that was bothering Coren could now be told and dealt with. The stresses of this trip and of meeting the Prince were perhaps a bit more than a young girl like Coren had been prepared for. Lady Butler pondered the wisdom of her choices. After all, Coren's life at Butler House had not prepared her for the sorrows and rejections that life so often sprang upon the unwary. "Coren? Please tell Mother what is troubling you." Lady Butler's voice became soft and gentle, putting Coren at ease.

Coren began, "Mother, while Jenny and I were out shopping this morning, we happened upon Prince Albert at Madame La Fleur's Parfumerie."

"How nice for you, dear," Lady Butler nodded at Coren to continue.

"At first I didn't think so..." Coren hesitated, as if she were reliving it all again. "Then the Prince told me that I was the only one whom the Queen had invited to the dinner this evening." She stood now and spoke animatedly. "I'm the only one, Mother. There are no others."

"Oh, that is wonderful, dear. I told you the Prince would take a liking to you." Lady Butler hugged Coren tightly, then held her at arm's length. "Now perhaps, you will listen to Mother."

"But Mother, I have done something terrible." Coren shook her head. "How could I have been so foolish as to have you send a message of refusal to the Queen. Oh, Mother, what will we do?" Coren collapsed onto the bed in dramatic despair.

Lady Butler looked at Coren, remembering with fondness and a bit of embarrassment her own impetuous decisions as a young girl. She recalled now how her own mother had, on many occasions. saved her from a great deal of embarrassment. An incident, not very unlike the one that Coren found herself in at the moment, came back in vivid humility to Lady Butler.

A young Lord Butler, not yet master of his title, had shown great interest in the young Catherine at the picnic gathering in the early summer, at the small but delightful Ballyseede Castle. The soft summer breeze, the abundant greenery and the nearby woods, lent an air of fantasy to the day. Brocade carpets and damask cloths were spread out upon the grounds for the younger attendees, while tables complete with fine bone china and crystal were set among them for those who were less inclined to lounge upon the land.

The young Catherine hovered near the dashing young Lord Butler, trying nonchalantly to catch his eye. When that didn't work she began to stroll among the patchwork of carpets and cloths, fanning herself in a semi-coquettish manner, her eyes all the while never leaving her prey. He still didn't seem to notice her and she didn't notice the tree.

Crash!

She noticed the tree! And he noticed that she was now in a heap upon the ground. At once Catherine's mother, who had been following her antics, was at her side, beckoning to the young Lord. "My young man, would you be so kind as to bring a cool cloth for my daughter's forehead. It appears the excitement may have been a bit much for her."

"It would be my pleasure, my lady." The young Patrick Michael Shea Butler, not yet a Lord, dashed off. He quickly returned with a water-cooled cloth. He placed it upon Catherine's forehead. "The sun has also been a bit much for me. Perhaps, Lady Eleanor, I should rest here with your daughter while you enjoy the remainder of the day."

"How gallant. I thank you." The young Catherine's mother, Lady Eleanor, nodded and then gave a conspiratorial wink to her daughter.

Lady Butler smiled at the long ago memory and then looked to her forlorn daughter. "Coren, I have to admit something to you." Lady Butler waited for Coren to face her. "I have not been the most trustworthy mother that a child could have."

"Mother, I'm not sure why you would say that?" Coren said. "You are everything that a mother should be and more."

"Perhaps. But then, perhaps not." Lady Butler enjoyed this. She was into their game once again. And now, she got to play out her hand. "I must confess that I did not do as you asked."

"Did not do what?" Each word was said deliberately. Coren's attention was now riveted on her mother.

"I did not send word to the Queen..."

"Oh! Mother!" Coren screamed before Lady Butler had finished the sentence. She sprang to her feet dashing to her mother. "You are perfect, Mother! Simply, perfect." Coren squeezed her mother, reverting to the little girl that loved to get lost in her mother's embrace.

Memories of infant cries and first words flooded Lady Butler's thoughts. And now as she felt the adult arms of her only child surround her, she longed for those days. Her child had grown, faster than she would have liked. But then, they always do.

Lady Butler eyes glazed over, as tears formed in the corners. She looked into her daughter's eyes and . . .

Emeralds sparkled.

CHAPTER THIRTEEN

"You'll feel much better after a couple hours of rest, my dear," Lady Butler said, drawing the curtains closed.

"Oh, but Mother there is so much I need to do! My hair, my bath and whatever am I going to wear! Mother, I need a new gown, immediately!" Coren bolted to her feet and just as rapidly sat down, her head spinning.

"I see the brandy, which you so vigorously imbibed in, has taken its effect." Lady Butler's tone carried with it more than a hint of irony.

"Oh, Mother, my head." She massaged her aching temples. "Why didn't you stop me?"

"I think you should ask your uncle that question. Now, lie back and rest a while." Lady Butler kissed her daughter lovingly on the forehead and exited the room.

As soon as the room stopped spinning, Coren found herself adrift in sleep.

Dreams of the upcoming dinner plagued her slumber; She jostled and thrashed about as visions of: Blood-red wine, spilling from a broken hand-cut crystal glass, soaking into the Queen's favorite linen table cloth. Silver knives, bearing the royal seal, slipping through her fingers and falling to the floor. A footman that tripping over her foot. Pheasant from the royal hunting grounds at Windsor, that wouldn't stay on her plate. Words that wouldn't flow from her lips. Sentences that wouldn't end. A jumble of ridiculous statements, said to impress ... that didn't. Laughter, at all the wrong places. And an incredible urge to excuse herself to the toilet, when she had only just returned.

Coren woke briefly from her troubled sleep only to drift off again. Visions of the dinner disaster were replaced by: Street urchins chanting, "Knives, sharp knives! Murder, fine murder!" Jenny, juggling bottles of perfume as she weaved among the children. The Prince, laughing amid the squalor of Whitechapel, dancing with Jenny around the faceless corpse of some tortured woman.

Coren awoke abruptly, lost for a moment in the space between being asleep and awake. She wiped the cold sweat from her dampened brow and slowed her rapid breathing. Realizing that it had all been a dream, she sighed gratefully and leaned back onto the chaise. The sounds of birds at play in the early afternoon sun, filtered in through the now opened window. Coren surmised that some caring soul, Jenny or her mother most probably, had looked in on her and determined that a little fresh air was in order.

The mere thought of what this evening could bring – no, would bring – sent her stomach tossing with anxiety.

Stretching to wake her still sleeping muscles, Coren threw herself off the chaise hitting the floor with a thump. She hopped to the carpeting covering a section of the bedroom floor, her toes immediately sinking into the deep plush wool. She lingered there for a moment, letting the weave entwine itself in between her toes.

Coren stepped around the four-poster bed and made her way to the window on the far side of the room. There, she pushed the shutters apart. An explosion of light burst into the room. Coren's eyes closed instinctively and she squinted to see through them, remnants of the brandy still vaguely apparent.

The day had already been filled with a trip to Whitechapel, a quick stop for perfume – that turned into a disastrous meeting with the Prince – one or two glasses too many of brandy, and an hours sleep.

A full day for some, Coren thought. *No for many*, she corrected.

Now, only a few hours away from tonight's dinner with the Prince, the early evening outside of High Gate Hall was glorious. There was warmth with the setting sun and sounds mixed with pleasant smells from the grounds below. It was a day for singing, for skipping and playing outdoors. A day for rolling in the grass and rushing through flowerbeds, chasing grasshoppers and butterflies. It was the kind of day that she adored as a child. It was the kind of day that brought memories of games once played, and now, replayed forever in her mind.

A loud thump and the sounds of glass breaking brought Jenny scrambling from the hallway to Coren's room. After a slight knock, not waiting for a response, Jenny shoved open the strong wooden door. There, on the floor before her, sat Coren, curled up holding her foot, grimacing in pain. "What happened?" Jenny said, unsure of how to react.

Coren looked up into the face of her maid and friend. "I stubbed my toe on that blasted bed!" Then continued through gritted teeth, "I was hopping and skipping around the room and I hopped and skipped right into that post!" She closed her grip tightly around her foot, as if that would stop the pain.

"Here now, let me see." A smirk spread across Jenny's face as she spoke.

"It is not funny, Jenny!" Coren's face betrayed her words. "I'm in pain. Perhaps my foot is broken, and you stand there and laugh at me!"

"Oh, it's not your pain I'm laughing at." A chuckle escaped from her before she could stop it. "It's the thought of you hoppin' and skippin' around the bedroom that has me in the giggles, miss."

"Well, get out of them and help me," Coren huffed.

The room was in a bit of a shambles, Jenny noticed as she stepped around Coren. A vase had fallen and smashed on the floor. The carpeting by the bed was twisted and the goose down-filled pillows on the bed had been tossed to the floor. "Whatever were you doing in this room, miss?" Jenny's eyes bulged with curiosity.

"I told you. I was hopping and skipping when I hit the post of the bed with my toe." Coren held her foot up to bring the point home. "See, here."

"And were you throwing vases to the floor, also?" The sarcasm in Jenny's voice did not escape Coren.

"No," Coren added a bit of her own sarcasm. "I was not throwing vases to the floor. It fell when I hit my toe."

"I see," Jenny said. "And what about the carpet, miss? It seems to have twisted itself all up?"

A long glare at Jenny followed, before Coren spoke. "I was spinning around in circles."

As if she didn't understand, Jenny repeated Coren words. "I'm sorry, miss. You were spinnin' around?"

"Don't act as if you don't understand me, Jenny. I was spinning around in circles. How much plainer can I be?" Coren said, her exasperation apparent.

"What for?"

"To become dizzy." Coren paused, realizing how silly it must have sounded to Jenny, but she also knew that Jenny knew her better than anyone.

"Apparently it worked." Jenny laughed aloud.

"My, don't you think you're funny." Coren pulled herself up from the floor, gingerly easing weight onto her foot.

"I'm afraid to ask, miss, but what caused the pillows to end up on the floor?" Her eyes glinted, awaiting the answer. "Did they also fall from the bed when you stubbed your toe?"

"You know bloody well how they got to the floor, Jenny!"

Coren tried to take a step forward, a twinge of pain traveled up her leg, causing her to limp. "Oh my toe!"

Jenny ignored her charges distress. "Oh no, miss, I don't think that I do." She paused for a moment, watching Coren limp around the room. "Unless of course the pillows took flight, or they may have fallen to the floor when you were ... "The dramatic pause caught Coren's attention, she stopped to look at Jenny grabbing hold of the bed post for support. "Unless that is," Jenny paused. "They fell when you were jumpin' on the bed!"

"I was not!" Coren, too vehemently denied.

"Ha!" Jenny shouted. "I think thou dost protest too much," Jenny said, imitating the finest of upper class English accents.

"Don't you dare quote Shakespeare at me!" Coren limped quickly to the other side of the bed. "I was not jumping on the bed."

"Oh, just think of how pleased the Prince would be to find you on your weddin' night, two glasses of honey wine laid out before a full moon, and you, bouncing up an down on the bed."

"Jenny, stop it this instant!" Coren picked the pillows up from the floor in an attempt to hide the evidence.

"Oh, my darling." Jenny's voice took on an affected tone, mimicking Coren as though she were speaking to her prince. "Oh, my dearest darling."

"Jenny, I'm warning you," Coren said shaking her finger at Jenny.

"My darling Prince, please join me here on our bed for a bit of a romp..." Jenny said, dramatically extending her arms in invitation as she sat upon the bed. "Oh no your Highness, I don't mean that kind of a romp!" Jenny beamed.

"Jenny!" Coren snapped, stomping her foot, causing her to wince, once again in pain. "Ouch."

Coren's protest went unheeded, as Jenny continued, "No, dear. Not that kind of a romp. What I mean to say is that I would like you to join me in a game of Bouncy-Bounce."

Jenny coughed out a gruff laugh. "Let's see who can get the highest. Yes, that's it my Prince – bounce"

"Oh, Jenny, you are vulgar! Vulgar, I tell you," Coren shouted. "And I can bounce higher than that prince anyway."

Coren bounced on the bed, to prove her point, bumping her head on the canopy above.

"You can not." Jenny affected the tone of the Prince.

"If I choose to, I could easily bounce higher than you," Coren said a hint of indignation in her tone.

"Then why don't you just show me, miss?" Jenny taunted.

"I would if I could but as you may recall, my toe is injured, and I am in much pain."

"That's just an excuse," Jenny shouted.

"Is not. Watch this!" Coren bent her knees and sprang up from the mattress, pushing hard. Instead of going up, she, Jenny and the bed went down. The support under the mattress gave way, crashing to the floor. The room rumbled with the sound. Jenny fell back and hit the headboard.

Coren bounced forward.

"Jenny, are you all right?" Coren screamed.

A bellow of hoarse laughter issued from Jenny, lying half on and half off the bed she continued to laugh uncontrollably. "I'm fine, miss," she gasped.

"Well now, look what you've done," Coren scolded. "Because of you we can not play Bouncy-Bounce anymore." She began to chuckle, unable to contain herself any longer.

"Me? You are the cause of this." Jenny's voice cracked with indignation.

"Is that so?" Lady Butler's voice boomed from the hallway. She pushed open the door and strode into the room. "What, the saints preserve us, have the two of you been up to?" It was a rhetorical question that neither Coren nor Jenny felt compelled to answer. "There has been such a clamor coming from this room. Why, one would think that someone was up to no good in here." Lady Butler glanced around the room, taking note of the disarray. "By the looks of it, one would be right."

"Why, Mother, we were just . . . that is Jenny . . . " Coren attempted to explain, feebly.

"Me?" Jenny interjected.

Coren shot a scornful glare in Jenny's direction. "We were just playing a little game, Mother."

"It was a game that has caused quite the mess, I see. I'll assume that it will be cleaned up promptly. Remember Coren, we are guests in Sir Robert's house." Lady Butler scowled at her daughter. "And Jenny?"

"Yes, ma'am?" Jenny's head snapped up in attention.

"I might be concerned about your further employment, if this were to happen again." Lady Butler pointedly stared at Jenny.

"Yes, ma'am." Jenny said, adding a slightly uncomfortable smile.

"Please treat this house and Sir Robert with due respect," Lady Butler said, looking from Coren to the Jenny and then back again.

"I'm sorry, Mother," Coren said, the hint of a child in her voice.

"I should hope so." Lady Butler turned to leave, hesitated, then turned back staring directly at Jenny. "Jenny, do get up!" she spoke in a perfect staccato rhythm.

"Yes, ma'am." Jenny struggled at once to remove herself from the bed, but found her foot had caught in the space between the mattress and the sideboard, "Right away, ma'am." She wriggled more rigorously, but her foot held fast.

Lady Butler shook her head in exasperation, mumbled "Oh the Saints please stay by my side," under her breath, then ambled off down the hall.

Jenny pulled again at her leg. "Now see what you've gone and done?"

"Me?" Coren said.

"Yes, you. Now please, help me up," Jenny said, struggling fitfully.

Coren yanked forcefully on Jenny's trapped leg, to no avail. "It won't move, Jenny."

"Try harder miss, I can't be stuck here forever."

"I am trying Jenny. I can't get it out. Whatever shall we do?" Then added, "I'm afraid we'll just have to amputate."

Jenny screamed, "We'll be needing some more of the brandy then, miss."

It seemed to Coren as if hours passed before she and Jenny had finished putting the bed back together. Surprisingly, it took all of their combined strength to lift the goose-down and cotton-filled mattress off of the frame and replace the boards underneath that supported it.

"We can do this, Jenny," Coren said through gritted teeth. "Push!"

"If I push any harder, I'm goin' to have a baby." The dry sarcasm of Jenny's comment sent both she and Coren into a fit of laughter and the mattress came smashing down once again. "We're never goin' to get this room back together," Jenny said exhausted.

"Yes, we will," Coren grunted, pushing at the mattress. "If it takes us the rest of day, we will!"

Jenny curled her fingers around the edge of the mattress. "Remind me to never play Bouncy-Bounce with you again. My poor old body can't take this."

Luckily, the boards had not broken, but had instead, slipped from their resting position on the side rails. It would have been much easier to have one of the men from the house staff come to the room and replace the boards, Jenny had suggested to Coren, who would have nothing of it.   In time, Coren and Jenny had the bed back into position, the carpet, table and chair had regained their places among the room's furnishings and flowers now filled a new vase.

After righting the room, Coren took to the bath, with Jenny's help. When she was finally washed and dressed, she realized that the energy used to restore the bedroom had made her extremely hungry, so she was eagerly anticipating tea and the huge array of foods that always awaited the guests at High Gate Hall: cold meats and cheeses, fruits and breads of every kind, puddings and pies -- her stomach growled as she scurried down the hall to the staircase and unceremoniously took the stairs two at a time. Whenever a maid or butler passed Coren, she would slow her walk to a respectable pace. She did not want her mother to hear of her running down the main stairway of this great house. She had caused quite enough of a stir this day and now her hunger was all she could think about. Lady Butler had taken a great deal of time educating Coren in proper decorum. Stairs were never to be taken two at a time. But, now, when no one was around to witness the act, Coren leapt from one stair to another in her eagerness to reach the landing at the first floor.

The doors to the dining room were only slightly open when Coren reached them. "Good afternoon, Mother." She spoke as though nothing out of the ordinary had taken place earlier. This tactic, Coren had learned, was the best way to deal with her mother, who would always forgive, but never forget.

"It is a fine afternoon, Coren," Lady Butler responded evenly. "I trust that everything is back in proper order?"

"Yes, Mother. Everything is quite in order," Coren countered.

"And it shall remain that way." Lady Butler cocked her head slightly to the side.

"Why, of course, Mother." Coren smiled beguilingly, and kissed her mother's cheek. "Now, if you don't mind, I am absolutely starved."

"Oh, that is a pity." Lady Butler smiled ever so slightly.

Coren studied her mother for a moment and then looked about the room. The sideboard at the opposite end of the dining room was bare, as was the buffet on the adjacent wall, except for the ornate tapestry that covered its center and fell to the ends. Was it later than she thought or had the servants simply not wanted all the food to go stale while they waited for her to come down? "What has become of the food, Mother?" Coren tried to remain nonchalant.

"Well, my dear, you may remember that tonight is the Queen's dinner?" It wasn't so much of a question as it was a statement.

"Yes, Mother, of course, I remember." Coren watched Lady Butler closely. Her mother was up to something and Coren needed to concentrate to find out what it was. The rumbling of her stomach kept pulling her thoughts away.

Lady Butler took a sip of tea from the hand-painted bone china cup that sat before her. On a plate just in front of the cup and saucer, two biscuits remained, uneaten. "You see, Coren, we have decided to forgo a meal this afternoon. We wouldn't want to spoil our appetites for the Queen's reception tonight, would we?"

If Mother asks me one more question that isn't a question, I swear I will scream out loud, Coren thought as she contemplated her next move. "Yes, Mother, of course, you are so right," Coren said, all the while deciding on the rules of engagement. "We would not want to upset the Queen by not enjoying the dinner tonight to its fullest." She smiled to disarm. "Thank you Mother, for thinking of it."

"You are quite welcome, my dear." Lady Butler relaxed a bit. "I'm pleased that you understand."

"Perfectly, Mother. In fact, I think I will even skip a cup of tea." She pushed her unused teacup away and rose from the table. "I'm going to my rooms to rest. We don't want me looking too tired for the Prince now do we?" Coren strolled from the dining room as if she had not a care in the world. Once she reached the stairs, however, she vaulted up them two and three at a time.

"Jenny! Jenny! Where are you?" Coren yelled as she

entered her suite.

"Right here, miss," Jenny said from where she lay on the lounge on the far side of the room. "Lord love a goose. Whaddya want?"

"What are you doing?" Coren eyed Jenny with disbelief.

"I was tryin' to sleep," Jenny said as she sat up making room for Coren. "You pooped me out with all of that liftin' an' shovin' an' pullin'."

Coren strolled over to Jenny. "Well, you can't sleep now," Coren said, shaking Jenny.

"I was afraid that was comin'," Jenny sputtered as she tried to take hold of Coren's arms.

"I need you to go down to the kitchen and ask cook to make you some thing to eat." Coren pulled at Jenny once again.

"Thank you, miss, but I'm really not hungry," Jenny spoke through a yawn and leaned back. "What I'd really like to do is to close me eyes for a few winks."

Coren pulled Jenny to her feet. "Not for you and you're not napping now!"

Jenny stepped back from her charge giving her a long look.

"The food is for me," Coren continued, "I'm famished!"

"I beg your pardon, miss, but didn't you just come up from tea?" Jenny motioned toward the door.

"Jenny!" Coren shouted, exasperated. "Come, you must get all the food that you can."

"Fine, miss, what is it that you want then?" Jenny said reluctantly.

"I don't care. Anything that Cook has will do." Coren feigned weakness. "I'm going to expire soon if I don't get something to eat." She clutched her stomach.

"Enough with the drama." Jenny dragged herself to the doorway. "I'll see what Cook has."

"A cake or two would be nice." Coren's tone lightened.

"A cake or two it is, then," Jenny said, humoring her charge.

"And perhaps some cheese … and the lamb from last evening, if there's any left over. Oh, and see if cook has some corned beef." Coren's list continued.

"Fine then. Cake, cheese, lamb and corned beef, it is." Jenny frowned. "It's enough for a brigade."

"Jenny, do hurry!" Coren shooed her hands at the maid.

"I'm tryin' to go, miss, but you keep addin' to the list." Jenny made it to the doorway.

"Potatoes. Jenny, don't forget potatoes!" Coren yelled as if her life depended on potatoes.

"Yes, miss," Jenny yelled back, stepping out to the hallway.

Coren dashed after her. "And soda bread!"

"And soda bread."

It took two trips to the kitchen and back, but soon Jenny had a spread of food placed on the table and it looked as if a full banquet had been spread out.

Coren was delighted as she devoured nearly everything. "Oh Jenny, I'm afraid that this is more food than I have ever eaten."

"I believe you're correct, miss." Jenny said, slightly appalled that not a crumb or morsel remained.

"Now, what was that all about?" Jenny had waited for Coren's feeding frenzy to finish before asking her.

"Mother decided that we shouldn't have tea today because of the Queen's dinner. "We wouldn't want to spoil the Queen's reception now would we?" Coren's voice and demeanor took on that of her mother.

"You had better be careful with that impression, miss," Jenny said through a smile. "It's quite good and it might just stick." She laughed at her own joke.

"I don't know what's wrong with me today, Jenny, but I could have eaten a horse."

Jenny smirked and said, "Oh, miss, please don't do that or you'll have to walk to the Queen's dinner." She laughed again.

"My, you are certainly enjoying yourself over this," Coren

said, searching the basket for any food that may have fallen to the side.

"Miss, I hate to ask this, but given your appetite," Jenny paused, apparently struggling to find the correct wording, "You're not with child, are you?"

"No!" Coren stood, indignant, tipping the basket as she did.

"I didn't think so, but I had to ask." Jenny grinned.

"That was a ridiculous thing to ask, Jenny." Brushing the crumbs from her lap. "I've never known a man, in that way. You always know my whereabouts. You should be ashamed to ask me such a thing!"

"Sorry, miss," Jenny raised her eyebrows. "Just havin' a wee bit bit of fun with ya.'"

Coren "hmphed" and felt her stomach. "Why, do I look..." she found the word hard to say, "pregnant."

"No. No." Jenny assured her. "You're just eatin' like one who is."

"Jenny, I don't know what's wrong with me." A frown crossed her face. "I could just eat and eat and eat!"

"It's simple, miss." Jenny picked up the plates and baskets. "You're nervous."

"I am?" Coren stopped to think about it. "I don't feel nervous."

"Tonight, you are going to be with the man of your dreams, dine with the Queen and quite possibly become a princess," Jenny spoke matter-of-factly.

"Oh my, Jenny!" Coren fell to the bed in the realization. "I'm so nervous!"

"Told you so." Jenny opened the door.

"Where are you going?" Coren sat up.

"I'm gettin' rid of the evidence," Jenny said, holding up the basket. "Wouldn't want your mother to find this here."

"No, you're right, Jenny. Thank you," Coren said absently.

Jenny whispered, as she stepped out into the hall, "I'll be back soon." And closed the door.

"Oh, Jenny! Jenny!" Coren shouted.

The door slowly opened and Jenny stuck her head in, apprehensively.

"See if cook has another pie. I'm still famished!"

CHAPTER FOURTEEN

Coren was pleased with herself for keeping up with the discussions about the weather and her sailing from Ireland to England. Much to her amusement, she found herself having a delightful time. Albert's father, Edward, the future King of England, was unexpectedly, a charming man. Coren could see where Eddy, as she found her prince was called by his family, got his charm and handsome face. Coren found the discussions of the Royal lineage most interesting. Prince Edward was to become, King Edward VII and would begin his own house, the House of Saxe-Coburg and Gotha. The establishment of the Royal House, she learned, was derived from the descendants of the father. Since Queen Victoria had married Prince Albert of Saxe-Coburg and Gotha, the House of Hanover that began with George I, would now end with the glorious Queen seated next to her. Albert's mother, Alexandra, Princess of Denmark was so gracious that Coren felt completely at ease with her. So much so, that the idea that this lovely woman could someday become her mother-in-law kept slipping into her thoughts. Princess Alexandra had a girlish air and the delightful lilt of her Danish accent charmed all that met her. Now, as Edward slipped his arm around Alexandra's shoulders, it was obvious to all that they were very much in love. Coren felt a slight catch come to her throat as she viewed the simple beauty of the romance before her.

The small talk that she engaged in had gone quite smoothly. At times, however, her thoughts turned away from the idle drawing room chatter to deeper questions on Irish Independence and of the poor that filled the streets of Whitechapel. Alas, they were not questions that she could or should ask, nor were they discussions in which she should partake, but that didn't stop her.

Seeing an opportunity with the Princess Alexandra, Coren moved to her side. "Excuse me, Your Highness?"

"Yes, my dear?" Alexandra smiled in query.

"Have you ever been to Whitechapel?" Coren asked bluntly.

Slightly taken aback, Alexandra replied, "Why heavens no. Why would one?"

"So that one could help those in need there," Coren intoned.

"Oh, but we do help them. We are always contributing to hospitals and the churches there." Alexandra rested a hand lightly on Coren's arm.

"Contributing? Contributing how?" Coren urged. "How does one know what is needed if one has never been to Whitechapel?"

"One does not need to be poor to know, my dear. Nor, does one need to be among the poor to know that there is a need," Alexandra spoke with a motherly tone.

"But wouldn't the situation be better served if one could actually see ..." Coren's plea was lost as the paneled doors to the drawing room slid open and a butler announced that supper was being served.

Following the Queen, they moved into the glorious dining chamber. It was a spectacular room. Saffron yellow brocade and silk panels trimmed in gold and turquoise adorned the walls. The table for this intimate gathering shimmered under the light of a hundred-candle chandelier. Silver utensils, gold trimmed goblets, crystal and china were all laid to exact specifications. It was all so perfect that Coren suddenly became slightly apprehensive that she would not know where to begin. Her stomach gurgled. Fortunately, Lady Butler was seated to her right. There she could take refuge.

To Coren's left, however, the Queen had placed His Royal Highness, Prince Albert Victor. In that, Coren took little comfort. He would be so close to her for the entire meal. It frightened her, for more than one reason, but her initial thought was that, by having him seated so closely, he would be able to watch her every move. What if she dropped a fork, spilled a glass or, heaven forbid, slurped her soup? What if her nightmares came true? Coren's stomach again gurgled with added nervousness.

The meal started with a clear broth of leek and apple. It was wonderful and Coren congratulated herself on not letting a drop fall. The evening was off to a perfect start and Coren relaxed slightly and fell into conversation with little effort.

The servants that stood behind each of the guests expertly removed the soup bowls. It was all performed so smoothly, without a sound. Not one plate ever clinked another. Not one piece of silver clanked against the crystal. It was enchanting. It would be easy to live like this. It would also be easy to forget the poor, living like this, Coren thought, and then chastised herself for the thought. In truth, she confessed, being in the highest of the classes seemed to place a spell of wonderment on everything. That brought a smile to her face.

"Do my tales of school amuse you?"

Coren's head snapped to the left, startled by the Prince's question. She flushed, as she realized she had not heard the story. "I'm so sorry, Your Highness."

"I see." Albert smiled wryly. "You must be preoccupied."

Coren nodded vigorously in agreement. "Yes! Yes, that is it. I was preoccupied."

Albert picked up a crystal goblet, keeping his eyes riveted on Coren. He sipped slowly, allowing the wine to caress his lips and linger on his tongue.

Coren swallowed, as if she too were consuming the wine.

What would the deep burgundy -hued liquid taste like on his lips, she wondered? This time the smile that formed on her face was not of amusement, but of something much more dangerous. Seduction.

The next course, a salad of nuts and fruits set around a plate of greens, was placed before the guests. It was a culinary masterpiece of arrangement, reminding Coren of the spectacular still life hanging in Sir Robert's dining room. A Pieter Claesz, she recalled. Coren instinctively picked up her salad fork. Then it struck her: a sudden rush of nausea followed by an urge to push the plate in front of her away as far as possible. She could not take another bite. This afternoon's bout of gluttony: the breads and cheeses, pies and cakes, fruits and puddings, suddenly threatened to come rising up. Not one morsel more could her stomach take. The very thought of attempting it, caused her to grimace in pain.

Lady Butler, never one to miss a trick, placed her hand on Coren's arm and leaned in so that her words would not be overheard, "Are you feeling all right, dear?"

"Oh yes, Mother. I'm fine," she said, smiling casually, hoping that Lady Butler would not see through it.

"You look a bit peaked." Lady Butler squinted slightly. "Are you sure?"

Stabbing her fork into the salad, Coren smiled broadly. "Oh, Mother, I'm fine."

"Perhaps, I was wrong to cancel tea this afternoon. It may have been better for you to have eaten something." Lady Butler shook her head. "This evening is so important to you. I should have given more thought to my decision."

"Mother, I'm fine. Really," Coren said this as she placed the salad into her mouth. She remained smiling as the chore of eating that single bite of salad nearly sent her over the edge.

"No matter now," Lady Butler determined. "With so much food before us and so much yet to come, I'm sure you will eat your fill."

Coren choked down a mouthful and nodded at her

mother.

Coren discovered that it was quite easy to push the salad around her plate to make it look as though she was eating. But when it came to the other courses, like that of whole baby swan stuffed with wild rice and peaches, she could do little to disguise the fact that she had not had one bite.

"My dear girl, is the food not to your liking?" For the first time during the meal the Queen was speaking directly to Coren and now everyone at the table was looking at her.

Why, no ... Yes! Your Majesty, the food is wonderful." Coren sliced a bit of the swan as though she was just about to eat it. A thin disguise, she thought.

"I have noticed that you have hardly eaten, my child," Her Majesty continued, "Perhaps it is only the fever of new love."

"Yes, Your Majesty, that is it," Coren agreed before she realized what she was agreeing to.

A chuckle of laughter made its way around the table as the guests all concurred with the Queen.

Coren was in love. She had just admitted it to ... everyone. Waves of hot embarrassment engulfed her.

"Would you mind terribly telling us who this man is?" It was Albert's voice Coren heard, whispering in her ear.

Coren was speechless. She felt all eyes around her penetrate into her soul, waiting for the expected answer. The Prince had made a game out of this, a dangerous thing to do with Coren. Yet, she was unsure of herself and of exactly how to answer. Of course, the man she loved sat to her left, she thought. He was the only one. No other could or would ever take his place. But how could he play with her like this, in front of the Queen and her guests?

Her Royal Highness came to Coren's defense. "Eddy? That is not very gallant of you to embarrass the young Coren in front of our guests."

"Quite so, Your Majesty. Perhaps you are right," Albert said, rising from the table.

"I should think so." The Queen laughed a quaint little

chuckle that rolled around the table as each of the guests joined her.

Albert scanned the room, apparently letting the guests enjoy the Queen's joke at his expense. His eyes lingered ever so slightly on each of them and stopped at Coren. "My dear grandmother, the Queen, is quite right." He cleared his throat, and while still gazing at Coren said, "I should not have asked you a question that I am not prepared to answer myself."

A sudden hush fell over the room. A slight breeze from the fire-warmed air caused the flame of the candles to waver ever so slightly, casting shadow dancers onto the wall, who swayed to a ghostly orchestra. Coren watched as, in her mind, the shadows transformed into likenesses of herself and the Prince.

"Dear guests, I am so pleased that each and every one of you could attend this evening," the Prince said graciously. "I must, of course, thank my dear grandmother, Her Royal Highness, for this dinner in my honor, or rather in the honor of the one who sits here beside me." Albert turned to Coren, and with a gentle urging, pulled her to her feet.

Coren immediately felt a veil of dread drape over her, as she immediately jumped to the conclusion that this was it. Doubt echoed through her mind. Surely, she thought, the Prince will tell everyone how sorry he is and that a relationship, although hoped for, will not be possible between us. The guests will express their condolences and tell the Prince to, "Keep a stiff upper lip." Oh, how she hated that saying! The shadows dancing, the unheard rhythm, all gone to waste. Only days of sadness lay before her. Her hands trembled at the thought. Her knees knocked. She wanted to bolt from the room, screaming at the Prince for this public humiliation. How dare he! How dare he! She grew furious at the thought.

She glanced around. Eyes from every corner of the room stared back at her, waiting for her to acknowledge that it was all worth it. It was better to have tried ... she thought and then abandoned the cliché. Everyone was smiling at her, even her own mother.

It was all playing out so slowly, as though time had agonizingly come to a dead stop. "What should I say? What should I say?" Coren heard the words, but did not remember speaking them aloud. What she had planned on saying only in her thoughts, had rung out clearly.

"Why dear, you must say," the Queen said, as she slowly stood, "'Yes,' of course,"

As if an order had been given, each of the guests followed the Queen's example and rose, taking up a goblet of wine.

Coren turned to Lady Butler, whose smile spread from ear to ear. She had never seen her mother so look so happy. Confused, having been lost in her thoughts, Coren whispered to her mother, "I'm afraid I missed something, Mother. Why are we toasting?" Coren looked about the room, noting that everyone was smiling. "What are we all so happy about?"

"Coren, you must have heard," Lady Butler said with hint of laughter. "The Prince intends to marry."

Coren affected an air of delight and turned to the Prince. "That is so wonderful, Your Highness. Who is this fortunate woman?"

All in the room erupted with laughter. Shouts of "Here, here," were raised by some of the men.

"You are an angel, Coren." Albert looked down into Coren's bewildered eyes. "But only the devil in you would make me ask again." He placed his goblet of wine on the table and with both of his hands took both of Coren's. "I would be eternally grateful, if you and Lady Butler would allow me to ask your father, the esteemed Lord Butler, faithful servant to the Crown, for your hand in marriage."

"Oh!" Coren's exclamation sent the guests again into a fit of laughter.

"Coren, dear." Lady Butler leaned onto her daughter's shoulder. "I think the correct response is, 'Yes.'"

"Oh!" And they laughed again. "I mean, yes, of course."

Coren swung her arms, exaggerating the response.

"You are marvelous!" Albert swung his arms, as Coren had just done, in playful mockery. As he did so, he jostled his goblet of wine, spilling the contents onto the white linen tablecloth. The stain spread out around the goblet, forming a blood-red that it seemed, only Coren took note of.

CHAPTER FIFTEEN

The guests crowded around Albert and Coren, congratulating them with true fervor. The swiftness with which the Prince had taken to Coren surprised everyone. Albert had been in search of a bride, or rather his father and mother had been, for many London seasons. A Royal of Albert's age, just barely twenty-four, who was not yet betrothed, prompted whispers of scandal.

Queen Victoria was aware of the talk of scandal among London society regarding her grandson. Now, at least some of the gossip would be put to rest with his marriage to this Irish beauty. Her grandson, would someday, like his father, be King of all Britain. That would bring hardships all their own. Now, with Coren by Albert's side, like Alexandra at Edward's side, the tasks ahead would be made easier.

Albert's father proudly espoused his son's proposal of marriage, not necessarily to assuage the gossip that surrounded him, but to see his son truly happy. Albert had confided to his father that he wished for the comfort of the middle classes, who only had themselves to worry about. Edward was hopeful that since Albert had found Coren, his son would also find the happiness he sought, just as he himself had, with his own lovely Alexandra.

Alexandra mused, "Our son has chosen a worthy match for himself." The gentle move of Alexandra's hand to

Edward's showed that she, too, knew of what he was thinking.

Coren was obviously lovely, yet underneath that beauty was a strong independent spirit that would be the perfect complement to her son's, she thought. In the brief moments that she had spoken to Coren, she sensed that this young Irish lass would possess an undying loyalty for the man she loved as she demonstrated a deep sense of caring for others as well. Yes, Alexandra smiled, she liked this girl, and knew they would be kindred spirits and fast friends.

Congratulations seemed a bit hasty, Lady Butler thought, and then decided for propriety's sake, she needed to speak. She cleared her throat and rose to her full height. The guests turned to her. "It is most kind of you to wish my daughter and His Royal Highness, Prince Albert the best of a future together." A murmur of agreement rose among the guests. "However," Lady Butler continued, "my dear husband, Lord Butler, has not yet agreed to the marriage. It might be best if we all held our heartfelt congratulations until Lord Butler has given his consent."

"Too true, Lady Butler. How presumptuous of us all," Her Majesty berated. "Let it be known, however, that the Crown will do everything in its power to assure that the gracious Lord Butler will give his heartfelt and most enthusistic blessings to my grandson and your daughter."

"Thank you, dear Grandmama. I am sure that the Crown has the ability to be very persuasive – as I know only too well," Albert interjected. A polite chuckle from the guests followed.

"You do! You do!" Her Majesty chimed in, obviously entertained by his aside. It was apparent she enjoyed humbling her grandson to keep him from becoming too sure of himself. "The Crown also remembers where the Royal whipping stick is. So you had best mind your manners."

Albert reddened as several of the guests laughed out loud.

"Perhaps Your Majesty should try using that well-worn stick on certain members of Parliament next session," Coren boldly volunteered.

Shouts of 'Bravo!' and "Well said!' echoed through the dining chamber, as once again laughter rang out.

Queen Victoria raised an eyebrow and gave a slight nod in immediate approval. "Lady Butler, I do like this girl!"

The remainder of the evening went splendidly. No longer were Coren's thoughts consumed with where she could possibly hide the next plate of food, but instead lingered on her prince. She giggled at the thought of that phrase, *her prince*. Was he really hers?

"Yes." Prince Albert turned to Coren and smiled.

"Yes, what, Your Highness?" Coren cocked her head, perplexed.

"Yes, to whatever it is you're thinking." His response was matter of fact. Only the thin smile that spread slowly over his face gave him away. "And I hope it was the same thought I was thinking?"

Coren's eyes widened and she bit down on her lip, more to keep a smile from forming on her face and mirroring his, than out of nerves. "Why I'm sure I don't know what Your Highness was thinking." She toyed with him. "I can, of course, only assume that it was good and kind thoughts of me."

He studied her for a moment. "My thoughts about you, Coren, are only and can never be anything less than, good and kind."

His eyes met hers and Coren was instantly taken back to the moment they first met, where soft music played and

Albert's arms were wrapped tightly about her. She melted again, swept away by the reflection of the lights, glimmering from the dark pools of his eyes.

"I hope that we will have the opportunity to spend a great deal of time together in the weeks before our marriage." Albert's words brought Coren back to reality. "That is if there are weeks before we marry."

Coren was about to agree when she took note of the latter part of what the Prince had just said. "What do you mean, Your Highness, by, if there are weeks." With caution evident in her tone she continued, "When was Your Highness thinking of ..." she stopped, not sure of how to proceed.

Albert leaned in so close to Coren's ear that his lips lightly brushed them as he formed the words. "Tonight, if possible?"

Chills, shivers, goose bumps, and every conceivable sensation coursed through her body. These sensations from the sensual sounds of his voice were so enticing, that Coren wished that he would read the entire folio of Shakespeare's works with his lips brushing against her ear.

"Tonight, Your Highness?" Coren asked, not sure of what he meant.

"I wish that we would marry, tonight."

Coren jumped to her feet knocking the Prince to the floor as she did. "Why Albert ... I mean Your Highness, that is impossible!"

All the guests in the room stopped in their mid-conversations and turned to see what the commotion was about.

"As you all can see," Prince Albert said, still sitting on the floor. "I can hardly stand. I am so in love with this woman."

Everyone laughed with relief, enjoying the Prince's good humor. Everyone that is, except Lady Butler.

Lady Butler had been keeping a close eye on her daughter throughout the meal. Now, while the other guests discussed and collaborated their stories for tomorrows' gossip, she strategically positioned herself on the chair so that either a sideways glance or a quick look in one of the mirrors that adorned many of the walls would let her see what Coren, and more importantly, the Prince were up to.

Lady Butler was delighted that the Prince wanted to have her daughter for his bride. Her slight reticence, however, lie in the fact that the Prince was considerably more worldly than Coren. Prince Albert was a world traveler with a six-year gap in their ages, and experiences, could make all the difference in their life together. Lady Butler was not sure what her daughter knew and did not know about life with a man. It was a conversation that she had intended to have with Coren, when the right time came. Apparently, it was now. She made her way around the room, purposefully directing herself toward her daughter and Prince Albert. She could not have the necessary conversation with Coren now, but she could see what the commotion was all about.

Prince Albert got to his feet as Lady Butler arrived. "I apologize if I have caused you any embarrassment, Lady Butler," Albert said, bowing slightly.

He's good, Lady Butler thought, as she prepared to speak. He had pre-empted what she was about to say, taking the power of her words away. *This prince might make a worthy opponent for Coren or myself*, she thought, and then said aloud, "Your Highness has caused me some concern, not necessarily embarrassment." Then, looking to her daughter continued, "I would just like to be assured that nothing is amiss."

Coren took a deep breath, as if to speak, and then hesitated. Would she start a scandal, when the Prince had just asked for her hand in marriage, by allowing herself to repeat the words the Prince had spoken? After all, the words were innocent enough.

I wish that we would marry tonight.

Now that she thought about it, she would like to marry tonight. No - this moment! And why should she wait? She had found the man of her dreams and couldn't think of any reason to wait a moment longer, except for the one that stared her in the face. Lady Butler.

"Mother, you needn't worry," Coren spoke up, afraid to let the silence linger any longer. "The Prince was being very forward and I could not let him get the better of me, so I – stood up to him. I'm sure you understand."

Lady Butler laughed slightly. "Of course, my dear."

Was Mother really dismissing the notion of a problem or had she actually believed her feeble excuse? Coren thought for a moment, then decided to believe the latter and determined it would be prudent to continue to keep as close a watch on her mother, as her mother was keeping on herself and the Prince.

Dinner was finished and the orchestra began to play in a small ballroom just off the dining chamber. Albert had arranged for the first piece to be the same waltz that the orchestra had played when he and Coren had first danced. He guided Coren to the ballroom and she once again found herself in the arms of her prince. "May I?" Albert smirked knowingly.

"Of course you may." Coren raised an eyebrow, cocking her head slightly. "But only if you can persuade the orchestra to play this waltz all evening."

"It's already taken care of, my dear." Prince Albert smiled.

My Prince is always one step ahead of me, Coren thought. *He will make a fine opponent for the game.* She studied his incredibly handsome face. *A fine opponent.* Her grin now mimicked his.

"We find something funny?" Prince Albert raised an eyebrow.

Coren slapped the Prince lightly on the arm, an action that surprised her. "No, your highness, I do not find anything funny. I find it a wish come true."

"Ah then, shall we?" Albert asked, offering his arm.

"We shall," Coren said taking the proffered arm.

The moment that Albert drew Coren closer into his arms and the scent of his Bayberry cologne swept into her nostrils, she was transported. She was lost in a vision of the mornings that she and her Prince would share nestled snugly in each other's arms. Coren surprised herself by the longing for those mornings when, she would wake to see the stubble on his chin and curl herself into the place between his arm and his chest. Those were the mornings she would dream of tonight and every night until they played out, just as she now realized, she wanted them to.

Father's blessings came as no surprise to Coren. She knew he would never let his politics get in the way of his daughter's happiness. Still, she found some relief in receiving them. What did surprise her, however, was the fact that he had decided to deliver his response in person.

Queen Victoria was quite insistent in her request that Lord Butler send word immediately. She too wanted his blessings and for the Crown, the sooner the better. This union would do more than just squelch the rumors that followed her grandson and the Royal Family. She wanted the union of England and Ireland, and what better way than through the marriage of her grandson to the daughter of the most outspoken of Irish Society.

Lord Butler never gave way in his quest for Irish independence. His relationship with the Crown was based on his refusal to give in to the Crown's demands to bring the Irish people and their sporadic leaders into the fold of English rule. The Crown could always depend on him to be fair, however, no matter what his feelings were. Thus, he had struck an uneasy alliance with the Queen. She needed him. He needed her.

"This is much too important to be sent by messenger," Lord Butler said adamantly, as Coren whirled to see her father a mere three feet behind her.

Coren was delighted that her father had made the journey to London. She missed him dearly, but his duties were of the utmost importance and she understood and supported him whole-heartedly. She threw herself into his arms as she squealed in delight. "Oh Father, I'm so happy to see you! Now everything is perfect."

Lord Butler fervently hugged his daughter to him, murmuring, "Ah, Macushlah, Macushlah." He held her at arms length and spoke, "My dearest, do ye truly love him?" He let his brogue thicken.

"Aye, Father, I do," she said, imitating his Irish lilt.

"Then with all my heart, I wish ye both well," his voice broke as emotion overcame him.

Coren hugged him tightly. Her eyes brimming with tears of joy and love that now, made emeralds sparkle brighter.

CHAPTER SIXTEEN

This would be a day made for making memories. Not the kind that would slip away into bits and pieces, crumbling after a few years like rotted wood, but memories that would form the foundation for all the memories to come. Whole pictures. Every thought, every smell and every sound would be locked away into the deepest crevasses of Coren's mind. There she could recall: special words whispered into her ear, a touch, a glance not seen by anyone but herself, and the gentle whoosh of the doves swooping close to her head. These memories, like the mighty stone forts of her Ireland, would stand forever.

Lady Butler wore a radiant veneer as she paced her suite, disguising the melancholy that threatened to overcome her. She was reviewing in her mind, all of the multitude of last minute details she had to direct throughout this morning. A morning that would see her daughter wed by afternoon. She was overjoyed that her daughter would soon marry a prince. Yet she could not help but feel a certain sadness, too.

This morning, she would bid farewell to the daughter she had known and *the game* as it had been for these last eighteen years. They had both won. The game, now, as well as her own life, would be changed forever. A satisfied smile came over her face. Lady Butler returned from her musing and noticed Jenny, bustling about the room.

"Jenny? Is everything ready?"

Startled, Jenny said, "Almost, ma'am."

"Almost? Almost?" Lady Butler frowned. "Jenny? What does that mean? Almost?"

"Ah, it means that we're . . ." Jenny hesitated then spoke the obvious. "Nearly ready, ma'am."

Lady Butler arched an eyebrow. "I'm quite sure that I know the definition of the word, Jenny."

"Of course you do, ma'am." Jenny said, innocently. "But why then did ya ask me to explain it?"

"Jenny would you like to remain in this employ?" Lady Butler looked at her sternly.

Jenny hesitated a moment. It was a well-honed threat. But one that Jenny never knew if she should take heed to.

"Well?" Lady Butler's voice thundered.

"Certainly, ma'am." Jenny took heed.

"Then see to it that everything is not simply 'almost' ready!" Lady Butler's eyes flashed in admonishment.

"Yes, ma'am." Jenny hurried toward the door. "She's in a right foul mood this morning," Jenny whispered as Coren passed, entering Lady Butler's suite.

Lord Butler had remained knowingly silent as Lady Butler and Jenny spoke, but now crossed the room and leaned into his wife, kissing her gently upon the cheek, as if a single kiss could wipe away her unspoken fears.

Though not usually one to allow public displays of affection, Lady Butler never gave the slightest hint of embarrassment from her husband's overtures. She, in fact, turned to Lord Butler as he kissed her and kissed him back, full on the mouth.

Lord Butler knew it was difficult for her, letting go of their child.

Bloody hell. It's difficult for me, he thought.

Coren witnessed this simple exchange of affection between her parents, as she entered the doorway of their suite. Her eyes moistened with tears. She wondered if she could really leave the two people who meant the world to her? Who were her world? Perhaps she wasn't as 'grown up' as she had thought.

Lord and Lady Butler parted their lips and looked at Coren lovingly. That was all Coren needed, this avowal from her parents, that she was indeed doing what was right.

Lady Butler had enlisted the Queen's personal assistance in the planning of the wedding. "In truth," Lady Butler confided to Coren, "with everything happening so quickly, I could never have put my plans together without the assistance of the Queen."

"Her Majesty has been most helpful," Lord Butler added as he seated himself in a worn leather chair comfortably placed near the fire.

"Such a short engagement period is . . . surley unheard of." There was a hint of apprehension evident in Lady Butler's voice.

Coren corrected. "You will recall that it was Albert's request, not mine."

"If not for Her Majesty, this wedding could never have been planned and acted upon so quickly. But, I suppose, when one rules the country," Lady Butler continued, "one can make the rules."

"Well put, my dear," Lord Butler added.

"Coren, it's time for you to dress," Lady Butler instructed.

"Oh, Mother, I have time," Coren pleaded. "Please, let me stay here with you and Father for just a few minutes more."

There was no reply, only a muffled sniffle from the leather

chair by the fire.

Saint Paul's towering steeple stood stark against the cloudless sky of that London afternoon. A silk carpet of pure white stretched from the great doors of the cathedral down the steps to the street below.

Swans swam carefree in the small pond that Prince Albert had had built just for the occasion, their plumage so white that their black beaks and yellow eyes looked as though they had been painted on. Thirty gilded cages, one for each day of their engagement were suspended from either side of the archway to the great edifice. Each cage contained two white doves.

Inside Saint Paul's, the long black and white marbled aisle that Prince Albert and Coren would soon walk together, was polished to a high gloss. Reflections from the candles that lined the aisle flickered off of the tiles.

Long processions of royalty and society strolled through the doors to bear witness to this momentous event. It had happened quickly. More quickly than either of the two families would have liked. What should have taken a year or so to plan had fallen into place in just weeks. Their love would not wait. It was scandalous.

But so romantic.

As Coren waited for her processional music to start, she was struck again by Albert's insistence on a quickly held wedding. At times it was just as distressing to Coren as it had been to Lady Butler. The Prince was a man that any woman would want and Coren was definitely no exception. But given the short engagement, she realized that she hardly knew him. She didn't know what foods he preferred or what colors he liked or what side of the bed he slept on! Oh no, Coren thought. A potential disaster. She always slept closest to the window, with a slight trickle of clean Irish, or now English, air wafting in. What if he hated fresh air? What if he wanted her side of the bed? What if he slept in the middle? Coren began to laugh, a laugh that threatened to grow to hysterics. How could she worry about these trivial matters? If Albert didn't see things her way, he would just have to change. She chuckled again.

"Miss! Miss! They're ready for ya'," Jenny chirped into Coren's ear. "Are ya' all right?"

Coren came out of her thoughts as a smile spread across her face. "I'm fine, Jenny. I've just been woolgathering." She kissed Jenny on her brow. "Thank you for everything. I do love you so."

Jenny burst into tears. "Oh, Miss Coren, I love ya' too," Jenny gushed, blubbering as Coren began her long promenade to the altar and her waiting prince.

CHAPTER SEVENTEEN

The wedding was perfect.

CHAPTER EIGHTEEN

The reception at Buckingham Palace, which followed the wedding, was just as perfect and lasted long into the night. "It was simply glorious," Coren said to everyone who asked if she'd enjoyed the ceremony. People from all over the world came to bestow their congratulations and best wishes on the enchanting bride and groom. Coren had been given a quick lesson in the proper decorum and etiquette for greeting all of these royal personages, but occasionally doubt lingered in the back of her mind as she curtsied and addressed each guest. She must be all that Albert expected, she thought. And more.

"Don't worry. You're doing just fine," Albert said in her ear. "Just keep smiling."

He really must stop reading my thoughts, she mused. It was most annoying! Coren would have to watch herself in the future.

"I canna move my face any more." Coren thickened her Irish brogue to add to the comedy of the line. "I'm afraid you'll have to live with me like this for the rest of your life, my husband." She turned to him and showed him a hideous grimace.

"Gladly." He leaned to her and kissed the grimace away.

"Buon Giorno, Your Highness. I see that the honeymoon has already begun." A bellow of laughter followed.

Albert turned abruptly. "Pasquale, my dear friend." He

embraced the man Then espying the woman standing next to Pasquale, he reached for her hand and raised it to his lips. "May I present the Italian Ambassador and his wife Antoinette," he said turning to Coren. "Ambassador and Signora LaFica, my wife, the Princess Coren."

"Ambassador, Signora LaFica, tu se mi piace." Coren held out her hand.

"It is our pleasure, I assure you." Ambassador LaFica took Coren's extended hand into both of his.

"La vita in Italia e differente da quella negli Britannia?"

"Si, si, Principessa," the Ambassador said. "Let us speak of the differences between our two nations later this evening."

"Si, dopo," Coren said with a nod.

"You speak Italian?" Albert said to Coren after reining in his surprise.

"Apparently." Coren batted her eyes at him.

"You surprise me at every turn, my Principessa." Albert smiled, then leaned into her ear. "And I have my own surprises for you later."

Coren's mouth fell open as the color flushed to her cheeks.

Ambassador LaFica cleared his throat.

"Ambassador, forgive us," Coren said regaining her composure. "My husband has spoken highly of you and your charming wife."

"If that is true I hope that he has only told you the good deeds that we have done," Pasquale chuckled.

"But of course." Coren smiled. "As I understand it, there are no others. I have heard how important your work helping the needy in your country has been to you, as it has been for me to help those less fortunate in my native Ireland."

"Ah, Albert, you don't deserve this woman. Intelligence and beauty are a powerful combination." The Ambassador chuckled again.

Albert's eyes glowed with new love. "As I am finding out. I am still surprised that she said yes."

"Your Highness, I had no choice," Coren demurred.

"You didn't?" Albert raised an eyebrow.

"No." Coren's eyes twinkled with mischief. "I promised my mother that I would only marry a man I loved."

Albert stared into Coren's eyes, lost for a moment, overcome with deep emotion. Then he wrapped his arms around her and kissed her deeply.

"Perhaps we should end the reception now, Your Highness?" The Ambassador nudged Albert's side.

The kiss did not end.

Pasquale chuckled and as he took his wife's arm said, "Ah, he should have been Italian."

The length of the receiving line continued to grow long into the evening. Coren greeted and met everyone with a jubilant smile and polite small talk, but her thoughts were far away. Her thoughts were on the end of the night.

Tonight she would go to Albert's home. Tonight she would fall into the arms of her prince. Tonight she would lay in his bed. *In their bed*, she corrected. Tonight she would become a woman. No longer would the little girl who lingered inside, wonder at what womanhood and love would bring. She would lie with a man: feeling him next to her, on top of her, his weight pushing down, his arms engulfing her, his face so close, his manhood rising. This would be the night that she discovered if what her mother had told her was true.

Oh, how she hoped it was.

"It will be." Albert read her thoughts once again. "I promise." She heard in her ear.

Coren knew by the rush of warmth she felt that she was turning scarlet.

CHAPTER NINETEEN

She wasn't quite the woman she'd hoped when their wedding night began. A nervous giggle escaped from Coren's mouth as Albert crawled into bed alongside of her. A strange sensation overwhelmed her as she came to the full realization that this was the first time she had been in bed with a man. He positioned himself on her left, away from the window.

What an accommodating gentleman, she thought. Even though she was nervous, she felt safe. Protected by this man. It would be this way from now on, for years to come, until they grew old. They would sleep and do ... who knew what else together!

Well, she thought, giggling again, *I guess I'm about to find out, what else.*

"Are you nervous?" Prince Albert asked propping himself up on his elbow, peering down at her.

"No," she lied. "Are you?"

He grinned.

Her senses were almost overwhelmed by all that she was thinking, all that she was seeing and all that she wanted to do.

Albert shifted closer to her, his musky scent filled her nostrils.

Their bedroom - just the thought of this place being *their* bedroom, was enough to send her back into nervous giggles – was enormous. It was filled with the most expensive and exquisite furniture. The room was dimly lit by two candles Albert had placed on each of the side tables that rested on either side of the bed. Shadowy figures flickered on and off Albert's face. The flames from the candles danced in his eyes. He looked more handsome than Coren could ever remember him being. For the first time she saw that his chest was covered with a thin mat of dark hair. It swirled around his chest, which flexed as he shifted his weight. Even in the dim light she could make out his muscled torso and arms. They begged her to touch them. She giggled again.

"I amuse you?" A thin smile and arched eyebrows accompanied the question.

"Oh no!" Coren thought about it for a moment. "I mean, yes, but in a good way."

Albert's eyebrows arched again.

"Truly," she said trying to convince him.

His naked torso so close to her made it difficult for Coren to keep her eyes off of his chest. She tried to look only into Albert's eyes, taking in the darkness that pooled there, but her eyes, as if on their own, kept falling back down to his chest and the dark swirls of hair that she ached to touch.

Albert flexed his chest, causing the muscles to bounce. First one side then the other. Coren's gaze shot back up to meet Albert's. He smiled. "Can you do that?"

Caught off guard, Coren laughed out loud. "No!" She looked down at her own chest. Her breasts were full, taught and upright. She considered herself to have a fine bosom - not too big nor too small--but she had never consciously tried to make them bounce. She laughed again. "I couldn't."

"One never knows until one tries," Albert said, with a hint of curiosity.

Coren closed her eyes and concentrated. She thought hard. Nothing happened.

"There. Look. You did it." Albert's eyes darted back and forth from Coren's chest, barely covered by a wisp of material, to her eyes. "See, I knew you could do it."

Coren looked down at her breasts and watched as she thought about them again. They did not move. Only the loud laughter that poured from her mouth caused her chest to bounce.

"Ha! Now you're doing it again," Albert teased.

"Where?" Coren said looking at herself and pulling at her neckline to see if she missed something.

"Well, it is hard to see," Albert said. "The garment you are wearing makes it difficult, but I assure you that you made them bounce, just like this." He flexed his chest once again, bouncing his pectorals simultaneously.

"I can not do that, Albert," Coren spoke, a little scolding in her voice.

"I assure you, you can. I saw you do it." He reached out and touched a spot on her breast just above her neckline. "There." Sudden waves and rushes of chills sped through her body. She shuddered. For a moment, she lost control. Her stomach tightened and she could not breath. Her legs kicked out in convulsions. Her foot rubbed up against his. Coren immediately pulled her leg away and then wished she hadn't. Slowly, in an attempt to be nonchalant, Coren eased her leg back toward Albert's. She shifted in the bed, pulling the covers up to her neck. And then realizing what she was covering, she pulled the sheet back down again. Her toes touched his shin. She hesitated a moment and then moved her leg closer. She stopped, resting now, just slightly touching Albert's leg.

And then it struck her. She hadn't thought of it before. But now it hit her full on. She was not just lying in bed with a man for the first time in her life, but she was lying in bed with a naked man! When had this happened? How had he gotten his clothes off without her seeing? She wanted to recoil, to pull away . . . and she wanted to move closer, to feel him. Cascading random thoughts came into her mind and then fled away. The mere thought of him, so close to her and naked! It was enough to send those unrelenting same series of shocks and chills through her once again.

But then was he really completely naked? She could clearly see that he did not have a nightshirt on. His bare chest and arms lay just before her. Her toe lightly caressed his leg, moving up and down. It too was bare. Only one portion of him remained unseen, untouched, covered by the bed linen. Coren glanced at Albert's mid-section trying to see if the outline of the sheet draped over his body gave her any hint of what lie underneath. The dim light of the two candles was not enough to allow her to see what was there. The dancing shadows that fell and moved over the bed made it even more difficult to see what the sheets concealed.

Coren took in a deep breath and stretched her arms and her legs. She fidgeted in the bed, trying to maneuver closer - in as discreet a way as possible. Her leg could not move up high enough past Albert's calf to feel if he was wearing some kind of covering. Slowly she eased one arm under the sheet, arched her back raising herself up and with her hand, untwisted the bedclothes covering her.

Satisfied that Albert did not yet know of her intentions, she rested, leaving her one arm under the sheet. Again she feigned restlessness and stretched, even faking a yawn. Then quickly considering, she wished she hadn't done that, lest Albert think she was too tired or too bored to do anything other than sleep. But the fake yawn happened so naturally. She silently congratulated herself on her bit of trickery. Now her arm was just inches away from him. She could feel the heat radiating from his body. She could feel her own heat begin to rise.

He stirred.

For a moment Coren was afraid that he would turn away from her. Instead he settled, closing the gap between himself and Coren's hand. Albert laid his head on the pillow next to Coren, smiling so lovingly. He made no attempt to touch her, to kiss her or to move upon her as she so desired him to do. He just lay there, his eyes sometimes open, sometimes closed. Coren feared that her first night with a man would consist only of him sleeping by her side. She considered this, wondering if that would really be so bad. After all, there would be plenty of other nights, hundreds of nights, when she and Albert would have the opportunity to be together as man and wife.

Opportunity?

This was not some game of chance played by the farm hands in a potato field. This was her wedding night! A night all brides were supposed to look forward to. She would not let it slip away into the wee hours of the night, when both she and Albert would be too tired to do anything.

Coren knew that she had to do something and she had to do it now. Without so much as a moment's hesitation, Coren reached her hand out, stretching her fingers and grasped at where she thought he should be.

A gasp. A very loud gasp escaped from Albert's lips, as Coren's fingers wrapped around his stiff, taught manhood.

The gasp was followed by a scream from Coren as she felt the searing heat from him pulsate through her arm and into her groin. She felt a rush of dampness and warmth in her loins. There was a searing heat in her hand. Yet, she did not release him.

Albert's mouth instantly covered hers, his arms sweeping her to him, enfolding her.

They kissed for what felt like hours, his tongue and hers dancing. Her neck was nibbled, soft words were whispered into her ear, and the tops of her breasts were caressed until she thought she would burn up with fever. It must have been hours, or could it have been days? Coren did not know. Time had sped by or had it stopped? She wasn't sure. There were no cognizant moments, no times when she calculated what to do next. It just happened. Hours or days, it did not matter. She was here with the man she loved.

He held her. Arms wrapped around her shoulders.

And she held him! Her hand wrapped around his . . . Her eyes grew wide as she realized that she had not let go! He stood hard and full . . . and still in her hand!

And then everything moved on in waves of emotion and no more rational thought. Soon Coren was surprised at how she felt no discomfort by the weight of Albert who now lay on top of her. When had he done that? She didn't remember him moving on to her. And now with his lips and tongue earnestly covering her breasts - when had she removed her nightdress? It was all happening to her, and yet she was seemingly unaware. Had she helped him untie her nightdress and slip it over her head? Had she willingly exposed her bare breasts to him? The linen sheet was pulled down to her waist. His hard torso locked between her legs. His lips moved slowly, marvelously over her nipples. Hard, erect nipples that ached for the touch he so willingly gave.

Methodically, he moved down from her breasts. Kissing, licking, lightly rubbing her stomach. She convulsed and writhed in ecstasy. Her breath seemed to have left her. She was gasping for air, but could not get enough. Her mind reeled, at first wanting him to stop. To continue. To move down. She grasped the linens, twisting them tightly around her hands. She pulled them to her mouth and bit into the soft cotton fabric. She was afraid that she would scream, stop.

Stop, Stop. The words echoed in her mind, but he did not obey. Gloriously, thankfully, this time he did not read her thoughts.

Albert raised his head, eyes twinkling. Or had he?

Another surge of emotion struck her and she gently laid her hands upon his head, stroking his hair, which now fell around his face. She pushed on him, urging him down.

He moved. He moaned. He complied.

The movement alone caused her to arch her back upwards, tightening the muscles around her buttocks. Searing racks of joy sped through her. She could not control herself. She wanted more.

Albert's lips lingered, hovering above her. He brushed her mound with his hair and then lightly blew on the soft wetness there. She felt his lips brushing over her coarse hairs. She thought maybe she should tell him to stop, but couldn't think of reason why, especially when it felt so incredibly wonderful. His arms dipped under her legs and he pulled them apart. She didn't resist. She couldn't. She glanced down, mesmerized, watching his biceps bulge, the muscles flattening out against her thighs.

Coren giggled ecstatically as the dark hair under his arms splayed out, tickling the underside of her thighs in excruciating delight. With his teeth he tugged at one of the hairs covering her most intimate possession. The slight sting, mingled in with a sheer bliss that overwhelmed her.

Now she knew. After eighteen years she knew what it meant to have pleasure beyond dreams - or so she thought. Albert tossed his hair back with a flick of his head and brought his lips down on Coren's leg. Every inch of her leg: thigh, calf, ankle, foot and toes felt his tongue.

An unbelievable bliss.

And then he moved to give the same attention to the other leg. As his tongue slowly made its way back up to the apex where her legs came together, she was racked with spasms of uncontrollable tremors. His lips and tongue danced in perfect harmony over her. A symphony of sensations played out, overlapping one another, lingering, and then fading back so that new notes could solo. The winds, brass and percussion built up to crescendos of immeasurable proportions. What would be the climax of the piece?

She found out.

The sun rose and the morning sang before he had finished with her.

Coren lay in their bed, watching Albert sleep. She gazed into the dawn's slight umber, wishing the sun would set again before he woke.

CHAPTER TWENTY

The days that followed the wedding between Prince Edward Albert Victor and the now, Princess Coren Catherine were filled with never ending duties. There were lists of tasks to be carried out, and this list did not include the many daily greetings with various members of royalty, heads of state and society. However, Coren did have servants, secretaries and a full entourage to keep her going where she was supposed to go and guiding her to whom she was supposed to meet. In her mind, she really wasn't all that important a personage. Why don't they all want to meet Albert, she thought? And yet the lines continued, they all seemed to want an audience with her.

Her eyes drifted around the sitting room as she mused. I have already met so many of the elite that there cannot possibly be anymore. She knew she had met more people in a week than lived in all of Ireland! This gave Coren slight pause. Here in London wealth seemed so abundant, but in her beloved homeland so many seemed to be struggling.

Some Duke or other brought her out of her reverie. He held her hand and smiled. She returned his smile graciously, hoping he hadn't said something important. She could be safe with that. No one ever seemed to say anything important. She sighed. Would she never finish meeting those of society who called upon her every afternoon? Dozens, or so it seemed, of dignitaries would fill the sitting rooms of the palace, all waiting for a chance to meet the new Princess.

Most had come to give their congratulations to the newly wed couple and most would find a way to work into their conversations a slight favor or two that perhaps, Princess Coren could help them with, or mayhap her husband could help them with. Dear Mother of God! Did they truly think she was that inane? Apparently. Well, she and Albert could amuse themselves that night in bed going through the list of 'small' favors of the day. Lord 'so-and-so's' west wing could use just a tad of renovation. The Duke of 'somewhere' has been trying to buy this magnificent stallion. And on it went.

Then they would pursue the truly important matters.

Coren had scarcely seen Albert in the last day or two. He was just a voice down a distant hall or footsteps echoing as he crossed the courtyard in the garden below their window.

As Lord 'whoever,' rambled on, Coren began to reminisce about this particular morning. Each morning she would throw open the windows and gaze out over the incredible sprawling gardens below. And more often than not she would catch a glimpse of her husband as he went from one duty to the other.

As Albert made his casual stroll through the gardens, Coren's gaze followed his movements. *I love to watch my husband walk.* She flushed at the thought. His finely tailored clothes, hugged his body as he strolled, revealing broad shoulders and powerful arms.

Arms that can engulf me. She flushed again.

Now, as he strode away from her came her favorite part of his walk. Dear God, what would her mother say if she knew of her wanton thoughts. She was sure it was all Jenny's fault. Jenny had trained her incorrectly. She would have to reprove her for it . . . or perhaps thank her . . . Ah, well, what's done is done and he does have the most incredible . . . Jesus, Mary, and Joseph! He was bending over.

Coren did not just flush. She broke out in a sweat. She was sure she was about to collapse.

And then he did it.

He slid his left hand over his backside and sensually caressed it.

Coren almost screamed. Her mouth was agape. Her knees had buckled and she was forced to hold onto the window frame for dear life.

Albert, still bent over, slowly glanced over his shoulder and met Coren's eyes.

He knew! Again! How could he? Coren wanted to . . . to . . . to exchange her hand for his. She ached for him desperately. Would he come to her?

Albert straightened and as he did, he smiled lasciviously and slowly nodded.

When Coren and Albert's duties had subsided and they had the rare chance to meet, it was only for a fleeting moment before one or the other was whisked away by the hordes of staff and well-wishers that surrounded them both and tried to cater to their every need.

The lingering memories of that first night together held fast in Coren's mind. She played and replayed every detail she could remember. She wanted it all to be completely ingrained into her thoughts, etched into her mind, so that she would never forget a single moment of it. Then she replayed every moment of every night with him for the past two weeks, recalling all she had learned and enjoyed, and fantasizing on all she had yet to enjoy.

Even now, while she carried out the duties of her newly assigned life, sitting and making polite chatter, she could only think of Albert and his touch. She found herself floating back to their bed, feeling every tingle, every rush of shock coursing through her body. The anticipation of tonight was too much to bear. Would she never get enough of him?

Tea was served. Thank God!

As Coren occupied herself with her tea and some truly delicious little cakes, she could escape once again into her thoughts. She did find the incessant small talk and innocuous gossip with the ladies of society rapidly becoming boring. It dulled her senses to sit and listen to endless hours of talk about the weather and polo and the tea.

She wanted more from this new life. Her plans did not include wasting away in tearooms and music halls listening to the children of society parents play endless notes and recite meaningless poetry. Her plans brought hope to people. They did not put them to sleep!

As a child of one of London's wealthier businessmen droned on and on about a toad and a princess, which was intended to amuse Coren, her thoughts turned to her own musings.

Sitting here among opulence and royalty, visions of squalor and despair in her own Ireland collided in her mind. Here she sat, Princess Coren, her every need filled to overflowing, while just beyond the waters that surrounded this island, lay her beloved island of Ireland.

Ireland, a land that rolled green with the grasses of summer and red with the blood of her people. It was where she began and it would be where she would end. She had not forgotten her pledge to herself and those she had left behind. She knew that it was her destiny to fulfill the needs of her people who struggled daily for independence from England. This had now become her own struggle. Coren . . . the Princess Coren, through her marriage to Albert, had become an intricate part of England. She and Ireland were tethered to England much like Siamese twins. Conjoined, yet seeking separate identities. She loved her new home and life with Albert and everyone she had come to meet had been most gracious and helpful. She would need time, however, to work her way into the Queen's favor. The Queen had taken an instant liking to Coren, the intended bride of her grandson. But Coren wanted more. Would the Queen's feelings for

Coren continue as Coren pursed her own ideals for Ireland? For that she would need the aid and support of her new husband and she would need to convince the many who wanted favors from her that they must be willing to give back what they receive. This, she vowed once again, would be done.

But that was in her future plans. First, she must lay the groundwork and prove not only to Albert, but to the Queen, just what she was capable of. It needed to start here in London, where all eyes could witness the difference she could make. Would make. Where the newspapers would celebrate her triumphs, not for herself, but for those who had lost all hope. She would make the unreachable Royals reachable and bring the plight of the commoner to the eyes of the throne. She would be their herald within the great walls of the Royal Palace. She would not be afraid to reach out to quell injustice. She would venture into a place that cried out to deafened ears.

A place that she had been before.

Whitechapel loomed in her mind. It was an area just blocks from Saint Paul's Cathedral, where she and Albert were wed. Where the happiest moments of her life had begun. But images of the best that life had to offer were now replaced with the portraits and images of the downtrodden, the children, the stink and filth of it all. It was all so close and yet so far removed from the splendor of these gardens and the grandeur of these brocaded rooms and the people who indulged in them. It was the place for her to begin.

A sudden noise brought her back. Polite applause surrounded her. At first confused, Coren smiled as she glanced around the room. And then remembering, Coren put her hands together as a young child bowed and smiled in her direction.

"I hope that you found Lancelot's little story amusing, Your Highness." A smiling older woman peered into Coren's eyes awaiting approval.

"Why, yes, of course. It was splendid. It was one of the

best readings of that story I've heard in days." Coren silently prayed the woman didn't detect her hint of sarcasm. Her response seemed to please the woman, however, and the women turned to her child and kissed him on the forehead before hurrying him off to be congratulated by the others.

The remainder of the afternoon tea could not have been drawn out any more slowly. Perhaps, she should have the mantle clock removed? She mulled it over in her mind. She had already nodded off once this afternoon but had quickly brushed some invisible crumbs from her gown to cover her faux pas. Through the remaining conversations that afternoon Coren had to force herself to listen and respond, until at last, the final guest departed.

"Jenny! Jenny!" Before the door had closed behind the last of the departing women, Coren was up on her feet calling for her maid.

Plans had been made. During the course of this afternoon's dreary conversations, Coren had thought it all out. Playing with every detail until it was honed to her liking. Yes! It was a good plan. Whitechapel was the perfect place for her to begin. It would work perfectly. She would change lives, which would help her to gain many favors among London's elite. They would have no choice. They would have to support her. As soon as she had the Queen on her side that is.

Jenny!" Coren yelled down the long corridor that led to the kitchen. Where was that woman? "Jenny! Jenny, come quickly."

The outer door to the room, the one intended for guests, popped open. "I'm sorry, miss, this blasted house has so many doors and hallways that I canna' find my way around. It's like a bloody maze in here, it is."

Coren spoke, not paying any attention to Jenny. "I need you to find me some old clothes. Nothing very nice. It must look tattered and torn. Something stained and dirty."

Jenny stopped dead in her tracks. Her face at first took on an inquisitive look and then melted into concern with a bit of fear. "Ya' know, miss, I truly hate to ask. And I mean that most sincerely . . ." Her eyebrows arched, tightening the skin on her forehead. "What would you be needin' clothes like that fer?" Jenny paused, not wanting to go on, afraid of what the answer was going to be.

"Jenny, I cannot stand it any longer. I must do something!" Coren's speech animatedly poured forth. "I will go crazy sitting here day after day attending endless teas and receptions that mean nothing. There is much more here for me to do. I will not be a princess trapped in a tower." Coren looked to Jenny without giving her a chance to respond. "I've scarcely seen my husband. His Royal Highness is so busy with his own affairs of state. And let me tell you, Jenny, I would trade places with him in an instant. I must have a life of my own, one in which I make a difference." If Coren could tell anyone these thoughts and feelings, it was Jenny.

"You don't mean to be tellin' me we're goin' back to Ireland?" Jenny fell down into a chair like a rag doll just tossed aside. "Miss, I've just gotten everything unpacked from High Gate Hall."

"No. Not yet at any rate." Coren circled around Jenny like a cat onto her prey. "Ireland is where we will end. This is where we will begin." Coren knelt at the foot of the chair. "Find me the most worn, tattered clothes you can. I want to look like a poor slattern of the street."

"Yes, miss." Jenny rose from the chair exhaling her breath loudly as she did. "I'll see what slatternly rags I can find." She reached for the door.

"And Jenny?" Coren called to her without looking in her direction. "Find some nice rags for yourself. You'll be going with me."

"I was afraid of that, miss." Then she added petulantly, "An' what'll we be tellin' His Highness, when he sees you're not around?"

"Albert will be at his club. He hasn't been there since the wedding, and his friends have been badgering him to make an appearance so that they can all congratulate him in private. I'm not sure what that means, and I'm not sure that I'd like to, they are all just boys when they gather, but he did say that he might be very late. So, there you are, Jenny. I've thought of everything." She bobbed her head to punctuate her statement.

Jenny sighed. "I'm sure ya' have, miss. I'm sure ya' have." She slipped though the door not wanting to hear any more.

Coren stared off after her.

Emeralds ignited.

CHAPTER TWENTY-ONE

"What do you mean it's not dark enough?" Jenny shrieked.

"Jenny, please be quiet," Coren said, closing the door to the dressing room. "It is still much too light out. The sun has barely set. We need the concealment of the dark of night. I'm concerned that we will be recognized."

"Too light? Mary, Holy Blessed Virgin. Miss Coren, five suns could shine all at once on that wretched part of London and it still would not be light enough for me." Jenny said.

"I'm not going to argue with you, Jenny." Coren turned her back to Jenny emphasizing the point that the discussion was over. "You do not need to accompany me if you truly do not want to, but it is something I must do."

"Och! Give a girl some credit. You canna believe that I would just let you traipse off by yourself to that godforsaken place. And what would the Prince think of me?" Jenny said, as she threw her hands into the air.

Coren did not answer, prompting Jenny to go on. "I can just see it now. 'Yes, Your Highness, I did know that Princess Coren was going out to walk the streets of Whitechapel dressed up like some common tramp, but I thought nothing of it. Why, does it concern Your Highness?" Jenny went on animatedly, "He'd have my head if they still did that around here." She paused, then quickly added, "And he just might have it anyway!"

"You exaggerate, Jenny," Coren said tossing her hair about her shoulders. "But that is one of the reasons I love you so dearly."

"Now don't think them soft words is goin' to change my thinkin'." Jenny folded her arms across her chest to emphasize the point.

Coren ignored her and twirled about. "Now, how do I look?"

"You look like a rich, well fed woman dressed in the clothes of the poor," Jenny said, still indignant.

Coren took a long look into the mirror over her dressing table. "I do, don't I?" She did not wait for an answer from Jenny. Instead, she peered as closely as she could at her reflection in the silver-backed glass of the mirror. The clothes Jenny had found in the collection bin of the local church did fit both she and Jenny well. Much too well. So she and Jenny had worked for the better part of the day to make the garments look worn and dirty. They had had to dodge many servants and guests as they had made their way to the gardens to roll the clothes in the grass there and then had moved on to the stables, where Jenny once again had become quite vocal.

"Absolutely not! Miss Coren, this is the last straw. I am not rolling in piles of ..."

Coren had to laugh at her poor maid's plight. "Oh, Jenny. We're not going to go in the stalls. We'll just roll around a mite outside of them." Coren waited a moment to see if Jenny would react. "But mind you, there may be a stray pile or two lying about." Coren had laughed again. Maybe a bit too much.

Jenny had not been amused.

Back in Coren's rooms, the ripping and stitching had begun. After tearing the garments in precise places, she and Jenny had then sewed them back together. The odd stitches and seams made the garments look much like those that Coren had seen the women of Whitechapel wearing the day she and Jenny had stolen through that depraved section of London.

Now, as Coren looked into the mirror, she realized that Jenny was right. Despite the attempt to make the clothes look worn and dirty, she still carried herself like the well-bred woman she was. Her hair still glimmered in the gaslight and rays of crimson bounced off of each strand. Her complexion gleamed and her skin was taught and wrinkle free, something that no hardened eighteen-year old woman of Whitechapel would have the luxury of. Coren only hoped that the cover of darkness would hide these traits and that she and Jenny would be able to pass among the population of Whitechapel without being noticed. Maybe some type of scarf or head wrap would help and some more dirt on her face.

"Jenny, come help me, please. I'm too clean." Coren inspected her arms and hands.

"Yes, miss," Jenny sighed heavily.

Coren wanted nothing more than to be able to help the poor people of Whitechapel. It was in her plan and as she thought about it perhaps, her destiny. By disguising herself and mingling amongst the street dwellers of the night, she hoped to glimpse the worst of what life had meted out for them. She needed the cover of darkness to allow her to see the total depths of despair that lurked around the corners, making its way into the boarding houses where children and vermin shared a bed. Coren grabbed a piece of fabric from the bottom of the dress that she was wearing and ripped it off. She tied it around her head. "There, now doesn't that help?" Coren said, as she turned and modeled the new addition to her garment.

Jenny sighed another long breath and cast her eyes skyward, but did not answer.

"I'll assume that means yes," Coren retorted. "Now, come along."

Jenny, reluctant but ever the resourceful, had managed to find several discreet passageways and exits from the palace during her days of exploring and of questioning the other household servants. Now, she and Coren could slip away from the palace with little fear of their actions or absence being discovered.

The hansom cab stopped just shy of the intersection of Leman and Whitechapel Streets. Despite Coren's concern for the downtrodden of Whitechapel, she did not want to venture too deeply into that forbidden area, especially at night. The day trip that she and Jenny had taken some time ago had brought them far into Whitechapel, farther than she dared go now.

"Thank you, driver. We will walk from this point on," Coren said as she handed the driver a sum of money, more she knew, than would cover the fare. "Keep the extra, if you please."

"Yes, ma'am. Most happy to, ma'am," the driver said, pocketing the bills. He slapped the reins on the horse's back and the cab moved forward. After just a few steps the driver pulled the horse to a stop. He turned to look over his shoulder. "Ma'am, if you don't mind me saying, it's not safe for you ladies to be here now ... or at anytime." There was a clear note of concern in the driver's voice, one that Coren could not dismiss lightly.

Coren stood frozen for a moment. Had the driver recognized her? "Why I don't know what you mean. We live here." She tried to make the lie sound truthful.

"I doubt that, miss." The cabby shot long hard stares at both Coren and Jenny. "You dress like the ladies that walk these streets, ma'am, but you sure don't talk like 'em."

He was right. It was one element of the night that Coren had not thought of. She silently chastised herself for forgetting about it. In her best imitation of the worst cockney she had heard, Coren replied, "I don' know wha' it is you're bleedin' talkin' 'bou. On you're way wit' ya, 'fores I calls the cops, on ya', I will."

The cabbie, with a perplexed look on his face, shook his head, paused, as if to say more, and then slapped the hindquarters of the horse with the reins and was off, quickly swallowed by the darkness of the street where broken gas lamps stood as vigils to the night casting no glow, but instead standing guard to the blackness.

Coren stood, watching the cabby disappear into the night, suppressing a nearly overwhelming desire to scream out for him to return. She clenched her fists in an effort to control the urge.

"I'm so pleased that all of our years of practicing accents and play-acting have finally benefitted us. Well, let us go," Coren said, tugging on the sleeve of Jenny's rags.

The streets of this dreaded, God-forgotten area were not nearly as crowded as they had been when Coren and Jenny had last traversed these broken cobblestones. Gone now, were the merchants and children who had filled the air with their plaintive cries. Taking their place were the grunts and groans of drunken sailors and whores who spilled out of the many pubs that these streets bore. Lewd comments were flung at Jenny and Coren by several male passersby. When she and Jenny ignored the sailors, drunkards and cutthroats with their crude comments, they were then taunted by the women of the street. The odors of the day gave way to the putrid smells of the night: rotting flesh, sewers swarming with mice, rats and cockroaches the size of rats and the garbage that attracted them. An occasional pack of young boys would run up to Coren and Jenny, tearing at their clothes, teasing them with cries of what a 'real man' would do for them. Then they would run off, leaving their unchildlike laughter to echo behind them.

"What would Prince Albert think if he caught us here?" Jenny spoke, as though her guilty feelings for accompanying Coren to Whitechapel demanded it.

Coren gawked at the site of a dead pigeon being devoured by rats. "He would say that we are fools and that we deserve a fate no better than that pigeon's, I fear."

Coren did not believe this of course, she knew very well that Albert would all but divorce her if he found out about these two escapades into Whitechapel, but then, he wasn't as interested in helping the poor as she was. Coren would change Albert's thoughts on the poor and lower classes. She was sure of that. Like most of the upper classes, Albert was raised to believe that the poor were victims of there own making and that there would always be poor and that there was little one could do about it. Coren, however, thought differently. She knew that she could not change the lives of all the poor, but she could help them to better themselves. Once, of course, she knew more about them herself.

Prince Albert, luckily, would not find out about this night, if everything went as planned that is. The Prince was at his club, playing cards and smoking cigars, Coren discovered. This, he would do late into the night. It was a ritual that he had carried out ever since he had left prepatory school. It was what all the young men did. Coren figured that she and Jenny could spend several hours in Whitechapel and still be home, bathed, and in bed fast asleep before the Prince returned.

"This way, Jenny." Coren pointed down a side street. Above them a weatherworn sign hung askew from an equally weatherworn building. It was dimly lit by a nearby soot-covered gaslight, one of the few that were lit and working, she read the sign aloud, "Osborn Street."

This street, like most of the others in Whitechapel, was narrow, dark, and foreboding. Nevertheless, Coren hurried Jenny along. A sobering thought occurred to Coren. Here she was, royalty, walking among the lowest of life that London had to offer, and with her maid no less. Prostitutes and drunken men scurried about looking much like the four-legged, furry creatures that a local rat catcher seemed to be having a field day with. Jenny shied away from him, and bumped Coren's arm causing her to squeak, "Jenny, please!" In a doorway a man and a woman fornicated. Few looked. No one cared.

Jenny spoke so softly, it was hardly a whisper, "Miss, we shouldna' be here."

Coren stopped, pulling Jenny to her side. "You are right, Jenny. We should not be here."

A glimmer of hope lit itself briefly in Jenny's eyes, before being hopelessly snuffed out by Coren.

"We should not be here and neither should any of these people. Look around you, Jenny." Coren's arms displayed the wretched panorama before them. "This is disgraceful."

"But what can we do, miss?" Jenny conveyed her concern for the poor, frustration at not being able to help, and fear at being there at all in one phrase.

"I don't know." Coren tried to remain strong, but the slight quaver in her voice gave away her fear.

Coren stepped forward without saying another word. The fear that was building steadily in her chest kept her from speaking. If she did dare to speak, the sound would be that of a scream.

Halfway down the street a woman sat cowering, leaning against a building. She held tight to a child, bundled in rags. The dim light of the only working street lamp cast an angelic glow around the mother and child. Coren saw it as a sign. *An angel in hell!* "Come this way Jenny," Coren commanded.

"Don't worry, miss. Whatever way you are goin',' 'tis the same way I am," Jenny said, holding tight to the hem of rags that Coren wore. Rags that, compared to what many of the women in Whitechapel wore, looked like fine cloth.

Coren approached the woman and the child slowly, cautiously. "Why are you sitting here amongst the trash?" Coren said, forgetting to use her mock, lower class accent.

The woman looked up at Coren with eyes that were much too old for the time the woman had spent on Earth. She pulled the child in closer to her chest. "Not from around these parts, are ya', miss?"

Coren knew it was too late to try and fool the woman. She

had already given it away. "You are correct in your assumption. I am not from this area."

"Not even from England, are ya'? I ken tells." The woman smiled slightly, showing a mouth of rotted and missing teeth. Coren could see she was quite pleased with herself. Chuckling, she went on, "I'd say from America or some'eres close to 'at."

"No. Actually, I'm from Ireland," Coren said, slowly kneeling down to the woman.

"See there, I's right. I said some'eres close to America." The woman slapped her hand against her side and let out a loud squawk, then abruptly muffled it for fear of waking her child.

Her breath, pungent and putrid from rotted teeth, nearly sent Coren reeling. Coren stood quickly, her hand unconsciously covering her nose and mouth. "Why don't you go into one of the common houses to spend the night with your child?"

"Ain't got no money, miss. Simple as 'at." Tears started to well up in the woman's eyes.

"What will you do?" Jenny spoke out of concern for the woman and her child, but she also spoke so that Coren would not forget about her, leaving her lost among the passersby.

"Spend the night out 'ere, unless I can picks me up one of 'em sailors from the docks 'er." The woman paused a moment, looking at the child she held in her arms. "'Cept they don't take kindly to a baby." The woman's voice trailed off as waves of sobs overcame her.

"Here now. We'll take care of you," Jenny, who herself had started to cry, piped in.

"Not from around 'er either, are ya'?" A glimmer of hope and curiosity shone in the eyes of the woman.

"No, I'm not. I'm from America, just like you said," Jenny lied to the woman.

Coren took a handful of bills from a pocket she had fortuitously sown into her garment and handed them to the woman. She did not count them or care to. She just handed the bills over. "Here take this."

At first the woman just looked at the money, disbelief apparent. Coren was sure it was more money than the woman had ever seen at one time. She knew it was a small fortune, as she had taken care to bring a large sum of money in the hopes of just such a situation as this. It would be enough, she hoped, for the woman to buy herself a small house and not have to worry about food for herself and her child ever again.

The woman reached up with a slow hand, seemingly not sure what these two other women were up to. She closed her fist around the money and gently drew it toward her.

"Now, that money is yours, but you are not to go on drinking and spending it on frivolous items," Coren said, wondering if the woman would even know what frivolous meant. "Spend that money on you and your baby. Get yourselves out of here."

The woman didn't say a word. She just looked up into Coren's eyes and smiled that toothless grin, eyes filled with tears.

It was all Coren needed.

"Miss, if you don't mind me saying . . ." Coren cut Jenny off before she could say it.

"I know. Come, we'll find our way back and hail a cab." Coren was just as relieved as Jenny to be leaving this place. As overwhelmed as she was, she had at least succeeded in helping one – this one – and that would be enough . . . for now. She had changed a life.

No, two lives, she corrected herself. She smiled softly, her eyes glistened with unshed tears. She glanced at Jenny. Jenny's face mirrored her own.

"I know, miss."

Jenny and Coren walked hurriedly with their heads bent down until they reached the intersection of Whitechapel and Osborn Street. There the light was somewhat better and the street was a bit more crowded with people. The numbers of people milling about, despite their despicable and regrettable actions, gave Coren and Jenny a false sense of security.

"Look, Jenny. Here comes a cab now," Coren said, glee almost filling her voice. "We'll be back to the Palace in no time, Jenny." Then, to reassure herself, "No time at all."

The cab, which had been clipping along, began to slow as it neared Coren and Jenny. Both stepped back from the gaslight, into a shadowed doorway and away from the edge of the street to avoid getting hit by the horse or the cab. The cab slowed more, almost coming to a complete stop. As it did, a voice from the interior of the cab called out to, "No driver. Do not stop here. Continue down Osborn."

Coren was immediately disappointed. With this cab it had seemed as though their journey was coming to an end, but now it appeared that this would not be the cab that would see them home to safety. They would have to linger among this crowd awhile longer, hoping that another cab would not be too long in coming.

And then something began to gnaw at Coren. An ominous feeling began in the pit of her stomach and threatened to rise up into the back of her throat. The hair at the back of her neck rose and chills chased up and down her spine. She shivered in an effort to try to stop them and to banish the thoughts from her mind. But the notion lingered. Somewhere she had heard that voice before. It was familiar to her, yet she could not immediately place it. As seconds ticked by, her mind raced through the countless acquaintances, servants and merchants she knew or had recently encountered. It was all out of context. She was in the wrong place and so was the sound of the voice. Coren strained to hear the words in her mind again, *No driver. Do not stop here. Continue down Osborn,* trying to make them linger longer in her mind, hoping they would spark some hint of recognition.

And then Coren had it. Like a resounding punch to the stomach. It took her breath away. She gasped, turning to look after the cab. It rounded the corner from Whitechapel to

Osborn Street. As it did, the interior was briefly lit by the dim gas lamp. At the same time, the man inside leaned forward, just enough to reveal his profile.

Coren screamed silently, the sound of her inner voice deafening her. The sound of his name darkening her world. Her eyes closed as she fell against the decaying wall of the building. The name was blasting through her mind and yet it was only whispered from her lips . . ."Albert!"

CHAPTER TWENTY-TWO

Coren wrapped the silken sheets around her tightly, as though that would comfort her. She had bathed quickly and dove into the bed so that Albert would find her fast asleep when he returned. The problem was that she could not sleep. Each moment of what had happened to her and Jenny earlier this evening kept playing itself over, endlessly repeating in her mind. She closed her eyes tightly, wishing for sleep, instead, images flashed, awakening her senses. It began with the rotting stench of Whitechapel's decaying streets and ended with the bare glimpse of a man she thought – no, knew – was her husband. She turned over in the bed, grasping the comforter even tighter in her grip, but the scenes continued to flash before her, seen now in her mind's eye as if she had been an observer from a distant corner, hidden in a darkened doorway.

As the memory replayed, Coren saw the man in the cab move forward into the brief halo of light. Again the image which bore into her was that of Albert. The image faded leaving her with the same unanswered question: Why was Albert there? Why would he be in Whitechapel? Time and time again she searched for the answer. She dizzied herself with so much thought. Her mind pained at every notion. She longed for sleep. And when sleep finally came, she was not aware of it, drifting off unconsciously, losing herself gratefully to the silent slumber: a slumber, which could not last.

At first she was not sure of what had brought her out of her sleep. How long had she been sleeping? She didn't know. She scanned the room. It was still too dark. No light tried to steal its way through the shutters and the heavy fabric that concealed the window. The candle, left alight on the bedside stand, had now burned itself down and was out. She touched the wick searching for a slight sign of heat. There was none. Then she cocked her head, listening intently for a sound. There was none. All was still, silent and dark. Coren breathed out a long breath, letting the tense muscles in her arms, chest, and neck relax.

Out of the corner of her eye, a movement caught her mid-breath. Her eyes opened wider, her breath stopped. The dark corner of the room had her full attention. In the blackness of the corner a shadow moved. It was darker than the room. It was a blackness, which possessed shape and form where the black of the room did not. Its movement was slow and methodical. Each move a command of precision. Each move nearly undetectable.

Coren did not move. She dared only to breathe the slightest of breaths, and kept her eyes all but closed, lest the whites of her eyes give her away. Sounds emanated from where the figure stood. She could not make them out. And yet, they were oddly familiar.

Movement. The figure crept silently, moving toward her – slowly, inching its way. Outside of her suite, down a long spacious hallway, the ancient clock started to chime. A scream nearly slipped from her throat, but she caught it in time to swallow it and her fear. After the hammer had risen and fallen onto the strings of the chimes for the fourth time, the clock fell silent.

Suddenly, Coren realized that the air about her had changed. The scent of the figure in the darkness caught her. She sniffed quickly at the air. There it was again. There was an oddly comforting scent to it, one that she knew.

One that she knew very well.

Faint at first, but now ever present, the odor of bayberry fell upon her. It was the sweet, enchanting smell of the man she loved. She could feel the bed coverings being peeled back and the undeniable weight being added to the bed.

Albert climbed into the bed that they shared. Quietly. When the boards creaked, he stopped and waited a moment, then continued. Coren breathed again, not sure when she had last taken a breath. Albert draped his arm gently over her, the bayberry cologne, mixed with the smell of sweat and cigars, slid soothingly into her nostrils. And then a slight hint of something else. She couldn't place it, familiar, but distant at the same time. A scent that stood out slightly by its rough metallic notes.

Copper.

Her mind suddenly latched onto the scent, placing it firmly into her mind. The smell of copper . . . the smell of blood.

It was hours more before Coren would find sleep again, and then it would only last for minutes as the morning burst forth.

As soon as Coren had dressed, she crept out of the room, not wanting to wake her sleeping prince nor the demons that may be hiding within him. She headed straight away to the rooms Jenny occupied on the floor above her own.

Jenny was still in bed, caught in the space between sleep and awake. "Jenny," Coren whispered not wanting to startle the woman.

Jenny mumbled something incoherently and turned away from Coren. "Jenny, Jenny." Coren tried the gentle approach once again. When the sleeping maid would not rouse, she shook her. "Jenny! You must wake up this instant. Jenny! Get up!" Coren shook the maid with more fervor.

"Oh, all right!" Jenny spoke turning to Coren. "You're about to shake the soul right out of me, you are."

"I'm sorry if I startled you awake, but I must speak with

you." Coren sat down on the bed beside Jenny.

"Can we at least have a proper cup of tea first?" Jenny said, brushing the hair that fell from her sleeping cap out of her eyes. "I didn't get much sleep last night. The whole night kept playing itself over and over like a bad dream."

Coren stood and backed away from the bed, her face flushed.

"What is it, miss? You don't look well," Jenny said, pulling the covers off of her.

"Jenny," Coren hesitated. "I had the same dreams last night." Just the mention of them brought the sights and sounds flooding in torrential waves back to her thoughts. "I could not stop thinking about it."

Jenny studied her charge for a moment, watching as the light from the window surrounded her like a halo. "I tried all night to figure out how the Prince knew that we were going to Whitechapel. I swear I didn't tell a soul, I didn't."

Coren looked up, her face holding a puzzled expression. "What do you mean found out about us?"

"Well, miss, it's the only explanation that I can come up with." Jenny waited for Coren to respond. When she didn't, she went on, "The Prince must have a source in this house who told him what our plans were."

"A spy?" Coren said, incredulous.

"Someone knew that we were going out on a late night rendezvous and they must have informed the Prince." Jenny sat back onto the pillows of the bed.

"You may be right..." Coren hesitated.

Jenny leaned forward, arching her eyebrows. "No maybe about it, miss," she broke in and proudly announced, "It's the only explanation. Kept me up all night trying to figure that one out, but I did it."

Coren felt the tension begin to ease. With quick steps she started to dance around the room excitedly, twirling, smiling, her eyes lighting up brightly. "Oh, Jenny, this is wonderful!"

"It is?" Jenny asked, doubtfully.

"Yes!" Coren spun around. "Don't you see?"

"No, miss, I'm afraid . . ." She couldn't finish before Coren cut her off.

"Yes. Yes. What you said is right." Coren sat down next to Jenny, slightly breathless. "The prince must have a spy in the house. And somehow that spy found out about us going to Whitechapel."

"You agree that we were followed?" Jenny asked, excitement entering into her own voice.

"Oh! Oh, how wonderfully exciting this is. A spy following us around." Coren giggled at the thought.

"But who do you suppose it could be?" Jenny said, now fully engaged. "I swear I did not say a word to anyone."

"And neither did I." Coren searched her thoughts as she said this, looking for the one slip up, the one time she may have spoken when others may have heard her. Finding none, she continued, "I'm sure of it."

"We'll have to be more careful a' them around us." Jenny glanced around the room as if someone might be listening.

"You are so right," Coren whispered. Then she burst into laughter.

Jenny joined her enthusiastically.

Later that morning as she sat quietly in the garden sipping her Earl Grey tea, her favorite mid-morning blend, Coren thought about the spy and what the Prince would have done had he caught Jenny and her. It was a perfect stroke of good luck she told herself, when she had stepped back into the shadows, pulling Jenny with her, perfectly timed, just as the cab that the Prince was riding in drove by. He obviously had not seen them. In fact, she had barely seen the Prince himself. Had he been in his own carriage, she would have instantly recognized him. And so would everyone else. Why hadn't he been riding in his own carriage?

Suddenly the taste of her favorite tea grew rancid in her mouth. She swallowed hard. Why had the Prince rented a cab when his own driver was available right here? *Because everyone recognizes the Royal Carriage*. It was one of many thoughts that perplexed Coren about last night.

Should she just ask Albert?

No. Then he might discover where she had been. So many questions. And just when she thought she had the answers, another question rose up to take the previous doubt's place. It was all too much. She would have to talk this all out with Jenny. Only then, when she had the answers to all of her questions and had discovered who the spy was, would she and Jenny dare to venture once again into Whitechapel.

CHAPTER TWENTY-THREE

"Murder! Murder, I tell you."

"Murder! Oh my!" Coren turned in disgust. "Jenny, must we speak of such things?"

"I read about it in the morning paper, miss." Jenny moved so that she was again facing Coren.

Coren turned away from Jenny, not wanting to discuss the details. "Jenny, would you please?"

Jenny stood motionless for a moment, then turning with a huff, proceeded to the doorway. "If you only knew, you would want to hear about it," she continued, standing half in and half out of the doorway. Waiting.

Coren knew what Jenny was up to. This gambit had actually been taught to Coren by her mother. Lady Butler would stand at the door, as if she were about to leave, or about to enter. It all depended upon how one looked at it. Coren knew all too well how to use this tactic and Jenny had now put the ploy into full effect. "Oh, all right," Coren said "If you must."

With less than a second's time, Jenny was at Coren's chair. "It's not just any old murder, miss," she paused.

"Would you get on with it?" Coren spoke restlessly.

"It was a terrible murder." Jenny's voice took on a sepulchral tone.

"All murders are terrible, Jenny. I see no point in this."

Coren tried to rise.

"Well, if you're going to take the fun out of it, I might as well just tell you straight out," Jenny said exasperated, all pretense of the mysterious air she was trying to conjure, suddenly gone.

"Fun? Are you mad?" Coren shouted.

"Not 'fun' in the murder." Shaking her head and rolling her eyes, Jenny went on, "In the telling."

For a long moment neither of the women spoke. "Well, go on then. Tell it how you will. Go on," Coren said, breaking the silence.

Jenny once again lowered her voice to create the proper ominous atmosphere. "It happened on the same night that we . . ." Jenny paused, looking theatrically around her . . . "that we were in Whitechapel." Standing she leaned in close to Coren to emphasize her words. "And that's not all. It took place right on the very street we had visited!"

"No! It couldn't be," Coren exclaimed, taken in by Jenny's theatrics.

"Yes, miss. I wouldn't make up such a thing," Jenny said, as she clutched a fist to her heart in indignance.

"Oh, this is terrible, indeed." Coren thought about that night, letting it all flash quickly through her thoughts. "We could have been hurt or what if one of us had been the victim?" Her eyes lit up as she realized the complications of it. "Then how would I have explained it to the Prince?"

"We needn't worry about that. It didn't happen . . . And just a gol' darn minute! If you had to explain it to the Prince, then that would mean that I was the victim!" Jenny shouted, realizing what Coren had just said.

"Well, Jenny, it could not have been me," Coren stated simply. "The murderer only kills prostitutes."

"Och! So that's what ya' thinkin'? I'm a common street walkin' . . . " Jenny paused, as she watched Coren fall into a bout of nervous laughter.

Coren blushed with embarrassment. "No . . . Jenny . . . I

mean . . . That is . . . You're certainly not . . ."

"When you're through tearin' down my character, I'll finish my story," she said, crossing her arms and pursing her lips.

Coren tried to wipe the rouge of embarrassment from her cheeks. "I'm sorry, Jenny." She stifled another nervous chuckle. "Please continue."

"Hmph. Now where was I?" Jenny gathered her thoughts and leaned into Coren. "The murder took place very early in the morning, long after we had left the area, so we weren't in any danger. I should say, in any more danger than we already were. You know what I think of that place."

Coren didn't respond. She was lost in the thought of that night. She allowed it to play again in her mind, watching carefully to see where she had been and if she had, perhaps, walked in the footstep of a killer. That thought shook her. She trembled with both fear and exhilaration. "Think of it, Jenny. We may have walked right by the murderer. He may have been right where we stood!"

"If you don't mind, miss, I'd rather not." Jenny frowned.

"Tell me all you know," Coren demanded.

Jenny reached into her bosom and proudly brandished the newspaper article, from the London Times, she had stumbled upon that morning. The paragraph was not very long. There was, sad to say, nothing terribly uncommon about a murder in Whitechapel. It was the headline that caught Jenny's attention. *Murder on Osborn Street.* Then as Jenny read on into the article, the gruesome facts of the event were detailed.

Murder on Osborn Street

Emma Elizabeth Smith, of 18 George Street, reported to police constables that she had been attacked on Osborn Street, Whitechapel, by a man dressed in dark clothing and wearing a white scarf. The attack took place between the hours of 12:15 and 1:00 in the early morning of August the 3rd. The woman was brought to London Hospital by a local deputy, where she gave the brief description of her

*assailant and then died soon there after of peritonitis. A Coroner's
report and police inquest is to take place.*

Jenny reached for a book on Coren's nightstand and placed
the newspaper article between the pages of the book. "We
were actually there, miss. Scary, isn't it?"

"Jenny, you do have a way with understatement," Coren
said, playing a finger through her hair. The foolishness of the
foray into the night at Whitechapel began to make its way into
the thoughts and fears of Coren. She wanted to help those
who lived there, but she did not want to lose her own life in
the process. What good would that do to her plans, she
thought, then frowned.

"Something wrong, miss?" Jenny said, replacing the book
onto the nightstand.

"Sorry, no." Coren twisted the end of her hair so tightly it
hurt. "Jenny," Coren paused collecting her thoughts and
unfurling her finger. She did not want to lose Jenny's support
in her quest to help those in Whitechapel, yet, she did not
want to lose her own life or that of Jenny's either. Still, there
was much work to be done, and to do it, Coren knew that she
must go again to that part of the city where despair and horror
reigned. "Jenny, I know how you feel about us going into that
district again . . ."

"No, miss." Jenny started to rant. "Not for all the pots a'
gold at the ends of all the rainbows that there ever was in all
of Ireland would you drag me there again. It's too scary. It's
too dangerous. It's too . . ."

"I know, Jenny," Coren said, trying to calm her. "Indeed it
is and . . ." An idea came to her. "Because it is a dangerous
place, we must work to help those that live there." Coren
watched Jenny for a reaction. "Especially, for the children."
Coren tried to look plaintive.

There. That should do it.

And it did. "Miss, that's not very nice of you," Jenny said,
shaking her finger in shame at Coren. Coren watched Jenny

purse her lips and furrow her brow, for what had to be the tenth time.

"Fine. I'll go back there with you. But . . ." She pointed her index at finger at Coren's nose. We must wait a little while at least. Maybe then the police will have captured the mad man who killed that poor woman --What was her name?"

"Emma Smith," Coren said, the name firmly engraved in her mind.

"Right. Right. Smith," Jenny said, nodding.

"A mad man you said?" Coren did not expect an answer. It was more of a question to herself. Some nagging thought, a dark spot in her mind gnawed at her. Something inside her felt cold. It lingered briefly and then fled away, leaving her with a chill, the kind one cannot chase away.

"I'll be going now, miss. Is there anything I can get for you?" Jenny had made her point, and so, ambled toward the doorway.

"No. Thank you." The chill in her bones remained. "I'll be in the garden, Jenny. I feel a need for the sun to warm me."

"Are you feeling all right, then?" Jenny came back into the room and walked to Coren. She reached up, touching her hand to Coren's forehead. "You don't have a fever, miss." Jenny always knew when something was troubling Coren and she clasped her hand for a moment in reassurance.

"I didn't think I had a fever. But thank you for checking just the same." Coren squeezed Jenny's hand in return for a long moment. "I'll be fine, Jenny, dear." Long fingernails of icy chills trailed though her veins even as she said this. A bright smile came over her face, reassuring Jenny.   Jenny smiled in return, gave a final squeeze to Coren's hand and headed off down the hallway.

A moment in time played again in Coren's thoughts. A carriage. A darkened shadow of a man. A glimpse of something familiar. "I wonder," she spoke out loud. "I wonder."

Emeralds clouded.

CHAPTER TWENTY-FOUR

Albert repeated the words for the third time. He was not sure that Coren comprehended anything he was saying. She just sat perfectly still in her chair, staring forward. Her face blank. A stone-cold countenance.

"Coren, darling, you must listen to me." Albert knelt in front of Coren, watching her eyes as he spoke.

The same blank stare greeted him as before.

"It can not be." Coren's whisper roared through the utter silence of the room. "It can not." Her lips moved, but eerily, no other part of her face.

The words were simple, yet through them Albert knew, or hoped rather, that she was beginning to understand, or at least acknowledge what he had been saying to her. "My dear, it is. I'm so sorry." He held tightly to her hands, afraid that he might lose her. Coren seemed to be at an emotional brink, tilting toward some bottomless crevice in her mind.

"Why?" Coren spoke the single word not knowing that it would, in all likelihood, be the hardest question that Albert would ever have to answer.

Albert took in deep breaths preparing to speak, yet the words would not come. A heaviness filled his chest, sucking from him the strength to speak, as if by defying the words, it would make it all seem to be a bad dream. He swallowed hard and spoke thorough tightened muscles in his throat.

"The ferry broke up off the coast. The seas were very rough. A sudden gale hit them as they neared the deep waters. There was nothing anyone could do. Believe me, darling, Lord and Lady Butler and Sir Talbot did not suffer. The disaster struck while all aboard were asleep."

There was no movement, no sounds, nothing to let on that she had heard the words this time, either, only the slow silent tears that fell from her face.

Coren lay in her bed well past noon. Everyday for the last few weeks she would surrender to the comfort of her bed and stay until Jenny or Albert forced her to rise. Even then, Coren would just stare in the mirror of her dressing table for hours without attempting to comb her hair. She would not bathe or change from her nightclothes. Her despair grew at each thought of her parent's death. Depression had seeped in and taken control of every nook and cranny of her mind. Light fell nowhere now. Only the darkness of cold, deep waters that filled every waking image she had of her parents' and Sir Talbot's last breaths. Even in her dreams she could not escape the sounds of water, splashing against the wreck of the ferry, gurgling through the now gaping mouths of the scores that perished. It sickened her. Her once vibrant and clear complexion became sallow and dull. She cared for nothing. She cried for everything.

"Come now, miss," Jenny spoke in lively tones, accenting her words with colorful exaggerated movements. "We've got to get out of this mood." She looked at Coren and fought back her own tears. "It's a wonderful summer day. We have humming birds in the garden and the flowers have bloomed so brightly. You wouldn't believe how sweet the air is, what with all the flowers."

Jenny words made no impact on her charge, yet she

continued. "Oh! And we have babies about, too. Chicks really. That peacock is strutting around like he's the one that did all the work. Typical male, I must say. You should see him with his tail feathers all spread out as the peahen parades the chicks by. It really is a sight."

Jenny continued, but her voice grew faint in Coren's mind as Coren remembered a vision of her own: a garden at Butler House filled with blooming flowers and the sounds of life, a peacock courting a peahen. The past images flooded her thoughts. It wasn't that long ago that Coren watched the peahen tease the peacock, letting him get just so close and then she would move off. Coren's own plan to find her prince had been premised on the same tactic displayed by the peahen.

It worked for them both.

Albert. Coren thought. How has Albert been though all of this? Her own selfish thoughts had consumed her so that she couldn't remember thinking about anyone but herself, including her prince. Still, throughout it all, she would find him every night lying beside her. She had not once, since the death of her parents, slept alone. She recalled how Albert lay with her every night, yet he had never moved upon her, although, she had thought, that his need must be great. She remembered him slowly rubbing his hands over her back as she once again cried herself to sleep. She could feel his arms surround her, protecting her from the outside. She could hear his gentle breathing in her ear and the comfort of the faint bayberry cologne that he wore.

She longed for him. Albert. Her prince.

It came to her suddenly. A growing yearning spreading along the muscles of her stomach. An emptiness that needed to be filled. A desire that quietly grew and became overwhelming. A need to live.

"Jenny?" Coren caught Jenny off guard causing her to stop her incessant monologue in the middle of a word. "Would you please prepare a bath for me?"

Jenny's gaze bounced back and forth from the image of Coren in the mirror to Coren's face. "I would be glad to, miss. Right away." She scurried off with a renewed vigor of hope in her step.

Coren emerged from the bath wrapped in a thick cotton towel. Her hair was piled in a damp heap upon her head. Once the door to the bath had finished its arc, swinging fully open, Coren saw the darkened silhouette of a man standing by the window. He was backlit by the streams of dusty sunlight. He turned from the window toward Coren. She could not see his face, hidden in the shadow, but knew at once that it was Albert.

She could feel his smile radiate warmth. She could feel his love penetrating the darkness. And she could feel his heat awakening her own.

She watched as Albert took in the site of her covered by little more than the towel she was holding, and she saw his passion for her grow instantly. His eyes followed as she dropped the towel and shook her hair down, letting the wet strands fall about her face and shoulders. Her hair stuck to her cheeks and forehead. Albert's eyes darkened even more, reflecting her own intensity.

She had never felt more wanton.

He turned slightly, the full rage of his desire for Coren becoming very apparent. His silhouette bulged with his wanting.

Coren moved slowly toward him, knowing that her naked body glimmering with undried droplets of water from the bath.

As she approached him, their scents mingled, a concoction of his bayberry and manly smell and her sweet clean smell of rose soap and the faint teasing scent of her needs.

Coren fell upon him gently, fighting the urge to devour him instantly. She proceeded methodically, wanting instead to savor each moment with him.

No words were spoken.

When their lips met, currents of raw heat bolted through her. It had been weeks since they had lain together as man and wife and the absence of it caused her senses to reel with every movement that he made. A simple, stifled groan from his throat almost sent her over the edge.

Her hands found his shirt and unbuttoned it. Then found his belt and removed that as well. They next found his manhood and caressed it.

Hours passed as Coren led her prince on a trip of bountiful pleasures, of pure passions and unabashed desires. She knew he'd wanted to fulfill his pleasure many times, but she would not let him. Instead, Coren made him wait. He burned at every touch she laid upon his body. He brimmed at her gentle, circling tongue, but she knew he held back, until she was ready.

Her own lust for him was narrowly under control. Her battle to keep herself from letting go and surrendering to him was immense, but Coren needed him more now than she had ever thought imaginable. In moments, what had taken hours to work up to was over. They both lay spent, tired and fulfilled. Fulfilled, not just in body, but in mind and spirit as well.

Coren felt the reassuring arms of her prince slowly wrap around her as she cried herself to sleep once more.

CHAPTER TWENTY-FIVE

The gloom that surrounded Coren lifted, and as the days passed, she returned to the life that she had now become accustomed. All but the faintest whisper of sadness had disappeared. Albert noted this to Jenny.

"It's nice to have her back, Your Highness," Jenny said, a bit of glee in her voice. "I don't know what you did to get her back, but it worked quite well."

"Some things need a man's touch, Jenny," Albert said, the innuendo obvious.

"Or a woman's desire, Your Highness." Jenny curtsied to the Prince as she exited the room, running straight away to Coren, the echoes of his laughter resounding behind her.

The curtains were pulled wide open, fresh flowers from the abundant gardens filled several vases, their perfume floated through the air mingling with the early late summer breeze. "I can tell you're up to something." Coren greeted Jenny with laughter in her voice.

Jenny stopped quickly. She tilted her head as she took in her charge. "How do you always know?"

"Your walk gives it away," Coren said.

"My walk?" Jenny turned around trying to get a glimpse of herself in the mirror. "What in heavens do you mean?"

"Ah, Jenny, just something I've learned." Coren let out a squeal of joyous laughter.

"My, but we are in a good mood today, especially at someone else's expense," Jenny huffed.

"Oh, come now." Coren moved through the room in great sweeping motions. "It's much too nice of a day to be taking my words so seriously." Coren put her arms around Jenny's shoulders. "Now, tell me what you have been up to. I know there is a little mischief in you just begging to break out."

"I've just left the Prince. You might like to know that he's in a very good mood today, as well." Jenny paused for a moment, continuing only when Coren did not take a bite of her linguistic bait. "The Prince seems to think that he is responsible for your good mood."

Coren watched as a hummingbird darted from one of the window pots to another taking in the sweet nectar from the fragrant flowers that cascaded there. As arrogant as the Prince's feelings may be, they were also quite the truth. The loss of her beloved parents and dear uncle in one accident made her realize how much she loved and needed Albert. Their night of long, slow lovemaking brought back the feelings to Coren that she had hidden, feelings that she had locked away after the sinking of the ferry and the death of the three people whom she had loved so dearly. Albert was all she had now, besides Jenny. There were a few cousins, aunts and uncles back in Ireland, but they were all but strangers to her, seen only on the occasions of holidays and weddings . . . and funerals. The thought crept in. Coren pushed it away, but not before cold images of her mother, father and Uncle Robert slipped before her mind's eye. Albert and Jenny were the only family she truly cared about. Albert was right then, in his thinking that he was the reason she had come out of the darkness which consumed her. He was right. And honestly, she loved him the more for it.

"And what did you tell the Prince to set him straight, Jenny?" Coren knew that Jenny had to have said something; otherwise this conversation would not be taking place.

"I did set him straight, I did," Jenny proclaimed loudly. "I told him that whatever it was he did – he did it because you wanted him to!"

"How right you were," Coren said, as she uncharacteristically stamped her foot in agreement.

Jenny beamed. "We ladies must stick together."

"How right again. " Coren raised an imaginary glass high into the air.

Jenny mirrored her. "To us."

"To us," Coren said, tossing the imaginary glass into the fireplace. A comfortable silence fell upon them before Coren spoke, "Jenny, do you recall that last night that we went to Whitechapel?"

"Remember?" Jenny began to pace. "How could I forget, miss?" She paused mid-stride. "It was terrible!"

"Wasn't it?" Coren said vaguely, as she sat down on the chaise, motioning Jenny to join her. "I've been thinking about that place and the people who live there."

"I don't think I like this." Jenny started to rise from the chaise.

Coren pulled at her, forcing her to stay. "Now listen. I've been thinking about those poor children and what all my money could do for them."

"Miss, I don't know that the prince would approve of you spending your inheritance on a lot of poor children in Whitechapel," Jenny admonished.

"Ah, but think of what the people of London would say of me and my dear husband if we made this our cause. It would look well for the Queen's grandson to be so concerned with the lot of the poor. And, hopefully, it will help convince others to do the same." Coren explained.

"I feel that there is an – and – here," Jenny spoke smugly.

If her plans were laid out and played properly there would

be an – <u>and</u> – there. "You are right, Jenny. My, but it's getting difficult to get things past you." Coren meant it as a slight-- Jenny took it as a compliment.

"Thank you, miss." Jenny bobbed her head.

Coren smiled. "If all goes as I expect, Jenny, then you and I will be back in Ireland in a year or two, fighting for Irish independence." Coren cocked her head a tad. A crooked smile grew, as she waited for Jenny to respond.

The independence of Ireland was as important to Jenny as it was to Coren. It mattered to Jenny's family and her class more, in reality, than it did to the upper classes. It had always been a common bond between the two women. And she knew Jenny would have to admit that her plan was a very worthwhile idea. After all, how could anyone condemn her after she had gained the confidence of the Royals and the people of London. Her plan would help both the Irish and the poor of London's Whitechapel and many others along the way. It was a good idea, yet she knew Jenny could not help but suspect that there was something more.

"Is that all, miss?" Jenny waited.

"Certainly that's all. It is not for me, Jenny. I don't want anything from this, only a free Ireland," she spoke sharply, as though she had just been wounded by a knife. Coren looked pointedly at Jenny. "It will mean that we will have to travel to Whitechapel again."

"I don't mind," Jenny said, almost apologetically.

"You don't mind? Really?" Coren's voice rose with the questions.

"Of course not. Why with the prince and all his attendants surrounding us, perhaps we should have the Royal guard go in before us to scare away the hoodlums and such--that is if they linger there during the day." Jenny paused, as Coren gave no reaction. "What is it, miss?"

"Jenny, we can not possibly go into Whitechapel with a complete entourage. Why the entire area would be vacated and we would not be any help to any one. No, Jenny. We must do this quietly. Perhaps later, after we gain the trust of the people who live there, we can go in en masse, but not yet."

Jenny was quiet a long moment before speaking. "Do you mean to say that you would like us to go there again? Unaccompanied."

"Well, yes. That would be most effective," Coren said, a note of condescension in her voice.

"And does it need to be at night to be this effective?" Jenny asked, the rhetoric obvious.

"It would be best." Coren responded. "If we travel with an entourage, in broad daylight, in royal carriages, we will certainly garner attention, Jenny. But attention is not what we want. We do not need to be noticed. We can not possibly attend to the needs of others, if we are surrounded by onlookers and such." Coren waited for a response from Jenny.

"I was afraid that you would have thought it all out." Jenny grimaced.

"Come now, Jenny. You are the only one that I can take with me." An idea sprang to Coren as she said this. "Unless, of course, you would prefer that I go it alone?"

"I knew that was coming before ya' even said it, miss. You don't fool me. No you don't." Jenny pointed a finger at her charge shaking it at her in shame.

"Then you'll go?" Coren smiled hesitantly.

"Of course I'll go. Who else would be fool enough?" Jenny added under her breath.

"We will make a difference, Jenny. You will see." Coren's smile brightened now, her eyes lighting up with an inner radiance.

And emeralds sparkled once again.

CHAPTER TWENTY-SIX

"Jenny!" Coren's whisper carried down the long hallway, drifting off somewhere into the moonless night. She pushed slowly on the door to Jenny's room, trying in vain to avoid the steady creaking of the old worn wood and hinges. "Jenny? Where are you?"

"I'm here, miss, "Jenny spoke from just the other side of the doorway, her form totally concealed by the inky blackness.

"Oh!" Coren stifled a shout. "You scared me half to death. Why didn't you answer me?"

"But, miss, I just did," Jenny said.

"Yes, you did, and you nearly gave me an apoplectic fit." Coren stepped inside and closed the door, a slow steady creak echoed into the darkness. "Jenny?" she whispered slightly louder, feeling more secure now that she was inside the room. "Jenny!"

"Well, I'm afraid if I answer you, you're going to die right here in front of me," Jenny snorted with a laugh. "Ye're bein' a mite dramatic."

"Don't try to be funny. It isn't becoming." Coren tried to be stern but her smile belied the gruffness in her voice. "Light a candle, Jenny."

Jenny moved cautiously around Coren easing herself to the other side of the room where she had placed a candle at the ready. "Oooh! Oow!" Jenny let out a yell from somewhere on the other side of the room. The darkness filled every void, cloaking her in its velvet curtain.

"What is it?" Coren did not care anymore and raised her voice to a near shout. "Jenny? Where are you? What is it? Jenny. Answer me!"

"Oh my, that hurt!" Jenny's voice came to Coren racked in pain. "Oh my, oh my. That bloody hurt."

"What, Jenny? What is it?" Coren spoke with concern, and a hint of exasperation in her voice.

"I'm sorry, miss, but I stubbed my bloody toe on this bloody bloomin' bed post. I'll limp for the rest of my life from this one, I will."

"Well, light the bloomin' candle so I can come help you!" Coren said, mocking Jenny's indignance.

A scratch, followed by a burst of light, then the rotten smell of sulfur filled the room as Jenny drew the match across the striking paper. She leaned over a small table, took hold of the bare candle and lit it. A warm, comforting light began to eat away at the darkened corners of the room.

"Can you walk?" Coren reached a hand out to her maid.

Jenny took several tender steps forward and then back, as if she were trying on a new pair of shoes. "Yes, I can walk."

"Oh, good." Coren clapped her hands together. "I was afraid that we might have to call the whole foray off."

Jenny's lips curved into a scowl. "Why I thank you for all your concern."

"I'm sorry, Jenny." Coren extended her hand once again. Jenny took the proffered hand and stepped forward, wincing slightly from the pain of her bruised toe. "I should have shown you more compassion," Coren offered, as Jenny continued to play up the injury. "My, you are hurting aren't you?" Coren guided Jenny to the far side of the room. "Maybe if you walk on it a bit."

Jenny stepped along, limping on the injured toe, adding an occasional gasp of breath for effect. "You see, miss. I'm limping like an old, worn woman."

"Yes, I see. And isn't it wonderful!" Coren clapped her hands again. "Everyone who sees us will think that you're just another street walker plying her trade."

Jenny stopped abruptly, turning to Coren. "What do you mean a *street walker*?" Her Irish ire began to rise. "I do not look like a street walker." Her voice rose even more. "A common prostitute! Is that what you're calling me?"

"Don't be so contemptuous." Coren shook her head at Jenny in disbelief. "I said you look like one, not that you are one."

"Oh, now that clears it all up." Sarcasm dripped from every word.

"Come now, Jenny. We haven't the time for this." Coren said, waving her off. "Where are the clothes that we wore the last time?

"I threw them into a heap at the bottom of the trunk," Jenny said indignantly.

Coren spun around, a wide smile filled her face. "Why how clever of you, Jenny. Now the clothes will look even more like the rags that the ladies of Whitechapel wear." She propped open the top of the trunk and rummaged around for the torn dress and old outer coats that had accompanied she and Jenny on their last trip to Whitechapel. Coren pulled the wrinkled, tattered dresses from the trunk, shook them out and tossed them onto the bed. "Why now they are absolutely disgusting." Coren hugged Jenny. "How very clever of you. Very clever indeed."

"Thank you," Jenny responded, her lack of enthusiasm apparent.

"Now, where are the bundles that we were going to give away?" Coren looked around the room.

"I've placed them near the alley gate, right where the driver is to be. If he shows up, that is," Jenny added.

"He'll be there. He's reliable. Isn't that what your Mr. Dolittle said of his friend?" Coren raised an eyebrow.

"If Mr. Dolittle said it, then it must be," Jenny avowed.

"He's a right honest man, he is."

"Of course he is." Coren smiled, knowingly. "And a fine gentleman when you're out together, I understand."

"Don't tell me," Jenny paused. "You've had a spy on me?"

"Of course not," Coren winked. "I feel perfectly comfortable with Mr. Dolittle."

"He's a right gentlemen, I tell you." Jenny spoke as to defend him.

"It's just that the Prince does not really know your Mr. Dolittle and he was a tad concerned so he . . . "

"You did have a spy on me." Jenny snorted.

"Not, me, Jenny." Coren paused, as she opened the door to the alley. "The Prince did."

The carriage Coren had ordered some days before was waiting for the ladies in the alleyway, exactly where Coren had told the driver to be. The pound and a half that she had given the driver secured his employment and the promise of several pounds more insured he would make his appointment.

The slow ride up to Whitechapel took them past the same roads they had seen on their previous trips. Nothing had changed. The street lamps, those that were lit, cast shadows upon the sidewalks, darkening the doorways and courtyards hidden behind rotting wooden fences.

Coren and Jenny sat silently, as they had done on the previous trips. They stared in disbelief at the scourge before them. Even at this late hour, well past midnight, the streets of Whitechapel were busy with drunken women and men, groping each other as they walked.

Men could be seen holding women up against the wall of a factory or common house, their hips thrusting, their voices grunting. Young boys passed by, taunting the men to let them have a way with the ladies after the men had finished. The cursing, graveled voices of the 'ladies' shot back at the boys that, 'They were not man enough or moneyed enough.'

Up Whitechapel Road, passing, Plumber Street, New Road,

and Barkers Row, they continued. The scene outside the carriage, however, remained the same.

Just up ahead, London Hospital, offered a slight respite to those who could make their way there – or a final resting place for those who couldn't.

Coren was the first to break their silence. "I think that this is the right place for us to start. Don't you, Jenny?"

Jenny responded with a voice that could not disguise the fear. "I don't think that anyplace here is the place to start, miss."

"Driver. Stop up ahead," Coren said.

"Yes, ma'am," the driver responded, slowing the horses.

A line of women and children mostly, fronted London Hospital with an incongruous anticipation, an almost giddiness, like those waiting a turn on a carousel. Some of the children darted in and out of the line, playing a counting game as they moved closer to the doorway. This line, however, did not end at the joyous "oom pah pah" of an ever revolving, painted carousel. It brought them to a bed for one night. And like the carousel, this endless circling would begin again tomorrow evening. A common practice of the hospital, for those who could afford it, was to rent out unused beds for six pence a night. For the majority who couldn't afford the six pence, the options included a boarding house, a common room, or for the men, a room containing a rope, tautly stretched from one side of the room to the other on which one could purchase a spot to lean against for a night's sleep. But here, one could sleep without the fear of losing one's possessions or one's life. Thus, many paid the high price for a bed, forcing a long queue to form outside the hospital doors every evening.

Coren stepped down from the carriage, motioning Jenny to follow her, and with bold determination strode toward the hospital entrance. Jenny followed closely behind, bundles in tow.

Jenny paused a step or two after she had passed a pale,

thin child, huddled against her mother. "Miss Coren? Jenny said. Coren turned.

"Here child," Jenny said, as she pulled a garment from the bundle.

The child took it, and at once put it on.

"And one for you." Jenny handed another garment, heavy with brocade to the woman. Coren watched Jenny's distribution to the two indigents.

What an odd contrast, this poor woman and child wearing silk and brocade.

Those in line outside of the hospital began to swarm Jenny.

Cries of: "For my baby. My baby." and "Give it 'ere. Give it t' me," assailed Coren's ears as Jenny tried to push the grovellers back.

"Get back, now. Get away," Jenny shouted above the tumult.

Coren stayed her hand. "Jenny, let them have it all. That's what we brought it for."

Without a moment's hesitation, Jenny threw her hands aside and let the bundles fall from her arms.

Immediately, the throng fell upon the bundles, tearing at them. Garments tore, food spilled, bottles fell to the gutter – broken. Gnarled fists began to tear at Coren's and Jenny's clothing.

A hand fell upon Coren's shoulder. A deep voiced boomed, "Get back. Get your filthy hands off 'em." The driver dragged Coren and Jenny back to the safety of the carriage.

"I really think that it would be best if we went back now," Jenny said, nodding all the while.

"Don't be such a worry wart. We are perfectly safe. Jenny, our purpose here is not just to help them with a few scraps of clothing, but to speak to them, listen to their plight, and try to discover a way to help them in the future. We can't be like the rest of the uncaring nobility, just ignoring them. We have to make a difference!" Coren was almost yelling, she felt the color heighten in her cheeks.

This. This was what she was born to do. And do it she would. Jenny or no Jenny. Prince or no Prince. This was her mission and nothing was going to deter her.

Coren took a large step forward, then slowly eased into the crowd. She brushed the locks from the forehead of a young tow-headed waif. She couldn't tell if it was a boy or girl, but it didn't matter. As the child turned to her, he or she beamed a smile so bright that Coren thought she would be blinded by the simple innocence radiating there. "Thank you, mum," the voice whispered.

Tears immediately sprang to Coren's eyes, momentarily blurring her vision. Why would God in all his glory allow this to happen? Was there some divine reasoning? Were these young innocents put there for a purpose? Yes, they were. She knew that now. She knew this as well as she knew that someday her beloved homeland would be restored to all its glory and independence. In the simple eyes of a child, her future awaited.

Coren gently patted the child on the head and said, "No. Thank you."

Then with all her determination, Coren strode to the head of the line, leaving Jenny's plaintive cries to trail behind her.

Several people tried to stop Coren's progress and when she reached the head of line, those who would soon be summoned in for a bed, pushed her back.

"'Ere now, waits your turn," a female voice growled behind her.

"My dear woman, you will be most heartily rewarded, momentarily," Coren reassured.

The woman, quite taken aback by Coren's manner of speech, closed her mouth and slowly nodded.

At the head of the line, stood a towering woman, dressed in a nurse's uniform. She must be six feet or more, Coren thought, as she compared her to the doorway's entrance. This was the first hurdle and she would not be intimidated.

"Excuse me, my good woman, who is in charge here?"

The burly woman sized her up. And looking down her rather bulbous nose said, "Who wants to know?"

"I do!" Coren said, bringing all the haughtiness into her tone, which her mother would have used when speaking to someone trying to get the better of her.

The woman, now slightly unsure, in spite of her stature, ventured, "Whatta ya' want?"

"I would like to procure all the available beds for the night. And for the rest of this week. To whom should the money be given?" Coren said, now being as gracious as possible.

The woman, stunned, took a faltering step back and sputtered, "I'll gets the superintendent, ma'am."

The woman disappeared into the hospital and returned scant moments later, barely allowing Coren to ready her next plan. The doorway was then filled by a tall, kindly looking gentleman of elder years. He removed his spectacles and gazed into Coren's face. "I understand that you would like lodgings for the night, Madam?"

"No, my good man. I would like to secure lodgings for all the good folk in this line for the duration of the week," Coren corrected.

"This is a hospital, Madam, not a lodging house. Our first priority is for the sick and the injured."

"Well, if you would take a look about you, I am sure that you would see that there is not a healthy person among them – especially the children," Coren chided.

The superintendent apparently did not know what to make of her. He studied her, as she met his gaze with effrontery. "Madam, do you realize that a week's stay for all of these people does not come cheap?"

Coren hesitated a moment. She could play her ace and announce who she was, but that would arouse unwanted discussion and have Albert possibly finding out about her mission. No, it would be best, she decided, to fold now, even with an ace high, laying down a sure win for the uncertainty of the next cards. Her mother's game had taught her that losing a hand is not necessarily losing the game. "I haven't the money at the moment," she stated.

"As I suspected." The superintendent nodded.

"But I assure you I will return with it tomorrow," Coren continued, "You have my word."

The superintendent turned with a huff and started to walk back into the building. Coren made to follow, only to have her way blocked once again by the Amazonian guard.

Coren shouted, "Wait! Wait!" after the superintendent. "What if I leave you this?" Coren reached beneath her layers of tattered clothing and unclasped a necklace that lay hidden there, a buried treasure. She held it out to the superintendent. "Here. Take this. It was a wedding gift from my mother. It should secure the needed lodging for a week's time and leave a handy profit for yourself."

The superintendent paused, then snatched the proffered necklace from her hand. "Done!" he exclaimed, then hurried back into the building.

The overgrown woman opened the door, stepped aside, and shouted down the line, "Ya have a bed for the night. And give your thanks to this 'ere woman." But when she turned to gesture toward Coren - Coren was gone, well on her way back to the waiting carriage.

By the time Coren reached Jenny and the carriage, the line of people was flowing steadily and rapidly into the hospital.

"Miss Coren, I don't know what you said or did over there, but it sure did work. The people are pouring right fast into that building," Jenny noted out loud, shaking her head in amazement.

"Yes, for the moment we have taken care of many," Coren wistfully replied. "But I realize, Jenny, that there will always be poor and what little we have done for them today, won't guarantee them a tomorrow. We can help a few, but it will take much more than us to aid the many. We need a better solution."

"Aye, but can we discuss this inside the safety of the carriage?" Jenny said, motioning toward the carriage. They climbed in.

"Jenny, we are perfectly safe," Coren assured her, as the carriage started up. Coren leaned toward the driver to make the point. "Is that not so, driver?"

"I beg your pardon, ma'am?" the driver spoke, obviously startled.

Raising her voice to be heard above the clank of the horses' hooves, Coren said, "Are we not perfectly safe with you?"

"If you don't mind, ma'am," the driver began, "you're safe with me. It's the Ripper I'm not too sure about."

Coren sat back in the chair of the coach. "What is this . . . Ripper?" Then, turning to her maid said, "Jenny, do you know anything about this?"

"Remember, miss," Jenny said, a slight whisper in her voice, "the woman who was found murdered here the last time we indulged in this folly?"

"Of course, one does not forget such a thing, Jenny. And 'tis not a folly," Coren chastised.

"Well, miss." Jenny cleared her throat hesitating. "There's been another."

"Another?" Coren asked, a slight anxiety rising in her voice. "When? Why did I not hear of this?"

"It was when you were recovering from your loss," Jenny said. "Just about a week after, actually, from the time when that first poor woman was murdered here." Jenny looked around outside of the slow moving cab, as if she had spooked herself with her own words. "I wanted to tell you, I did. But the Prince thought it would be best if you didn't hear of such things, with your parents and Sir Robert and all."

Coren sat quiet for a long moment, fingering the area on her chest where her mother's necklace had so recently been. "I quite understand, Jenny."

"I'm sure the Prince had your best in mind. That's why he didn't want anyone to say anything to you." Jenny tried to reassure.

"That was very sweet of him." Coren smiled wistfully.

Even as the words left her lips, Coren felt a sting as she considered her own betrayal of her Prince. How silly, she admonished herself, trying to control the thoughts that were now beginning to fly through her head. She couldn't possibly tell Albert of her deeds and plans. That was not a betrayal. Just as the Prince was only trying to protect her, she was only trying to protect the Prince. Love for him filled her. She wanted nothing more than to turn this cab around and have the driver run the horses as quickly as they could, all the way to him. Her Prince. But that would not be wise. She had her own goals and she must see them through. She had her Ireland to think about. Why then, were there dark niches in her thoughts?

A glimpse of a man in an unlit coach.

A profile that she knew.

A feeling of dread.

Their cab turned onto Commercial Street. The random journey through this island of despair continued. "What happened, Jenny? To the woman, I mean, and this . . . Ripper," Coren said, bringing herself back to the present.

"Are you sure you want to know, miss?" Jenny's voice pleaded with Coren to say no.

"Yes. Tell me," Coren stated.

"I don't know all the details. I wasn't there when it happened." Jenny's attempt at levity failed. "What I know is, that a woman . . ."

"They called her Siffey around these parts," the driver interjected. "Her real name though was Annie. Annie Chapman, it was."

"She was found very early in the morning by a man living in one of those wretched lodging houses, like those there," Jenny said, pointing to the row of old Spitafields weaver's houses that lined the street. "I hear that she was killed by a knife. Her throat was slit, they say." Jenny paused as she watched Coren turn away in disgust. "I won't go on, miss."

"Yes, you must," Coren said, her eyes beginning to tear.

"There's worse than the having her throat slit." Jenny waited a moment again, before continuing. At Coren's nod she went on. "The killer took out her stomach, they say."

"No more, Jenny. Spare me the rest. I need not imagine any more." Coren's voice grew cold and quiet. "This is why we need to help these people, Jenny. We must move them out of this despicable life."

Coren let the cab roll on for several more minutes before she spoke up again. "I think we have seen quite enough, driver. Please take us back."

"Gladly, ma'am." The driver's voice eased, as he began to slow the horses to a steady walk and readied to make the turn from Brady Street on to Buck's Row, which would take Coren and Jenny back to the more respectable areas of London.

Just as the carriage completed the turn, a scream pierced the night.

CHAPTER TWENTY-SEVEN

It was a scream so sharp and piercing that Coren thought it must surely not be human. The horses immediately became jittery, stamping, pacing, ears perked in the direction of the horrific sound, then flicking from one side to the other. Their nostrils flared and they snorted as though a predator lurked in the nearby shadows. The cabbie spoke to them in gentling tones, urging them to calm down. "Easy there. That's right, easy."

Then, just as the horses began to settle, a second scream. Horrific and panicked. One horse reared, standing tall on its hind legs, kicking forth with his front hooves at some phantom danger in the night. As the horse came down he lost his footing, slipping on the damp, slime-covered cobblestones of the street. He fell to his knees, violently pulling the carriage to the side. Inside, Coren was thrown hard against Jenny. Both let out screams of their own.

The carriage again lurched in the opposite direction as the horse pulled itself upright, this time throwing Jenny into Coren and in so doing knocking Coren's head against a protruding piece of window trim. A slow trickle of blood began to meander its way down her cheek as the cut in her skin opened up.

Again the cabbie spoke in gentling tones to calm the horses who continued their uneasy movements. He jumped from his seat and gently ran his hands along both horses, checking the old gelding's knees for any injuries. Assured that the horses were safe from injury and that his livelihood was secure, he called out to the women, "You ladies all right in there?"

"Yes, thank you." Coren straightened out her dress and outer coat, righting herself in the seat.

"No!" Jenny exclaimed. "You're bleeding!"

Coren reached a hand to her face where she had bumped her head against the window trim. Drawing her hand from her face, she noticed a slight trace of blood upon her fingers. "It's nothing. Just a scratch, really.

"Perhaps we should be gettin' you to hospital, miss?" Jenny cautioned.

"I'll be fine, Jenny," Coren said, dabbing at the blood with a portion of her over coat.

Distant whistles from the many side streets and squares began to sound as Bobbies dashed toward Berner's Street and the apparent location of the screams.

Shouts of "murder", "killer loose," wound their way to where the ladies and the cab remained, motionless.

"Murder?" Jenny's voice quivered.

A Bobby, whistle shrieking, hurried past the cab, his lantern swinging in a wide arc, unsettling the horses once again.

Chasing after the Bobby, were two local urchins shouting with almost demonic fervor, "Murder! Murder! Murder!" The tatterdemalions' voices crescendoed with each word in gruesome glee over their grisly anticipation of witnessing the upcoming sight.

"Did you hear that? Murder!" Jenny whispered now, as if the mere mention would make it that much more real.

"Yes, Jenny, of course I did," Coren said with an eerie calmness, as she leaned toward the side window calling to the driver. "If you don't mind we would like to move on."

"Right away, ma'am." Before the driver had finished speaking, the cab lurched forward, horses still anxious they moved at a heady trot.

"Murder! Murder! Murder!" Jenny repeated the words in the same sing-song patter as the street gypsies.

"Jenny, must you?" Coren said, as she once again checked her brow for traces of blood.

"If you don't mind me saying, miss, you're none too good for this place."

Coren drew the rag of her sleeve, from her face, noting that the bleeding had stopped. "What do mean?"

Jenny looked around as though someone may be within in earshot. "Every time you come to this godforsaken place, someone gets murdered."

A gasp of air escaped from Coren's wide-open mouth. "How can you say such nonsense?"

"Well, miss . . . 'cause it's true."

"Don't be absurd!" Coren said, incredulous.

Jenny gave Coren a look of worry. "Maybe there's a curse on you."

"Oh for the love of all your blessed saints. There is no curse on me or anyone else for that matter. Murders happen in this part of London more frequently than we would like to imagine. It just so happens that we, Jenny, we, were here for two of them." Coren raised an eyebrow hoping that her point had been made.

"Ahh, you're right! I've been here with ya' when there were these murders." Jenny swallowed hard.

"See, Jenny?" Coren said, widening her eyes. "I have nothing to do with these grussome happenings."

"I do, miss. I see it all too well now. I see that I must be the cursed one!" Jenny clutched her chest at the declaration.

"Jenny, please. Do not start talking of curses. I'll have none of it." Coren tried to be stern. "You're scaring me half to death."

The carriage turned away from Berner's Street and back out to Commercial Street heading toward Whitechapel Road. The horses finally settled moved a clipped pace. The now faint sounds of people in the distance faded as they drove on allowing the darkened corners of the many side streets, alleys, and squares to slowly drift by. The streets here were empty, except for the occasional passed out drunk or prostitute who leaned or fell, littering a doorway, lamppost or gutter. Others who normally wandered these foreboding arteries of Whitechapel who were not too drunk, drugged, or passed out, had now moved up to Berner's Street. The screams of "murder" calling to them like a moth to the gaslight. The anticipation of a grisly sight of murder occupied their time and filled their minds, perhaps taking them out of their own miseries for a while or setting them up for an opportunity to pick pocket those crowded around the bloody scene. The now deserted streets had a strange calm to them, almost a peacefulness, that was only disturbed, Coren noted, by the incidental pack of rats that would scurry by the horses as the cab moved on.

Neither Coren, nor Jenny, nor the driver spoke for several minutes as the horses were pushed to move along at a steady pace out of the area and away from death.

The carriage turned down Whitechapel Road, and the stale air of fear in Coren began to ease. It would now be only a short drive, just past Miter Square, then down Leadenhall Street and finally back to the more respectable areas of London. Once there, Coren and Jenny could relax once again.

"It will not be much longer, Jenny." Coren spoke in an effort to reassure herself and to fill the need to say something, more than for Jenny's sake.

"Right miss."

Niether turned the gaze from the street to look at one another. The street lamps burned more brightly on this section Whitechapel Road. Most, Coren noted, were lit and working, unlike the last visit she and Jenny had made to this part of London. Then, the street lamps were in much disrepair. Most were broken, falling apart and had not been lit in years. Then only the occasional lamp had been in working order, yet the dirt and grime from the smoke the gas produced, obliterated much of the light. Had the lamps been repaired as a result of that last murder? Of that prostitute? Coren thought . . *What was her name.?*

Although murder was not uncommon in Whitechapel, the particularly gruesome way that that woman – *What was her name?* Coren tried again to recall – was killed was something that even the jaded, streetwise population of Whitechapel feared.

Emma. That's it! Emma Smith. The name came to her.

Almost there. That thought kept making its way into Coren's mind. She was more frightened than she wished to let on. She knew now that she had seen enough of Whitechapel at night. It wasn't fair, she decided, to place Jenny's health and her own at risk coming here during the darkness of night.

Health! she silently giggled. *Her life was at risk*! From this point on, she decided firmly, she and Jenny would only venture into this area through the church or with a police escort. A different tactic was in order. The idea of coming to Whitechapel in full entourage, as the wife of the Duke of Clarence would draw the much needed attention to the downtrodden who scraped life out of these cobblestone streets. It wasn't necessarily a bad idea to have come to Whitechapel at night to see the vast difference in the lives of these people versus her own only strengthened her resolve to help all those she could. Actually, trying to find the silver lining to her clouded trips to Whitechapel, working here with the poor and forgotten would be the best education she could ever receive, she justified, better than any university or Royal position. When she finally made it back to the green rolling hills of her Ireland, Coren would be prepared for anything. And when she ultimately fought for the independence of her native land, she would know what . . .

A sudden glimpse of a shadow moving quickly from a darkened doorway caught Coren's attention bringing her out of her thoughts. At first she was not really sure that she had seen anything. She squinted trying to find something in dark. Then the figure moved again and Coren opened her eyes widely. The figure moved sure-footedly, with the silence of the deadly black panthers Coren had heard about in the wild jungles of some far off lands. The figure darted from one darkened doorway to the next. The hairs on the back of Coren's neck and on her arms stood straight up. Chills, the kind that one cannot shake, permeated her body. She was sure that the figure, hidden in the blackness that the gaslights could not chase away, was staring at her. Instinctively, Coren sat back, tight against the rear of the carriage's seat, attempting to hide her own image in the same blackness that the figure, used to conceal himself.

"Jenny?" Coren whispered so slightly that Jenny did not respond.

As Coren was about to speak again, the figure abandoned his hiding spot within the shadows and darted into the street just ahead of the cab: He moved swiftly, cunningly, almost unseen.

But he had been seen. Coren stared directly at him, leaning forward out of her own shadows. She could clearly make out the deerstalker hat, pulled down covering his eyes. A black bag grasped by gloved hands swinging back and forth as he skimmed the street. A cloak that flapped behind him almost as though he was flying. Coren gasped, sure that the figure was coming for her. Screaming as loudly as she could, she grabbed at Jenny.

The man, the shadow, the figure--whatever it was--passed in front of the carriage several yards away. Peculiarly, the man payed no heed to the scream that escaped from Coren. Not even a glance a turn or slight hesitation in his stride. Even in her befuddled state, Coren's mind registered the oddity, as even the horses yielded, allowing the man to whisk by.

Coren's scream echoed through the empty streets, bouncing off of vacant walls and deserted alleys.

Jenny reached for Coren, startled. "What is it? What is it!?"

Jenny's own voice rose to hysteria.

The driver pulled the horses up tight. The cab came to a quick stop, tossing Coren forward. It was only seconds--less than seconds--but it played out in slow motion to Coren. The figure stepped to the side of the street and paused as the horses came to a complete but uneasy stop. The figure did not run off as Coren had expected him to. Instead, he moved slowly, deliberately, without hesitation, as if the cab, Coren, Jenny, the driver, and the horses were not there, acutely aware of all that was going on around him.

Coren was not even sure that the others had noticed the man. The driver had made no attempt to maneuver the horses to avoid the figure. Jenny had said absolutely nothing about seeing him. Only Coren had noticed that a figure had made its way up the street through darkened doorways and now had crossed directly in front of them. She paused in her thoughts. Was she dreaming? Was this real? She was suddenly not sure. As though time had stood still, Coren replayed the last several seconds in her mind. The figure, the doorway, the shadow, the chills on her arms, the hair at the back of her neck. It all flashed in quick succession, forming vivid images that only she could see.

But now the figure from the shadows had reached the side of the street. He stepped over the gutters, which during the day were filled with blood and sewage from the slaughterhouses, but now ran almost dry.

"Hold up here. Ho," the driver spoke in a calming voice to the horses. "Ho," his voiced trailed off.

Drawn from her thoughts and now positive that the figure was real, Coren watched as the man on the side of the street came to a sudden stop, stalled in mid-step.

And Coren froze.

"What is it?" Jenny said as she followed Coren's gaze to where the man had come to a stand still, just outside the circle of light from one of the gas lamps. "Your Highness?" The words escaped before she knew it and then Jenny caught her breath deep in her throat, as the words echoed off of the wet, grimy walls of the slaughterhouses and butcher shops.

The figure, caught by Jenny's words, turned ever so slightly toward the carriage.

The profile.

The movement.

The shrouded eyes.

Jenny knew him.

And so did Coren!

CHAPTER TWENTY-EIGHT

He came to her room in silence--like a phantom. Coren was only barely aware of him. It was the wafting air of his bayberry cologne, his natural musky scent, and a faint coppery smell that let her senses in on his presence. Silently, effortlessly, like the nightly fog that rolls over London, he slid into bed alongside of her and eased his hand down, slowly, softly upon her silk chemise covered breast.

Hot rushes pulsed through her body as she involuntarily sucked in a gasping breath. His fingers lingered lightly around her nipples, circling the now erect nubs at the tips of her breasts. She couldn't exhale. She was paralyzed with ecstasy. Down the center of her chest, between those taught, firm mounds his hand traveled. He rubbed the backs of his fingers straight down the center of her stomach. Through the thin fabric his touch caressed her, sending waves of chills followed by uncontrolled shivers. Each was more intense than the other. Her breath released now. It came hard, in spurts. At times she was totally unable to breathe and at other times she panted with quick light breaths.

Coren grew dizzy from his touch as his hand reached under her chemise and traveled up her leg to the spot that she wanted him to be most of all.

He found it in an instant.

Rubbing there gently, Coren began to moan. Her head

rolled from side to side, as his phantom fingers toyed with her moistened nub. She arched her back into his manipulations, as waves, like those of the torrential seas, collided within her. The waves began to swell and crest, breaking ever faster, as she was drawn inexorably to the rushing shore. Sounds, that she was unaware of, escaped from her lips. A final swell, then a crashing roar. And the tide ebbed.

Albert moved his hands once again up her stomach taking the chemise with them. It took all the strength that Coren had to raise her arms just over her head as he removed the garment. She could hear the soft whoosh as it fell to the floor alongside of the bed. He moved upon her. His legs effortlessly parted her own. He moved his body so that he filled the space between her legs. His nakedness collided with hers, as the heat of his untamed manhood grew hard against her inner thigh. His lips met hers in frenzied passion. Their tongues danced to primitive rhythms. He slid his fingers down her arms as they kissed. Upon reaching her hands, he clasped them and held them tightly. He raised them above her head. Pulling her hands up, he stretched her body so that it lay taut beneath him. He bit gently at her neck, just below her ear. Her head rolled into his caress. As he stretched her arms still tighter above her head, he entered her. His passion evident, hard and strong, he penetrated deeply within her. Slowly pushing in, and even more slowly pulling out, he moved. Coren wrapped her legs tightly around his. The muscles in his calves flexing against her smooth legs. The rough hairs on his legs oddly aroused her even more as he undulated against her. Rough and smooth. Hard and soft. Slick and hot. Every nerve ending in her body was on fire. She tightened her grip on him forcing him to find the inner most reaches of herself. He obliged by lingering there, flexing a muscle that she was unaware he could flex. It rose up slightly within her as he tightened his buttocks and then released. She arched her back to meet him in her own release and it was all they both could take. With explosions of ecstasy their bodies met for the final time. He cried out in primitive sounds, whose meanings were still understood. She screamed the silent inner scream that only lovers know.

For a long time, he laid there on her, his weight a comforting, strange sensation. She strolled her fingers down his dampened back, making spirals in the sweat pooled there. He sighed. She smiled. Soon, sleep came to both of them.

Hours passed, or maybe just minutes. An uneasy gnawing pulled at Coren while she slept. She tried to push it away. It nagged at her. It called to her in a voice both rough and tender to awaken.

She did.

Opening her eyes slowly, allowing them to adjust to the semi-darkness, a flicker of amber light caused Coren to turn onto her side.

There, in the glow of a single candle, Albert sat on a chair, staring at her. The candle cast its faint light across the side his face, illuminating a profile that immediately brought prickles of goose bumps to Coren's arms.

And nauseating surges of disbelief, mixed with waves of fear to her stomach.

That profile.

CHAPTER TWENTY-NINE

The morning sun rose casting its warmth over the garden below Coren's window. Birds of a multitude of species, along with insects too numerous for the mind to fathom, gathered at the ends of the sun's tendrils to feast and forage.

Coren, however, sat chilled to the bone by a coldness that even the sun could not chase. Only darkness reached her. The sun's warmth was lost. The vision of Albert, silhouetted by the candle at her bedside, sent the chills ever deeper. Despite the fact that she sat close to the window, bathed in golden rays and wrapped in a heavy linen blanket, she could not shake the chills from her body. She was not sick, not by a virus, but she was ill.

Ill at ease.

Ill with the thoughts that endlessly circled her mind, spinning a web so tight, so engrossing, that Coren was sure she would never find her way from its sticky silk confines. Like an insect from the garden below, she was trapped, bound in the widow's web.

It was Albert. She chased the thought out her mind, only to have it return with a vengeance. *It could not be.* She considered her fate. A fate that only time would tell.

A cyclone spun within her mind, kicking up whirling fragments of memories that blurred her vision and made her want to scream out primeval sounds of disgust and revolt.

Her stomach cramped with a pain that was unbearable. A pain that no one should ever feel. Yet, it was a pain that Coren was sure some had already felt, lying on the cold cobblestones, life flowing, ebbing, and then, stopping.

A malodorous scent assailed Coren's nostrils. That coppery smell again. She stood immediately, shook the coldness from her, grasped the blanket to her even tighter, and retrieved the vase from her nightstand that contained the now withered, flowers from her garden. Their fragrance once sweet, was now cloying, rotting and wilted. In sudden rage, Coren threw the vase against the wall. It smashed, sending jagged pieces of hand blown Venetian glass, about the room, desiccated flowers cast against the wall, sticking and then slowly sliding down, down to the floor. The water from the vase, brown and molded, splashed against the wall, staining a dark red. Not unlike the blood of the dead.

Coren screamed. Her throat opened and guttural sounds escaped from long lost places and from deep hidden fears within. She screamed again feeling the cleansing relief of emotions billowing up and out of her. Tears. Uncontrollable rushes of tears fell from her eyes, soaking the blanket that she had pulled as tightly as she could up to her, like a mother's arms to a child in need. Convulsions followed, racking her body with spasms. She clutched the blanket to her stomach and fell back onto the chair.

Coren's screams brought Jenny running. She covered the distance from the library to Coren's rooms in mere seconds. She paused at the door only long enough to knock. No. Pound. Once. Then, not waiting for an answer, she flung the door open and rushed in. In her mind, riled by the sensationalistic newspaper articles of late, were thoughts of Coren lying in pools of warm red blood, steaming from gaping wounds in her throat. She shook her head trying to remove the images, only to have them replaced by thoughts even more grotesque and gruesome. She did not want to think the thoughts that now spread throughout her mind, like the plague of days past, unstoppable. Jenny did not, could not, let her fears and doubts gain control of her.

She could not, she told herself over and over again, think what she was thinking.

Coren's body lay slouched over the arm of the chair by the window. Limp, it hung there. There was not the slightest of movements, nor utterances of sound.

Jenny screamed.

Coren jumped from the chair, arms flying. So caught up in her emotions, she was unaware anyone had entered the room.

Jenny spoke through tears of both joy and terror, "I thought that he'd done it to you, too, miss. I surely did."

Coren rushed to Jenny's opening arms. She understood what the "He" meant. Had Jenny been thinking darkly evil thoughts about the man that she loved? How could she!

At once, an anger grew inside Coren. The defense of the man she called "Prince" overwhelmed her. And then, after a second's thought, she realized with a sudden rush of insight, that she had been thinking these same grim thoughts.

It was true then. If Jenny too, felt the same, it must be true. She realized that her feelings were not the lone thoughts and intuitions of a doubting wife. Instead, they were real and completely plausible. "How could this be? How could it?"

When Jenny answered, Coren realized that her thoughts were not just internal, but that she had spoken them out loud.

"Now we don't know for sure that it's him," Jenny said, curiously defending the Prince, much as Coren had done. She hugged Coren and patted her back in assurance.

Even now, as deep thoughts of fear and anxiety racked Coren's mind, glorious moments of love and tenderness crept in along the edges to cast doubt and enormous amounts of guilt. It was clear now, as clear as it could be under these circumstances, that she and Jenny thought the worst of the Prince. That he could be the gentle lover who took Coren on journeys she could not possibly have ever imagined existed between a man and woman, and that he could be the same revolting killer who left women dead in the streets of Whitechapel, left her with such mixed, agonizing emotions that she wanted at once to run away from, and run to, the Prince. It chilled her even more.

"Jenny, I can not believe what I am thinking. This simply can not be." Coren hoped Jenny would again defend the Prince. When no defense came, she continued, "Oh Jenny, what do I do?" A wild array of thoughts collided within Coren's mind, confusing her more: run, hide, leave this place, go back to Ireland where she could escape this madness and be amongst friends.

"Miss, if I were you, I think I'd get out of this place. Go to where there are people. Lots of people, if you ask me. Perhaps there you'll be able to think more clearly," Jenny volunteered.

Coren mulled the suggestion over. It was true. She herself had thought that leaving this house would be for the best. But why, suddenly, when someone else had suggested that she abandon her husband, did the idea make her sick? How could she? She didn't have any proof that the man she loved was, after all, a . . . The word stuck in her throat, as if saying it would make it true.

"He's not!" Coren screamed, more at herself than at Jenny, who nonetheless, jumped back a step in fright.

"Oh, please, miss. Don't do that! We've got enough going on around here to give me the jitters. I don't need you shouting about," Jenny said, as she placed her hand over her heart as if to calm it.

"I'm sorry, Jenny. You're quite right," Coren said, nodding

as if all were settled.

"Thank you, miss." Jenny, too, nodded and moved to the settee by the window, where she sat, trying to calm her quaking emotions.

A long silence passed as each of the women found themselves caught up in a torrent of thoughts that ripped through their minds.

Jenny broke the silence. "It's not like we know for certain it's him who done it, miss."

Coren turned to face Jenny, tears rolled from her eyes. "Jenny, you don't believe it either?"

Jenny sucked in a large breath of air and let it escape slowly from her lips. "I don't want it to be. But I'll be honest with you, miss. I've been thinking about it for a while now. Ever since that first time we saw that dark cloaked gentleman in the carriage in Whitechapel. I thought it looked like the Prince then . . . "

"Oh, Jenny, so did I." Coren picked the blanket up from the floor and wrapped it around herself. "I thought it looked like him, but then I dismissed it. We only had a fleeting glimpse of the man and we don't know that he had done anything wrong."

"You're right." Jenny jumped up from the settee. "Just 'cause we saw a man in the street, doesn't mean that he's been up to no good."

"Even if it was the Prince?" Coren added the previously unspoken thought.

"Even if it was," Jenny finished.

"Then we must do something about it, Jenny." Coren stood upright, flinging the blanket to the bed.

Jenny's face took on a look of horror mixed with sadness. "You don't mean to say that we're going back to that wretched place?"

"No. No, that would be too dangerous," Coren assured her.

"Thank you, Lord." Jenny made the sign of the cross. "I

was prayin' you'd say that."

Coren sat on the bed, cocking her head slightly. She peered through the window. Beyond the slightly warped glass of the window, in places far off, life went on without skipping a beat. The weight of Coren's problems did not in the least affect it. It existed perfectly without any knowledge of the pain and terror that Coren was living at this very moment. Out there, nothing changed. Coren's eyes squinted at the sunlight and she found herself slipping into the memories of yesterday.

An orchestra played as a prince danced with a woman he had never met before. All eyes were on them. They glided across the floor. Or was it above it? She was unclear now. Bayberry cologne filled her senses as his dark eyes drank her in. She was as close to heaven as she ever thought could be possible.

Coren danced with an angel.

The profile of a darkly silhouetted man dashing across the cobblestone streets of Whitechapel, contrasting sharply with the visions of how they had met. The shadowed figure possessed a striking resemblance to the man she loved. Coren tried, as she had many times before, to wash the vision from her mind. She opened and closed her eyes in quick succession. The vision remained. She moved in close to it, studying every move the dark figure made. It was as if it was happening again, at this very moment. Her memories of him were clear and sharp. Coren relaxed and let the scene play out over and over again. From shadow to doorway to shadow again, the figure moved and then hid. She allowed her mind's eye to drift slowly down the figure, watching him, scrutinizing him. His step. His gait. The clothes he wore. The way he carried the black leather physician's bag in his right hand. The way the bag swung out far as he stepped. The posture of his body, arms and legs when he limped on his left leg. It was all so clear. Each second passed slowly in front of her. As the image started to fade in her mind, it left her with questions now answered and questions now raised.

"Jenny, do you remember anything about the man we saw those nights in Whitechapel?" Coren said, breaking the long silence and interrupting Jenny's own deep thoughts.

Jenny paused a moment before answering, her eyebrows arched up. "Of course I do. How could I possibly forget that, miss? It was the scariest night of my life, it was!"

"And what you recall makes you think that it was . . ." Coren stopped short of saying what it was that she and Jenny both thought. The Prince.

"I'm afraid it does, miss," Jenny quickly added to lessen the pain. "I tried not to think it, let alone believe it. But what else could I do? The man looked just like him, miss. I mean, you saw it, too."

"I did." Coren sunk back into the chair. "Even his walk, Jenny, his walk is . . ." Coren's words froze in her throat. "He limped, Jenny! That man limped across the street. I clearly remember it. He limped!"

"But the Prince . . ." Jenny started to speak, but Coren abruptly cut her off.

"The Prince does not!" Coren's eyes began to sparkle, as hope sprang back into her voice. "I can see him now. Again and again I've played this out in my mind. As the man steps across the cobblestones, he limps."

"Aye, that he does, miss," Jenny slowly ground out as the memory played out before her.

"Then it can not be Albert. It simply can not be!" Coren's exclamation filled the room. She bounced up from the bed. Life, once again, renewed within her.

"Oh, Jenny! We were worried for nothing. You and I both know that the Prince walks perfectly normally. He has never had a limp in his gait. It was someone else." Tears rolled down Coren's cheeks, as she reassured herself that the man she loved, the man she intended to remain with the rest of her life, the prince who would someday be king, was not the murdering maniac who roamed the darkened streets of

London's Whitechapel, in search of victims to rip apart. A simple limp in his gait made her sure of that.

She stopped.

No, it was more than that. It was an innate knowledge of him. An assuredness of who he was and what he was to her. He was her prince. Her Prince Charming, as it were. And she, his Cinderella. She giggled at the notion. She had always loved that fairy tale. And now the realization struck her. It was no fairy tale. It was her life. And it was to be her happily ever after. She was sure of it. This was her fate. She did love him so. He was her everything, now that her mother and father were gone. And she would be everything to him. How could she ever doubt him? How could she ever suspect him? What a ninny she was! Her age belied her intelligence. She felt she was all grown up, but apparently not. In matters of the heart she was just a babe. But she was learning quickly and loving it. It dawned on her now how much more in love with her prince she was than she had ever been. It surprised her that she could still be falling in love with Albert after all this time.

"I'm falling in love again with the man I love, Jenny." Coren moved once again to the warmth of the sun flowing through the windows. "All this because of a simple limp," she repeated the statement. "Isn't it wonderful, Jenny?" Coren beamed a bright wide smile at Jenny.

"It certainly is." Jenny forced a smile. "Except for one thing, miss."

Coren looked at Jenny, cocking her head slightly to the side. Emeralds sparkling.

"Everyone limps when they run across cobblestones."

Emeralds turned cold.

CHAPTER THIRTY

Ahhhhh!!!

Jenny's voice rent the air. "Prince Albert ye're choking me to death!"

Coren heard the scream through the thick plaster walls of the palace as if Jenny were standing in the same room. She dashed into Albert's neighboring dressing room, where she was sure the cries had emanated. Jenny's face was red, her mouth gaping. "Jenny!" Coren screamed.

Jenny's eyes bugged.

"Jenny! . . . Albert!" was all Coren could say.

Letting out a loud gasp, Jenny's faced relaxed. "My God! What is it?" Jenny looked quizzically at Coren.

Coren hesitated a moment, then said, "You screamed."

"The Prince here almost strangled me to death." Jenny spoke matter-of-factly. "I know it's called a choker, but Your Highness, I don't think they really mean you should do it."

"I am ever so sorry, Jenny," Albert said. "But I'm not very good at these sorts of things."

"Albert, whatever is going on?" Coren said, totally bewildered.

"You see, my dear. . . " Albert began.

"I need to get this darn necklace around my throat," Jenny interrupted. "But it's got this strange little thingamajigger in the back, and I can't reach it. So Albert here was tryin' to do it up fer me."

Coren spoke, now becoming exasperated. "Must you call him Albert?"

"He told me to," Jenny said, petulantly.

"Aye, lassie, it's true. I did," Albert said, affecting his best Irish brogue.

"Why Albert, I mean, Your Highness." Jenny glanced at Coren. "That there's as excellent a brogue as ever I heard in Dublin." And with another quick glance at Coren added, "Doncha think so, miss?"

Coren was speechless.

"Cat got yer tongue?" Albert again with that anachronistic brogue.

Jenny and Albert began to chortle, which soon turned into gleeful laughter as they watched Coren's discomfiture grow.

Coren, finally gathering herself up, said, "When you two are through with your most uncomely bantering, I would appreciate an explanation." She stared at Jenny and Albert, shaking her head slightly from side to side.

It didn't have quite the effect she had anticipated. The prince and the maid only laughed all the harder.

After several long seconds, Albert composed himself enough to utter, "My dear, surely you see the humor in all of this?"

"My dear," Coren mocked. "I would see the humor if I knew what was *bloomin' goin' on!*"

Laughter again. This time from all three of them.

Coren wasn't sure what had happened, but it seemed as though it wasn't what she had feared when she burst into Albert's dressing room, seeing Jenny's face red and Albert standing behind her. She chastised herself silently for such thoughts. Now, with Jenny and Albert caught once again in the throes of laughter, she had to agree it was humorous. Even if Jenny and Albert did make her discomfort into good-natured fun.

After several more squeals of Irish witticisms and bouts of

laughter, Albert attempted to explain. "It seems that our dear Jenny has herself an assignation this evening with a gentleman."

"Oh Jenny, how very nice." Coren smiled. "But whom will you be meeting?"

"A gentleman that I believe you know, my dear." Albert cocked his head inquisitively. "So Jenny has told me. A gentleman that now also wears bayberry cologne."

Jenny again, "Well I figured it smelled so nice on you. An' you bein' a prince and all, you must have good taste."

"Thank you, Jenny." Albert gave her a slight bow of deference.

Coren paused for a moment not understanding. Then comprehension dawned. "Oh yes. The garrulous Mr. Dolittle, I presume."

"The very same." Jenny nodded.

"And why was I not informed of this?" Coren tried to admonish her maid.

"An' seein' as you and the Prince here are goin' out tonight, I thought I'd give Mr. Dolittle the chance to show me the sights here in London. The *nice* ones," Jenny emphasized to Coren, who let the comment pass by, without so much as a raised eyebrow or sideways glance.

"I offered tickets to Jenny and this Mr. Dolittle, hoping they would join us at the play tonight, my love, but she graciously declined." Albert winked at Jenny.

"Yes, Jenny, why not join us?" Coren said.

"I don't want to be seein' any creepy old mystery plays. Thank you just the same. But I hope you and Albert – I beg your pardon, His Royal Highness, have a lovely time."

"That is too bad. It would be a pleasure to meet your Mr. Dolittle," Albert averred.

"Now if ya' wouldn't mind tryin' again to get this darn thing around my neck." Jenny held out the choker to Albert. "I'd be most grateful."

"Let me, Jenny." Coren stepped toward her. "Albert's

hands are most likely too large to work the clasp."

"I did notice that he had rather large hands, miss." Jenny winked at Albert. "An' if'n you recall, I told you that a man with large hands means . . . "

"Jenny!" Coren blushed crimson, and began to sputter, "I . . . I . . . never . . . "

"Aye, miss, you did." Jenny shook her head. "But it's all right. I'm sure Albert don't mind. In fact I'm sure he's kind of proud. . . "

"Enough, Jenny!!! Coren all but shrieked.

"All right, miss," Jenny said calmly. "Just see if ya' can get this necklace thingy on me," she continued as she jiggled the two ends of the necklace behind her neck.

Albert had fallen into a nearby chair in a fit of laughter so great that it would have made the Queen disown him had she seen it.

Coren could not look at him. She was sure even her earlobes were bright red. She could feel her face flushed with the heat and light beads of sweat start to form on her brow. Regaining her composure, she squeezed the necklace tightly around Jenny's throat and secured it in place.

"Awwk!" Jenny squeaked. "Yer' as bad as yer' husband." Jenny coughed out. "See now, if I ever borrow another one of your necklaces." She put a hand to her throat, inspecting it.

"What?" Coren said, not noticing until now what necklace she had just secured around Jenny's throat.

"This is your choker," Jenny said.

Coren turned Jenny around, facing her, a blank expression on on her face.

"So it is."

"The Prince offered it to me when he found out I had a date with my Mr. Dolittle. It was quite gallant of him, if I do say."

"Quite gallant," Coren repeated.

"An' he says you wouldn't miss one, as you got so many, he did," Jenny added with an air on nonchalance.

"Is that so?" Coren looked at Albert, one eyebrow now raised.

"An' he said, he'd just buy ya' a new one if I happened ta' lose this one." Jenny too looked to Albert. "Oh, I do hope my Mr. Dolittle turns out to be half the man yer' prince is."

Coren's expression changed from disapproval to one of absolute love. She took in the sight of her prince, now sobering from his fits of laughter. Yes, if others could only be half the man, she agreed silently with Jenny.

Albert had not told Coren that he had borrowed one of her necklaces to loan to Jenny. He was quite sure that she wouldn't mind, but in hindsight, perhaps he should have told her. Or better yet, he thought, I should have asked her.

Coren now eyed Albert as if to castigate him, then smiled and said, "Albert, why didn't you give Jenny the necklace with the big yellow diamond in the center? She could have slipped it over her head and not worried about a clasp."

Albert returned Coren's look with an overwhelming feeling of unbridled love. A feeling that she could clearly read upon his face. "Of course, my love, that would have been the better choice. Next time I will ask you which necklace you'd like to loan."

"Och. I don't need a big fat yellow diamond around my neck. This here is fancy enough and now that I've gotten it on, I can see that it brings out the color in my lovely green eyes," Jenny said, admiring herself in the nearby bureau mirror.

"Indeed it does, Jenny. I'm sure your Mr. Dolittle will be totally lost in your smoky green pools," Albert said quite seductively.

It was Jenny's turn to blush. "Oh, Your Highness . . . I . . . I hope so. He seems to be a fine man. And I would like ya' to meet him some time." Jenny winked. "An' give me yer' opinion."

"I would be delighted to, dear Jenny," Albert said.

Jenny blushed again.

"Now you had best be off and we," Albert reached for

Coren's hand, "had best be getting finished dressing ourselves or we shall be late for the curtain."

"Yer right." Jenny moved to the door.

"We don't want to miss the beginning, my dear. I hear it is quite chilling." Albert wrapped an arm around Coren.

Coren and Jenny met each others eyes briefly as Jenny sailed out the door with a quick "Ta."

Albert pulled Coren's hand to his lips, brushed them with a kiss and looked up to meet her eyes with his own. His look made the heat in Coren's groin flush. "Please wear the yellow diamond tonight. For me. You know it's my favorite and I want to spend the evening thinking of you later tonight in our chambers wearing nothing but that diamond."

The heat rose once again. This time from anticipation.

There was standing room only at the Lyceum Theater; even the slim cramped area behind the last row of orchestra seats, reserved for standing room was completely filled. From her seat in the Royal box, placed for perfect viewing in the center of the mezzanine level, Coren could see that every seat was taken.

"The Strange Case of Dr. Jekyll and Mr. Hyde", based on the novel by Robert Louis Stevenson, was very well received by the critics and the press in general. It seemed that most of London's society was here this evening. Coren had read the novel, a little too grim for her, and she had enjoyed several of the author's other works, especially *Kidnapped* and *The Master of Ballantrae*. She loved adventures and most of all – romances. The play version of Jekyll and Hyde, had just recently opened and Coren had heard much talk of it at various teas and soirees. An American actor named Richard Mansfield was playing both of the titular roles, as the story concerned a doctor named Jekyll, whose experiments on himself had gone awry and had changed him into an evil alter ego, Mr. Hyde.

Albert had been very anxious to see it and said that the subject matter was quite fascinating. Coren had said that it sounded disturbing. But here they were seated where they could see and be seen. And Coren noted, the glares and stares from those seated in the Orchestra seats below the Royal Box.

Coren smiled, produced a small wave to several audience members that she recognized, then turned to Albert and paused, he had never been more handsome than tonight, in his fine, black evening tuxedo and top hat. He took her breath away. Begorrah, she was lucky.

As they both waited for the curtain to rise, she took in how the fine fabric of his trousers molded to his muscular taut thighs. *Thighs that later on that evening would be pressed to hers*, she giggled at the thought. Then allowing her mind to wander into the slight future of tonight, she envisioned the tight curled hairs of him, rubbing over her smooth thighs. His muscles tightening on top of hers as he drove his body into her, filling her, giving her what she needed, what she craved, what she . . . Oh my, Coren's eyes widened. She glanced down to his groin and noticed the fine fabric around the juncture of his thighs was stretching noticeably. He shifted slightly as the pressure grew. She looked up to his eyes, which met hers anxiously. Had he read her thoughts? Again?

Albert suddenly grabbed Coren's hand and brought it to his lips in a caress. His tongue flickered over her knuckles. She drew in a quick breath as he then moved his mouth close to her ear. "Even your gaze can make me hard with longing," he whispered, and quickly darted his tongue to catch her earlobe.

Dear God, what had she done! She couldn't possibly sit here for the next several hours and not rip his clothes off. He must know what he was doing to her. Perhaps, they could leave at the interval, if she complained of a headache or some such ailment.

He still held her hand tightly and he was now . . . No! He wouldn't dare! He . . . He did. He put her hand right on top of the now very obvious bulge between his legs. The lights had dimmed she realized. Thank God! His hand rested atop hers on his very swollen manhood and he began to slowly and rhythmically squeeze her hand beneath his. She was sweating. She could feel the moisture now between her legs and she squirmed a little in response. He removed his hand from hers and placed it between her thighs. He started to press gently against the soft satin fabric. She moaned slightly.

"Sssh," Albert whispered. "It's about to start."

"What? Oh yes, the play." Coren blurted.

Albert chuckled softly.

Coren tried to concentrate on the play slowly letting his and her agony subside.

The story was quite involving and suspenseful and the American actor was amazingly convincing as both hero and fiend. But she found she really wasn't paying much as attention to the play as she should be. How could she? Albert could sense when the tension was becoming too great and he would stop his ministrations until her breathing eased somewhat, only to start stroking her once again a minute later. She thought she would die from such intense erotic frustration! And now once again she could feel the tension rising in her loins. With her hand still resting in Albert's crotch, feeling the pulsing there, and his hand between her legs, kneading her, stroking her, and making her more and more frantic. She could feel the pressure rising in herself again, the most intense yet. She couldn't stop him. She didn't want him to. The pressure built more as a young actress on the stage wandered a dark alley. The girl seemed frightened, as if there were a presence looming nearby. Coren became more and more agitated. She couldn't contain herself any longer. The pressure was too great. She clutched him. He clutched her. She couldn't stop. She couldn't ... A scream burst from her throat while the actress on stage also screamed as the madman, Mr. Hyde, choked the girl's life away.

There were several other screams from young women in

the theater. But only Coren's was from pleasure.

The interval.

Thank God! She had never anticipated an interval so much before. Relief. Finally. Relief from Albert's relentless torments. And now, she could not wait for the play to end and the return to the palace, where her torment would begin anew.

During the break in the play, Albert introduced Coren to a French Comte and his mistress. He asked her how she had enjoyed the play so far and she had responded with, "I can only hope that the second act is as thrilling as the first. Right, Albert?"

"Absolutely, my love." Albert raised her hand to his lips in a kiss and once again brushed her knuckles with his tongue.

Dear Lord! She'd never survive act two!

But she did survive – which is more than could be said for some of the members of the cast. There were several more murders, ending finally with the death of the evil Mr. Hyde and his misguided other self, Dr. Jekyll. The play was very disconcerting to Coren, especially in lieu of the recent Whitechapel events as well as her own forays into that wretched area. It made Coren stop to think. Could a person have two different sides to them that others around them don't see? Can one truly conceal a deeper darker self? Even Henry Jekyll's fiancée was fooled by him. Could even those closest to the person not see the other personality? Was Albert hiding another self? Was he two different people? One personality shown to her and the rest of the world and one...? Don't be ridiculous! Coren chastised herself. This was only a play. A fiction.

She knew Albert. She knew there was no darker side to him. How could anyone conceal such evil? It was impossible.

"Impossible. No one could have two different personalities. It's ludicrous to think that we could all have an evil dark side capable of murder or worse." The French Comte again was speaking to Albert as they began to exit the theater.

"Ah, you never know, my fine French friend, just what evil

lurks in people." Albert continued, as the entered the lobby, "Just look at that current rogue, butchering those poor young girls in Whitechapel.

Coren's breath caught. "Oh!"

"Yes, my love?" Albert turned to Coren.

"It's nothing. Just a . . . a chill in the air," Coren responded.

"Then perhaps we should get you home and remove the chill." Albert's eyes immediately filled with passion and intent. He turned back to the Comte and his escort "Adieu, mon ami, mademoiselle."

"Adieu, Your Highness," the Comte said, as he and his mistress bowed and took their leave.

The Prince took Coren's hand and helped her into the waiting carriage. "A chill? Or a shiver of anticipation, my love?"

Coren's eyes met his and she saw a darker side of him. A darker side filled with sensuous pleasures that only he knew how to draw from her. The side only she would have revealed to her in the dark confines of their chambers. There, new and exciting secrets would be unfolded and explored. There she would show him another side of her.

"Anticipation, my prince. Definitely, anticipation."

Emeralds blackened.

CHAPTER THIRTY-ONE

Albert lay there by her side, his soft rhythmic breathing lulling him into a deep sleep. Coren watched as his chest rose up and his lungs filled with air. The strong hard muscles that formed his chest expanded, twitching slightly. Soft curls of dark brown hair that covered his masculine form, untangled, and then fell back together as he exhaled. How could this be the man of so many nightmares? No. It could not be. Coren answered her own question. She traced the outline of his body with her eyes, traveling from the tip of his forehead, around darkly arched eyebrows, down past the now bristly hairs of his face.

An angelic face.

And her mind added . . . *angel of death*?

She pushed the thought from her mind, letting the question go unanswered. Her eyes continued, past his rising and falling torso to the flat expanse of his stomach and onto the place where his manhood lay, resting on its side. The silken covers lay atop of it, and yet she could trace the outline of its length and the ridge where it tapered to a round soft head. Albert moved causing the sheet to pull away from his leg, exposing the tight thigh and calf muscles that were also wrapped in the dark curls. Coren propped herself up onto her elbow, resting her weight upon her arm, where she could study him from a better vantage point. From there she watched him sleep as she had done so many times before. He dreamed, she hoped, of herself and him, lying tightly wrapped in each other's arms. A sudden urge overcame her and Coren reached out, pulling the silk sheet slowly, smoothly away from his manhood. It did not spring to attention as she thought or wished it might, but rather, it just lay there-- wrinkled and limp. Minutes passed, perhaps longer as she watched the man sleeping peacefully. Nothing happened. She had secretly thought that the mere fact that she had exposed him to the night air would cause some great reaction. It did not. Coren laughed at a crude thought, tried to stifle it and then burst out in uncontrolled giggles. She grabbed a pillow to cover her face and to keep from waking Albert.

Just as she calmed down, the same crude thought sprang to life again. *Both of my little men are fast asleep and I can not seem to wake even the smaller of the two!*

Coren buried her face into the pillow and shook with laughter. She was sure she would wake Albert. But he slept on, oblivious. Finally, she controlled her laughter. Reaching again for the silk sheet, she pulled it up slowly to cover Albert as he slept. As she did, Albert, in deep sleep, rolled to his side, facing her. Coren was so caught up in the shock of the moment, she did not have time to react, and froze with the covers halfway up. His legs caught her arm and twisted it under him. His full weight came down upon her arm, trapping it directly beneath him. In direct contact with his manhood! She felt it hot against her forearm, its softness molding around her. Instantly, tingles began to move up her arm as her circulation was being cut off.

Her arm was, like her prince, falling fast asleep.

She tightened the muscles in her arm, pressing down on the feather bed and tried in vain to move, to pull it out from under him. Back and forth she rocked her arm. It rubbed against Albert. He did not move. Her arm did not move. But . . . something else was moving.

Coren could feel the vital hardening of her prince's masculinity. It grew and stretched on top of her arm. At last, one of her men had awakened.

Emeralds in the dark, blazed brightly.

CHAPTER THIRTY-TWO

Coren walked down the long hallway rubbing her arm. It was sore from a night of crushing.

"Did you hurt your arm, miss?" Jenny seemed to appear out of nowhere.

"Why is it, Jenny, that you must notice everything?" Coren's tone carried with it a sharpness that Jenny was not prepared for.

"I'm sorry, miss," Jenny spoke, turning down a side corridor and calling after her, "I'll try to stop that."

When Albert had left for his day's duties, Coren returned to their suite. She was in search of something. She just didn't know what. She didn't know why. She had satisfied her doubts. Hadn't she? Then why was she here? She searched through his bureau and through the tallboy that he kept his clothes neatly hung in. There was nothing out of place. It comforted her in a strange way. By not finding anything, her confidence that the thoughts and doubts she and Jenny were having were not to be given any credence. But the lack of incriminating evidence also gave her pause to think that he had done a perfect job of hiding . . . anything?

How could she think this? Hadn't she already had this conversation with herself? What was she doing? It was insane. The thoughts were making her insane. It could not be. She would not let it be so. Images again flashed throughout her thoughts, the same images which she had seen over and over again. Her mind told her that her doubts were right. He is the one! It kept shouting at her.

But her heart would not let her believe it. She had watched him sleep and in his sleep he did not dream of dark and otherworldly things. She was sure of it. He did not thrash and claw about, as any man who could kill like the one they called "Ripper" must surely do as he slept. It may be only little solace, but it would do for now.

She need not be convinced that he was not the man. She needed to be convinced that he was the man. And no matter what, he was her man. And she loved him.

As the afternoon sun began to set, the butler called on Coren. "Excuse me, Your Highness, there is a gentlemen here to speak with you."

"Are we expecting anyone?" Coren placed her cup down onto the saucer.

"No, Your Highness, I do not believe we are. But I would venture that Your Ladyship would like to speak with the gentleman." The butler paused momentarily. "It is Commissioner Sir Charles Warren, ma'am, of the Metropolitan Police."

Emeralds clouded.

CHAPTER THIRTY-THREE

"Commissioner, please be seated, won't you?" Coren motioned to a large overstuffed settee.

"Thank you, Your Highness." He looked toward the settee but did not move. "I'm afraid this is not a social call."

"Oh! I see." Coren cocked her head slightly to the side. "Then what is it that brings you here, Commissioner." Inside, Coren had already answered all of her own questions, in saying them aloud she hoped, desperately, that the answers to them would change.

"This is not easy for me." The commissioner cleared his throat. "I mean, of course, for the Metropolitan police, ma'am." He looked around the room nervously, his fingers played over the rim of the odd-shaped, chimney pot hat he was holding.

Coren noted his discomfiture and said, "Commissioner, please, won't you be seated."

The commissioner smiled awkwardly and seated himself on the settee. "Thank you." He stared at the hat in his hands as he gathered his thoughts.

Coren dreaded what the commissioner was surely going to say to her, but apparently not as much as the commissioner dreaded saying it. She hoped he would be all right. Coren studied the man for a moment. An odd looking man, not at all like the policeman she would have thought would have come to take away her Prince . . . she paused in mid-thought as the realization of what this man was here to do sank in.

She studied him again from head to toe, starting with the old-fashioned policeman's chimney pot hat, to the monocle in his right eye, down to the enormous Prussian style mustache on his upper lip, which curled below the sides of his mouth, to the peculiar military general's uniform he wore, before saying, "Forgive me, Commissioner. I should have asked if you would like some refreshment. Some tea perhaps or a tall glass of cool water?" Without giving him time to answer, Coren pulled on the long corded tapestry rope, sending a dozen servants to scurry about in some far off corner of the house. It was a desperate attempt, she admitted, to try to stave off a few more moments before this man would tell her what she never wanted to know. Tell her what she knew could not be.

"Thank you, Your Highness, that would be quite nice," the commissioner answered, seeming somewhat relieved.

After only seconds had passed, an unassuming maid appeared at the door. Coren ordered tea and cucumber and butter sandwiches.

"So Commissioner, what brings you here? If this is not a social call then might it be something that, the Queen perhaps, has asked of the Metropolitan Police?"

"I'm afraid it is not, Your Highness. It is, though, a concern which is very important." As he spoke, he continued to fidget with brim of his hat, running his fingers endlessly over the smooth felt.

"Yes, I imagine it must be to bring you here." She wished suddenly, that he would just get on with it. Tell her that the man she loved was a murderer – that the man of her dreams was the vilest of villains.

That my Prince Charming is the Prince of evil. Coren was screaming inside.

Calmly, she said, "I imagine that the Metropolitan Police are very busy. Whatever it is, I thank you for taking the time out of your busy day, Commissioner." Torrents washed over, under and through her every thought.

Tell me! Her thoughts screamed.

Stall! Stall! They countered.

She took the action demanded by the first thoughts – foolish though they may be. "Well, Commissioner, perhaps you had best be out with it. If it is so important, as you say, we really shouldn't stall any longer."

"You are quite right, Your Highness." His voice quavered in anticipation. "It is not very often that the Metropolitan Police have to address a member of the Royal Family in a matter of this concern."

"That must be quite true, Commissioner." Coren tried to retain a regal composure to lessen the pronouncement that would soon come.

"You understand that the Metropolitan Police are very concerned with the well being of all of the citizens of London, but that we do take a special interest in the welfare of the Royal Family, as the Queen has decreed." His speech sounded well thought out and practiced.

"Yes, thank you, Commissioner. We are aware of the good you and the Metropolitan Police do."

"Then you must be aware, Your Highness, that it is not easy for the Metropolitan Police to come into this great home of yours with news, which may not be at all welcome." He stood then, adjusted his uniform and quickly sat again.

Coren watched the commissioner fidget, cough, clear his throat, and suck in a great breath of air. She steeled herself for the words that would most assuredly follow. *My love, my precious love, why should we end this way?* Her thoughts brought tears to her eyes. She quickly dabbed at the corners of her eyes, so the commissioner would not notice.

"Your Highness, we have been told by a constable on duty in the Whitechapel district ..."

Before he could finish a small, uncontrolled scream slipped from Coren's mouth. Odd, she thought, she had prepared for these words and yet the mere enunciation of them shocked her.

"Are you all right?" The commissioner, shaken by her outburst, sprang to his feet from the settee.

"Yes, quite, thank you," Coren assured him, regaining her composure.

The commissioner reseated himself and continued, "As I was saying, we have been informed by a very reliable constable, who works in the Whitechapel district, of an occurrence that has made us very concerned. Our concern, Your Highness, is for your safety, and we must appeal to you to do all that you can to remain safe. It would be a great loss to London and to all of Great Britain if we were to see harm done to any one in the Royal Family."

"Thank you, Commissioner, we again appreciate your concern." Coren had no idea where this calm in her voice was coming from, but she was grateful for it.

"You will understand then, when we say that it is of the utmost importance for you to be aware of what we have been informed."

The commissioner continued to fidget, and Coren tightened her fingers together, so as not to throttle the man! Couldn't he just come out with it! Instead, she said, "Yes, Commissioner, we are." Her hands began to shake so much that Coren had to tighten them even more.

"Your Highness," the commissioner began infuriatingly again and removed some papers from his inside jacket pocket. He unfolded them as if they were a priceless work of art. Then he began to read . . . "On the afternoon of June 28th on the corners of George Street and Whitechapel Road, near Aldgate Pump in the district of Whitechapel, I did take note of two ladies riding in a hansom cab for hire, stopped just outside of the scene of a murder. I also noted that one of the ladies in the cab appeared to be that of Her Ladyship the Princess Coren, Duchess of Clarence. The other lady was not known to me. I informed the driver and the ladies that the area was not an appropriate area for them and I suggested that they take leave of the scene immediately. The driver took heed and removed the ladies from the area."

The commissioner lowered the paper. "There is more. Shall I go on?"

A wide grin spread across Coren's face. "That is what you needed to say, Commissioner?"

"Why, yes, Your Highness, it is," the commissioner replied.

Coren's eyes filled with tears as her body shook with uncontrolled laughter.

"Oh, Your Highness, it is not as bad as it may seem," the commissioner spoke with a genuine air of concern at Coren's unusual response. "We know that exploring the unknown must be enticing, but we ask that if you wish to do so in the future, you let us accompany you." He added, "It would be best for all concerned."

Coren looked the commissioner straight in the eye. He seemed so small now, not a threat in the least. Relief flooded through her. "Commissioner, I cannot thank you enough for coming out here to tell me this. You are quite right though, that it is a concern . . . " She could not help it. Laughter took over and racked through her. Through wave after tumultuous wave and rush of laughter, she tried to speak. "We should . . . we should not have . . . done that." She composed herself again, briefly. "We are sorry." And she fell into fits of tears and laughter again.

"Apparently, Your Highness, you need some time alone," the commissioner sputtered, totally at a loss as to how to respond. He stood then, and moving to the door said, "Please call upon us at any time."

As he stepped out and closed the door, he could hear the room behind echo with screams of delight.

The maid returning with the tray of sandwiches curtsied to the commissioner and turned to open the door, as another peel of delirium sailed from the room. She turned, looking to the commissioner. He arched his eyebrows. The maid hesitated, then turned on her heels and hurried off down the hall.

CHAPTER THIRTY-FOUR

"Jenny, it was dreadful. Absolutely dreadful." Coren open her eyes wide to emphasize the point. "That poor Commissioner Warren must think me mad. But what was I to do?" A laugh crept from her throat and she fought to stifle it. "I occupied the conversation with trivialities just to keep him from telling me that my husband was a murderer, and in the end he admonishes me for being where I should not have been. I couldn't help it. I had to laugh." As if to stress the point, she covered her mouth in an ill attempt to stifle the oncoming current of laughter.

"You must have been petrified," Jenny spoke with a genuine air of concern in her voice. "I don't know how you did it, miss." She shook her head in disbelief. "I would have screamed and cried the minute the commissioner came to call." Jenny moved closer to Coren, taking her hand. "You poor child. What you don't get yourself into."

"Ha! I did not get myself into anything, Jenny," Coren said, as she flipped her head back in defiance. "I simply went exploring, and this is what became of it. We are none the worse for it."

"True, miss." Jenny let go of Coren's hand and flopped herself down into one of the overstuffed chairs that Coren liked so much. "Nonetheless, miss, you must take better care when venturing about. You are, after all, a princess."

"Jenny, I have not forgotten my station in life. And I did, as you may recall, take great care in my little escapade. It was you, I seem to remember, that made the commotion at every turn."

"Ah, miss, I think your memory is failing you in your old age!" Jenny turned on the brogue. "It was you who made the commotion over some little murder."

"Murder is not little, Jenny," Coren chastised. "Especially to the one who was murdered."

"You're right, miss. But it was you, now, who the commissioner said was recognized." Jenny clicked her tongue against her teeth, and then smugly added, "Not I."

"Jenny? Who would recognize you?" Coren said, pursing her lips.

Jenny pulled herself up where she sat and said very didactically, "There are a great handful of men I'd bet who would recognize me no matter how I was dressed!"

Coren couldn't help but laugh. "Oh! You are terrible."

"That I am, miss." She nodded in agreement. "And aren't you glad that I am?" Jenny laughed at her own joke, drawing Coren in with her. "Now, quit yer dawdlin'. Your handsome prince and all those dinner guests will be here soon. So get yourself fixed up in your finery as befits your station."

Coren strolled with elegant ease into the parlor where the guests had gathered. As she greeted each one by rank and formal name, they would bow or curtsey. Prince Albert had invited thirty guests to dine with them that evening. It was an affair to entertain some heads of banking and the usual crowd of friends mixed in with favor-owed acquaintances. Coren's mind was much at ease this evening and it showed in her manner and grace.

"Each time I look at you I am enraptured, as if it were the

first time I saw you from the top of those stairs," the Prince spoke in between introductions.

"Oh posh! You couldn't see to my hiding spot from up there. It was I who first saw you." Coren said through her smiling lips before greeting another of the guests, while she slyly brushed her hand up against Albert's leg. With one finger she drew small circles on the fabric of his suit, then traced the seam of his trousers up and down. Coren drew her hand away quickly to extend it to an ambassador and his wife, then just as quickly moved it back down to Albert's leg. This time she ran her fingers toward the back of his thigh, up his buttocks, across the top of his trousers, and then straight down between the valley which his buttocks formed.

Albert groaned.

"I beg your pardon." Coren's sly smile and arched eyebrows accompanied the comment. "Is the Prince in some . . . discomfort?"

"Not yet. But soon enough it will be all I can do to restrain myself." Albert cleared his throat. "I'm certain that these pants will not restrain me much longer, my dear."

Coren tilted her head to the side and slid her hand ever so lightly along the inner thigh of his legs, continuing up to and under his groin. Using just her fingertips, she let her nails trace the outline of his now taught muscles. She paused at the spot where none had ever touched him before. And tickled him.

"Oh, dear God in heaven!" When Albert could no longer hold the pleasure within, he reached back and took hold of Coren's hand, holding it tight. "You must stop, my dear, or I shall have to take leave of this party to change my trousers."

"Did the Prince spill something?" Coren said wryly.

He grinned in agony as he drew breath in through his clenched teeth. "Not yet, my dear. But touch me there again and I am certain to."

"Then let go of my hand." Coren dared him. "Let us see if you have the will power not to."

"Ah, you shall not win this one, my dear." Albert dropped Coren's hand and stepped forward. He announced to the multitude, "I would like to thank you all for joining us this evening." Albert glanced around the room. "I hope that you will enjoy it as much as I have all ready." He turned to face Coren. "Right, my dear?"

"Oh, but I am sure that there is much more pleasure at hand, my Prince." Coren batted her eyes and then widened them as they twinkled in the light from the lamps.

"One can only anticipate and hope." Albert's voice rose and quivered as he recalled the feeling of Coren's gentle stroke.

Coren watched as the Prince moved off to see to his guests. With his muscles still tight from her touch, he walked stiffly and with determination. She watched as he took each step, his torso and abdomen firm, his clothes falling against them in harmony with his body. The bayberry cologne lingered lightly in his wake. He turned, smiling, knowing full well that her gaze accompanied his every step.

And she melted.

The fear and anguish over her thoughts and yes, doubts, of him and the deadly rampage which had cursed this city for some time now, were gone. Her heart once again ached for his touch, his scent after long hours of love making, and the tickle of his pencil-thin mustache over her stomach and lower. She brought her hand to her outer thigh, gently tracing the area as she relived the sensation.

She had enclosed herself for far too long in a cocoon of ice to shield herself from the inevitable knowledge . . . even in her thoughts, she paused, not wanting to admit to herself the truth that her husband could be a murderer . . . and the pain from that knowledge that she was sure would come. Her love for him refused to allow her to believe in . . . that knowledge . . . those truths. But nevertheless, creeping doubts had long lingered, inching their way into her thoughts, causing her to believe that, within those doubts could be truths. Where her heart and her intuition had refused to allow her to believe, her eyes and her intellect only conspired to confirm those beliefs. Logic and love opposed one another.

A man with a gentle touch.

A man with a limp.

Seductive nighttime rendezvous.

Shadows in the dark.

Cries of ecstasy.

Screams of murder.

Her bed.

Whitechapel.

But no longer. How could she have ever questioned? This man, who she had given herself to totally, could never have been responsible for the cruelties played out in that dreaded area of despair and poverty. Her joy in watching him was replaced by anger at herself for doubting him. Now, questions of her own faith and love for this man filled her thoughts. Could she love him as she professed to and still have the lingering thoughts and doubts, that – try as hard as she may – she could not overcome.

Can one love as she loved, and still not know the answer? Perhaps her mother would have been able to tell her, but that, now, could not be. Coren missed her deeply. Thought of her often. Wished she were here.

Tonight, she would make up all of her doubts to her prince. Tonight, they would spend some time in heaven. Maybe, she thought, I can speak to mother while I'm there.

The evening's dinner was announced, and the regular, as well as new guests were seated around the ornate table.

The conversations of the gathered politicians, bankers and industrialists could not manage to keep Coren's mind off her prince. She instead kept slipping off to a private spot in her thoughts where: bankers were not allowed, politicians were banished, and industrialists never existed.

It was a quiet place, lit by hundreds of candles, a garden draped in soft silks and damasks of many colors. There, the only sounds were of the wind's susurration through the trees, and the splash of water over rounded stones. It was a quiet sound. The kind of noise one can still think in. The kind of noise that allows a single groan of ecstasy to echo a thousand times. Her breath, his breath, both coming hard, in spurts. Breaths, involuntarily held, and then just as uncontrolled, released in great sighs of pleasure. Bodies glistening with small beads of sweat, like dew on young supple blades of grass and entwined like the vines that hung from the trees. Coren's fingers trembled as she traced them down Albert's sides. He arched his back in spasms of pure pleasure. He slid into her and all was lost. She was his and he was locked within her, belonging only to her. There was no escape for either of them – prisoners of their own making.

Prisoners of each other.

There was no key to this cell, for it was built surely upon their raw uncontrolled feelings. Primordial savage ecstasy is what they shared. He whispered her name. It came to her from some far off place. Distant, yet familiar. He said it again, "Coren." It sounded strange to her, something was out of kilter, and yet, she could not place it.

"Coren! Coren my darling . . ." There was an urgency to his voice which was odd, inconsistent.

This place of peace and tranquility suddenly changed. She was confused. Desperation crept in at the edges of her mind. Lost again among the random horrifying thoughts she could not evade. Even here in her sanctuary, the doubts sought her out.

"I have heard that even one of the Royal Family is suspect." The voice came to her distant and almost unplaceable. Then came the sounds of laughter!

Coren came back. The comfort and safety of her thoughts

disappeared. She was once again among the dinner party. Her thoughts left nowhere to hide.

"I'm sorry, Ambassador LaFica. What did you say?" Coren said, slightly embarrassed by her lack of attention.

The Ambassador quickly gulped the crimson wine from his goblet. "I beg your pardon, Your Highness?"

"Just a moment ago I thought I heard you speaking about the Royal Family." Coren sat upright in her chair leaning in to him.

"Oh, that." Ambassador LaFica's Italian accent caused him to over enunciate each word, a trait that Coren would have thought charming at any other time. Now, she gave it almost no thought. "I'm afraid that is true," he continued. "I have heard that the Metropolitan Police have had a member of the Royal Family under surveillance."

"Could one of us be a spy then?" The Ambassador's wife, Lady Antoinette Josephine, spoke with a wry giggle in her voice, causing the rest of the guests to break into laughter and simultaneous small talk.

"Oh, it's me, honestly!" Sir Fenwick Anthony shouted waving his hands about.

Coren laughed at none of this. She sat straight-faced, waiting for the childish antics and banter to dwindle. After a moment, she again directed her attention to the Ambassador.

"How did you hear of this Ambassador LaFica?"

"I beg your pardon, Your Highness, but I am a diplomat and many such things come to me which I can not expound upon."

"I beg your pardon, Ambassador. I should not have asked you such a thing." Coren gently lifted her wine glass and sipped from it as all eyes watched. "Did the Metropolitan Police say who they thought might be a suspect, Ambassador?" Coren opened her eyes a little wider. "If, of course, that would not be giving away a national secret."

"No, no," the Ambassador assured, slightly flustered. "I believe that it would be safe of me to confide to all here the person that the Metropolitan Police have under suspicion."

"Pray tell us, who then?" From across the table, the elderly Austrian Princess spoke with a perfect British accent.

"Surely the Ambassador can not say who the Metropolitan Police are looking for." Albert's voice sliced through Coren. She turned to look at him. "That must be privileged. Am I right, Ambassador?"

Coren could not take her gaze from Albert. Sounds became distant as she studied him. Every slight twitch the muscles in his face made, every blink of the eye, and every gesture, she noted. There was not a move that the Prince could make that Coren did not know. If even the slightest hint of conspiracy showed in him, she would know. Then suddenly, she saw in him a move that sent her spine to chilling. Goose bumps sprang up on the flesh of her arms. Dizziness swept through her. And in an instant she knew!

Coren stared at this man, this prince and she knew.

She knew.

Albert winked at her and smiled a second time. She knew. Coren found in this flash of a moment that he, her prince, could not be the man that the Metropolitan Police were after. His smile, the same smile, which ignited the spark of love within her so long ago, brought the flames to a roar now. He was not what she had dreaded he could be. It wasn't a hard tangible fact that led her here. It was simple and honest. She loved him and that would not steer her wrong. A tear fell slowly down her cheek.

And emeralds glimmered.

CHAPTER THIRTY-FIVE

"Well, to be honest, Prince Albert, I am under no order to keep this a secret." Ambassador LaFica downed the rest of his wine. "As a matter of fact, I would have thought that you would have heard who the suspect is by now."

Albert arched his eyebrows. "Oh really, Ambassador? He leaned forward placing his arm on the dining table, upsetting a water glass, splashing some of the liquid onto the table. Albert ignored it. "Just why would I have heard of this suspect?" He spoke with a hint of irritation added to the sarcastic edge in his voice.

The Ambassador chuckled nervously. He too had picked up on the edginess to Albert's voice. The whole room had. A sharp splinter of thought caused the ambassador to hesitate. The guests remained silent. Even the servants ceased their movements in anticipation of the ambassador's words. Yet none came. The only clue that the Ambassador was about to speak was the changing mood on his face. The lines around his eyes grew darker, as a solemn look overcame his countenance.

"Perhaps, we should replace this talk of murder with something lighter, something the ladies would enjoy?" This came from somewhere near the end of the table. Coren could not see which gentleman spoke or ascertain who it was from the tone of his voice.

A non-descript politician, no doubt.

"Why there's nothing wrong with a little murder at the dinner table." Ambassador LaFica's wife spoke. "In my country, they do it all the time." She laughed, and then corrected herself. "That is, speak of murder at the dinner table, not actually commit it there." Polite laughter accompanied her statement.

"Yes, then. Let's have it, Ambassador." Albert tried to lighten his voice, despite his apparent growing feeling of frustration. Coren knew that he too, had heard rumors. Ugly rumors. But he'd told her he'd thought them just that, rumors. Apparently the Metropolitan Police did not.

Coren sat silent, watching, waiting. Her mind had been made up. She knew the truth, no matter what the Italian ambassador was about to say. She was sure. Yet, she could not help but feel a great sense of disappointment for her husband. He surely knew what the ambassador was hinting at, as did everyone at the table. Yet, to have it spoken aloud was almost as damning as if the Prince. . .

"Prince Albert himself is the killer." Ambassador LaFica seemed relieved to have finally said it. "That's right. That is exactly what I heard from the Metropolitan police directly."

A murmur filled the room as the guests tossed about their disbeliefs at the notion. Shouts of: "Cannot be!" "Preposterous!" "Zut alors!"

"And did you come to Prince Albert's defense, Ambassador LaFica?" Coren's look grew cold as she stared at the ambassador.

All eyes at the table darted back and forth between Coren and the Ambassador. Waiting for the first move to be made. All at the table knew of the deep love between the royal couple.

Ambassador LaFica rose from his seat and looked about the room. "I'm afraid we must be going now." He turned to his wife, speaking in Italian, "Vinaca, pupa." She moved to her husband's side, and taking his arm, strolled to the door.

The Ambassador turned back to the remaining guests. "Forgive me for ruining your dinner. And forgive me, Prince Albert, for delivering this news to you. I should have defended Your Highness. I did not."

Shame visibly overcame him.

"What if it had been true?" he added, almost ruefully.

"My dear." Ambassador LaFica's wife looked directly at Coren. "No matter what fools these men of ours make of themselves, and us, there is one thing that must remain constant, my very dear Principessa . . . our belief in them."

Coren allowed her gaze to follow the Ambassador and his wife out of the room. Silence resounded. Then with a blur of movement, Coren rushed to Albert's side, pulled him close and kissed him hard and strong on the lips. Her arms entwined with his as he responded. Passionately they kissed, oblivious to all around them. He groaned and she echoed his sounds. Then, just as quickly, Coren pulled away, turned to the stunned guests and shouted, "I love him, and I don't care what you or anyone, including the Metropolitan Police think!" Coren grabbed Albert's arm, holding tight to the silken jacket, and pulled him with her as she moved to the door.

"Coren, stop this! What are you doing?" Albert tried to hesitate, catching his balance as Coren dragged him, his feet sliding across the marble floor.

"We are leaving." Coren's words were firm and final.

"But we cannot. We have guests." Albert tried to cajole.

"To hell with the guests!" The door slammed behind them, leaving a stunned room of guests to silence.

"Jenny!" Coren bellowed, as she came bursting into her suite of rooms in a flurry. "Jenny, come here quickly!"

"Coren what is the meaning of this?" Albert tried to calm Coren as she dashed from one end of the room to the other, into and out of the adjoining dressing room, pulling out handfuls of clothes as she went. "Coren, please stop what you are doing and speak to me," the prince implored.

"I cannot, Albert. Don't you understand?" She pulled a gown out of a pile of clothes, which lay upon the bed. "I'm doing what needs to be done. Jenny!" Coren shouted down the corridor to her still unseen maid. "Jenny!"

"Have you gone mad?" Albert said, totally confused.

"Yes, Albert I have. Madly, insanely, hysterically in love with you. And I will not let them take you away from me. You didn't do it, and I will not stand here while they suspect and accuse you."

"Is that what you think? That at some moment now, a police constable will call upon this house to tell you that I am a murderer?" Albert pulled her close to him. "I know you would never believe such a thing."

"Oh, but Albert, I did!" Coren's eyes filled with tears, which quickly fell to her cheeks, "I did, Albert. And don't you understand, if I did, then what is to stop the Metropolitan Police, our friends, or the Queen from believing it?" She'd needed to be honest with him. She hugged him tightly, racked with tears from overlaying emotions of shame, guilt, and love.

Albert stared back into Coren's eyes with his own. Only his eyes were void, black, and empty. The words had taken their toll.

"Albert! Albert!"

She had lost him. Her disbelief in him had lost him. How could she expect him to understand? The woman he loved thought that he could be a murderer. Not just any murderer, but one who could kill in the most disgusting and vile manner. She had no right to have him. He, at the very least, deserved her faith in him, and she had not given him that.

She watched as he withdrew from her, physically and emotionally.

No. She would not accept that.

"Jenny and I were in Whitechapel when two of the

murders had taken place. We were trying to help the poor in that pitiful area. I so wanted to go back to Ireland with you and help my own people there, but I knew this would be a good place to start – helping your people. Jenny and I disguised ourselves as poor slatternly women and went to Whitechapel. It was all my idea. Please don't blame Jenny. I forced her to go. We did help quite a few – but there were so many. It's so sad and miserable. I was afraid you wouldn't understand." She knew she must sound crazed and hysterical to him, but she had to tell him all of it.

She had to make him understand. And believe her. And love her again.

"We were careful, and Jenny's Mr. Dolittle watched out for us. But we saw a carriage in the area of the first murder, and we thought we saw you in it, but we couldn't be sure. Then the second time, we saw another, a man again who looked like you, scurrying off into the shadows. It was dark, but for a second, under the streetlight – I was sure it was you. We were so scared and taken up with everything. The screams, the whistles, the horses, the people, the horror . . . we got caught up in it. I'm so sorry, Albert. I should have told you. I wanted to, but I didn't know how. And that night after our second visit, you came to me so late, and I didn't know where you'd been, and you were so different. I never even asked you why you were so late. I just condemned you. I'm such a fool. But then the constable came to the palace and told me that Jenny and I had been seen in the Whitechapel area, and that we needed to be careful. And if we were to go there again, they would escort us. But I couldn't have that. And I was so afraid he was going to tell you, but those poor people needed my help. I was so determined. So Irish. I thought I could do it all by myself. And now that I realize what an idiot I've been, I fear I may be too late and have destroyed everything between us. I could not live if that were true, Albert. You are my life. You have to understand. You have to forgive me. Albert. Albert, please..."

Coren's voice rose as she drew back her hand and slapped him hard across the face. "Albert!"

He came back. "This is no time to start thinking. Just do as I say." The Irish came back to Coren, strong and formidable. It welled up within her, taking over. And she knew that she could do whatever needed to be done. She held his shoulders. "You must believe in me."

Coren stared into his eyes. She saw in Albert the comprehension forming there. And then . . . love. Such a rush of love, that tears sprang to his eyes and poured down his face. His lips moved as he tried to speak, but as Coren watched, she could see the words would not come.

"Albert, what is it?" Genuine fear grabbed at Coren's voice. "What?"

Albert's throat finally cleared. "I do. My dearest darling. I believe in you. I always will."

"Oh, Albert!" Coren, now too was crying. Crying tears of relief and, yes, joy.

"Miss, you were calling for me?" Jenny now spoke, apparently she had been in the room for a while.

"Jenny, go with the Prince to his room and pack a few of his belongings. We are going away."

"Away, miss?" Jenny stood motionless.

"Do not repeat every word I say as if you were a trained parrot, Jenny. We haven't the time." Coren touched the side of the prince's face with the back of her hand. "Please, Albert, help Jenny with your things."

Albert turned without uttering a sound and walked out the door. Coren's eyes brimmed with, and then overflowed with tears. She thought again of her wonderful, perfect prince. Of his faith and trust in her and of the undying love he would always have for her. He was her fairy tale come true. And they would live happily ever after. Now she was sure of it!

Albert's voice echoed from down the hallway and into the heart of Coren. "Jenny? Jenny are you going to help me or must I do this on my own?"

"Go, Jenny! Help the Prince. Help my husband." Coren raised her hand and brushed the side of her face with the back of it.

Bayberry filled her nostrils and emeralds glinted in her eyes.

Epilogue

"Ya do know, my dear Mr. Dolittle, that you'll be makin' an honest woman of me when Miss Coren and Prince Albert get back from India." Jenny punched him in the arm, before re-snuggling herself in to his arms.

"I'm well aware my darlin' Jenny. I'd marry you this very moment if you'd let me. You're all the world to me." He stared into the fireplace and squeezed her into his shoulder even more.

"Aye. I'd better be, after all we've been through. I miss my girl so much though. I hope she's all right, and I hope she let Albert know that I never suspected him. Not for one moment I didn't. He's been charmin' and lovin' from day one, he has."

Mr. Dolittle turned to her, a quirk of doubt on his face. "Not for one moment?" His eyebrow cocked to her. "I do love the way you calls the Prince of England, 'Albert."

"Well . . . maybe _one_moment, you evil dastard, you. But who wouldn't be suspicious. We saw right into that carriage, and that man did look an awful lot like him. There was so much excitement and screamin' and yellin'. . . ."

"I know darlin'. Ya've told me. Many times."

She punched him again. "And I may tell you many more times, too. So don't be gettin' gnarly with me, Mister Dolittle, or I'll be cuttin' you off from yer fun, if ya get my meanin'"

"I hear ya. But could you do me a right favor, and punch

me other arm the next time. This one's gettin' a might sore."

As Jenny stared into the fireplace and basked in the love of this extraordinary man, she began to think back on her adventures with Coren. "It was sort of excitin', ya know. An' we did do some good for those folks at the hospital. It was so sad. I understand why Miss Coren wants to help them. I just wish I knew what was happening over there. I'm afraid of what kind of trouble she'll be getting' herself into without me there to guide her."

"I'm sure she's fine, darlin'. Your Prince Albert will protect her. She is a grown woman now. And before you get all misty-eyed on me, I got a little present for you. I probably should have given it to you sooner, but I was enjoyin' my time with you." He reached into his sweater pocket and pulled forth an envelope.

Jenny snatched it from his hand as she pulled back from him. "Mister Dolittle, I swear if you ever do that to me again, we're through! And I just might cut you off forever from me winsome charms." She hit him a third time. "Now, let's see what we have here." She stared at the envelope, caressing the exotic Indian stamp on the corner. "An elephant this time. She knows I love the stamps."

"Ya were so anxious a minute ago. Aren't ya gonna open it?" he said, rubbing his arm once again.

"I can't. I'm too nervous. Read it to me."

"All right darlin'."

Jenny gingerly opened the envelope and handed the letter to him. He took it from her, just as gingerly, knowing how precious it was to her.

She snuggled back into his shoulder and he began to read:

November, 30th 1888
Bombay, India
My dearest Jenny,
     Thank you for the note and for taking the time to send me the newspaper clippings from the London Times. We do receive some

news here in India, but it is frightfully slow in coming. As I suspected, the newspaper clippings demonstrate what I thought all along. Or perhaps, I should say in complete honesty, thought most of the time. There was great doubt in most of us. I am terribly sorry, however, that it took the death of another of those poor souls in Whitechapel to convince most that it could never have been Albert. It is a sad commentary on all of us.

And yes, we are very well, thank you for asking. Albert is busy as always with his service to the Queen for the Indian government. As the Ambassador, his duties are varied and many, for which I am thankful. Albert is occupied most of the day, as ambassador, and the nights are filled with dinners and dances and balls of many sorts. I have not yet gotten used to the food in this land. It is spiced and seasoned the way no good Irish woman would ever ruin a meal, but it does keep one entertained, especially at mealtime. Oh how I long for a good shepherd's pie, and I would love to fill the largest bowl I could find to brimming with apple soup. The weather here is atrocious. You would never believe how hot and humid it is. One must regularly change one's clothes just to keep from mildewing over. The countryside, however, is astonishing in its beauty. And there are animals here the likes of which I have never seen – even in the London zoo. I hope you like the elephant stamp. They are truly magnificent creatures. With all of that, I must admit, though, that at times, I am terribly lonely for Ireland and the company of my friends.

And more so, of you. I do hope that you are well and keeping all in place for our return.

We have received word, through the Queen, from the Metropolitan Police that the murders of those poor women in Whitechapel have stopped. Sir Charles Warren told Her Majesty that they had found a body of a man floating in the Thames some time ago and that he is believed to be the man responsible for the killings. It is sad that we will never know for sure who the culprit really is. I am afraid there will always be a stigma attached to the name Prince Edward Albert, The Duke of Clarence. I fear it will be many more lifetimes before this issue is put to rest. My hope is that our children will not hear of it and that they will live their lives *through, without one thought of 'Jack the Ripper.' It is a terrible thing what rumor and innuendo have done to Albert. But I let you know now, that we will return to London and I will see through my promise to myself and to my beloved Ireland. The Irish will walk free. They will no longer be ruled by an outside government. And that the name of the man whom I call "husband" will be spoken of in high places and with high regard. Let it be known, Jenny, that doubt will never more creep its way into my thoughts. For if I had only listened to my heart before I gave in to the doubt of my thoughts, I would have seen long ago that this man, my man, could never have been the murderer that some may have thought him to be. I will be by his side always and one day when he is king I will ask him to free the land of my birth and just as I have stood by him, all of Ireland will know that I have stood by her.*

My two great loves, Jenny, my husband and my country, will be free, and I will stand tall against any who tries to deny that. There is no truth to what they say about my Ireland and there is no truth to what they say about my prince. This, the world will know, if it takes me to my last breath – this they will know.

I will close now, Jenny. It is near time for Albert to return. The sun is setting and we have not missed a sunset together in all the weeks we have been here. Standing on the balcony of our bedroom suite, we watch as the sun begins to hide its face for another day, shimmering tendrils of rose and orange and purple reach out to caress us. And when they have all but given in to the black of the night, Albert carries me to the bed where we lie in each others arms and fill each other's passions, rising, falling, and drifting off to sleep, my arms wrapped tightly about his body – not holding him – but holding on.

Your dearest friend,

Coren

P.S. I am so happy that you and your Mister Dolittle are doing so well. When he asks you Jenny, say "Yes."

My dearest Jenny, I love you so, and you deserve the most happiness, for the truth is, Jenny, that I would never have found my prince and my happiness without you.

Coren dabbed at the paper with the ink blotter, as the familiar sound of Albert's footsteps climbing the stairs padded softly behind her.

The door to the bedroom slowly swung open, the dark, Indian mahogany creaky from the dampness of the air. Immediately, the sent of bayberry cologne wafted into the room. Coren turned in her chair. The figure standing in the doorway was ablaze in the colors of the setting sun. He stepped forward, throwing his waistcoat to the floor, unbuttoning his shirt. The dark curls of hair on his muscled chest, glinting like polished coal in the light.

"Albert, I've just finished another letter to Jenny that needs to be posted. She is going to be so excited to know that we will be back in the spring. And even more excited to know that we will be headed to Ireland." She rose from the desk and went to him, brushing back a silky lock from his forehead, and kissing him fervently and lingeringly on the lips.

"Oh my darling Prince, are you certain that you want to go to my homeland with me? You're not just saying it to placate me?" She held his face in her hands, staring into those beautiful, ethereal eyes, begging for sincere affirmation.

He reached out, stroked her hair, and traced the side of her face with his hand. Then, gently placing his hand under her chin he raised her face up.

"My darling Princess, how could I not want to see the land that spawned the woman of my dreams. It surely must be an enchanted place to have produced such a beguiling and extraordinary beauty. I've heard the legends of your land, and you're the living proof that they're true. I have always wanted to see – what do you call them? Ah yes, the "wee folk." Perhaps, we can even find a pot of gold or two to help your brethren." He brushed the bridge of her nose.

"Albert, you are going to love it. And if anyone can find the pot of gold at the end of the rainbow, it's you, my love. I'm so deliriously happy, I actually feel as if I've been enchanted."

He smiled rapturously at her. "I know you have enchanted me."

"I have also been thinking, my darling . . ." She slid her hand into his shirt and began to rub his chest. "I don't want to neglect those poor people of Whitechapel. They are so sad and pitiful. The thought of them just breaks my heart. I was thinking, maybe, if you like, we could spend half the year in London – or even just a couple of months – it's up to you, of course, my husband." She was tweaking and tugging his right nipple now. "But half a year would probably be best. There is so much work to do."

Albert's eyes were closed in bliss. She knew what he liked.

He muttered, "A witch. Yes, that is what I've wedded. An Irish witch. Whatever you desire, my love. I will always be under your spell."

He opened his eyes and as they met hers, he was captured, awestruck by her beauty and held by her love. Just as he was closing his eyes again to kiss her and she was closing hers, there was a glint of green as . . .

Emeralds sparkled.

Lance Taubold has been a Metropolitan opera singer, Broadway performer and Soap Opera actor. He currently lives, performs, and writes in Las Vegas. His upcoming releases include an anthology of paranormal romances, **Zodiac Lovers**, and a non-fiction work about the war in Afghanistan and at home, co-authored with Staff Sgt. Adam Fenner, **On Two Fronts**.

Richard Devin-LaFica is a contributing writer to Southern Nevada Equestrian Magazine, Envy Man magazine and is the published author of two business books to the showbiz trade: **Actors' Resumes: The Definitive Guidebook** (Players Press, 2002, 2006) and **Do You Want To Be An Actor? 101 Answers to Your Questions About Breaking Into the Biz** (Players Press, 2002). He contributed to two anthologies: **Tales from the Casting Couch** (Dove, 1995) and **Glory** (Sands Publishing, 2001). He is an award winning playwright, having received the Foundation for the Vital Arts Award for his plays, Deceptive Peace and My Mother's Coming (produced by Money Shot Productions, Hollywood CA) and is an optioned screenwriter. Find more at www.richarddevin.com

CPSIA information can be obtained at www.ICGtesting.com
Printed in the USA
LVOW12s1739311013

359481LV00016B/900/P